Bases Loaded

Roz Lee

DEDICATION

To my readers.

Without you, I would have chucked this
writing gig a long time ago.

.

ACKNOWLEDGMENTS

I wish to thank my friend, Kathy Bennett, who patiently listened to me while I brainstormed this story over a lunch, a dinner, and a drive to and from an event in Burbank. Her insight and comments helped me define the characters motivations and the plot and led to the story you are about to read.

Many thanks to my cousin Ellen who has become a valued beta reader for me. Your honesty is priceless, which is another way of saying I won't be paying you!

As always, I have to thank my editor, Laura Garland, who patiently corrects my grammar and sentence structure and does her best to keep me from appearing a fool. Since that is a monumental task, any errors are not her fault.

All my love to my family who put up with my crazy ideas and support my writing career no matter how embarrassing it might be to them.

CHAPTER ONE

He's here.

Being in the same room with Antonio Ramirez made Clare's skin tingle and her lady parts hum. She tugged on her skirt, wishing she'd tried on the dress earlier in the week when she would have had time to go out and find something else to wear. Being curvy was one thing, but being in denial about it was another.

Other women could get away with wearing last year's purchases, but not her. Nope. All she had to do was look at a salad, much less a dessert, and she gained weight. But even a too-snug dress couldn't keep her from attending Jason Holder's fundraiser—not once she'd learned the Mustangs' latest acquisition would be there.

She'd had a crush on the center fielder ever since he made his Major League debut with the Marauders back in the days when she'd been a student at Julliard. She'd used her family connections to get game tickets as often as possible and saved her allowance to buy even more. Of course, Antonio hadn't known she existed, and if he had, he wouldn't have given her a second look, but that didn't stop her from fantasizing about him. And her. Doing all kinds of things. Together.

And that had been before she'd heard the rumor.

But men like Antonio didn't fantasize about women like

her. Antonio preferred his women tall, slim, and cover girl gorgeous. In fact, every time he appeared in public he had a stunning woman or two at his side.

Clare scanned the room, looking for the tallest female. Runway types were always tall—and skinny. If she found the model or *models* in the room, she'd probably find Antonio Ramirez, too. It didn't take long to spot the lanky blonde and, as she'd predicted, the man she had come to the fundraiser to see. He was elegant in a tuxedo that had obviously been tailored specifically for his muscular build. The crowd surrounding him shifted, blocking her view.

Oh, well. The evening was young. Clare turned and came face to face with the last person on earth she wanted to see— Jessica Roach.

Well, shit.

As a rule, these sort of events attracted nice people—the kind who genuinely wanted to use their money or influence to promote a good cause. But they also tended to attract the kind that thought rubbing elbows with celebrities made *them* more important. Jessica was the worst of that bunch. For reasons Clare couldn't begin to comprehend, the society predator had made it her mission to remind Clare of her shortcomings at every possible opportunity.

"He's out of your league," Jessica said, nodding toward Antonio. She sipped her drink, her eyes sparkling with glee over the rim of the glass.

"Hello to you, too, Jessica." Clare forced a smile to her face.

Jessica smirked. "You aren't his type."

Typical of a shark. Not even a pretense at civility. Seek out your prey and get a bite in before they have a chance to flee. "Who are you talking about?"

"Tony Ramirez, of course. I saw you drooling over him."

Clare fought the urge to wipe at her chin, fearing she had done just that.

"He doesn't go for *earthy* women."

Tell me something I don't know. "He doesn't swim in your waters either." At least she hoped not. She blinked away a mental image from long ago she'd tried unsuccessfully to forget. Jessica was exactly the kind of fish Antonio kept in his aquarium.

Bases Loaded

"You'd be surprised." Jessica brought her drink to her lips, rimming the edge of the glass with her tongue. She winked at someone over Clare's shoulder.

Gross. Clearly, the shark had found tastier prey. "Nice seeing you, Jessica," she lied, and made her escape. She wouldn't let the likes of Jessica Roach ruin a perfectly good evening.

Clare acknowledged a few more people she knew then headed for the silent auction tables stretched like a jeweled necklace around the perimeter of the ballroom. Since taking the job as the organist for the Mustangs last year, she'd been invited to more of these events than she could count. No way could she afford a single thing up for auction, but that didn't stop her from bidding. In a room filled with the top echelon of Dallas society and franchise players from every major sports team in town, someone would outbid her before the night ended. They always did.

Having studied the bid brochure ahead of time and selected a theme for the night, she located the first item on her list, a his-and-hers massage package at an exclusive spa. There was no *his* to go with Clare's *hers*, but the bid item certainly qualified as a Romantic Interlude. In fact, she had highlighted each item on her list with Antonio Ramirez in mind. Even as she recorded her ridiculously low bid, she indulged herself in a little harmless fantasy.

The two of them, relaxed after receiving incredible full-body massages, would sink into a warm bath surrounded by candlelight. Lulled by soft music, they would sip champagne and learn the curves and planes of each other's bodies. Her skin would come alive under his touch while her hands explored his hard body.

She smiled to herself and quickly filled in her email address—not that anyone would be contacting her to say she'd won—and signed her name. With a sigh, she placed the pen back in its fancy holder and moved on to the next item on her list.

Antonio smiled and clasped the hand thrust his way. "Nice to meet you, Mr. Mayor."

Mayor Ryland pumped Tony's hand enthusiastically. "The pleasure is all mine." His smile added emphasis to his words. "You're just what the Mustangs need. I'd love to see the team bring the World Series to Dallas next season."

"We're going to do our best, sir."

"I know you will," the mayor confirmed.

A tug on his other arm drew his attention. "Tony," the sequin draped toothpick whined, "aren't you going to introduce me?"

"Um…sure." *As soon as I remember your name.* He searched his memory for the elusive name. Something unusual. Chloe? No, that wasn't it. Was it?

"No need," the mayor said, turning his attention to the woman. "Everyone knows the most famous cover model to ever come out of our little town." He reached for her hand and brought it to his lips for a kiss. "Welcome home, Dierdre."

She batted her eyelashes, and Tony could have sworn she'd purred. "It's good to be back. When I learned about Jason's new foundation, I knew I had to do whatever I could to help."

What a load of crap. Her publicist was his publicist, and the bitch of a woman had paired them up for the fundraising event for reasons that escaped Tony entirely. Dierdre had zero interest in the foundation his new teammate Jason Holder had established to aid children suffering from heart disease. She was here to be seen. Tomorrow, she would be on someone else's arm, thank God, at some other event. He just needed to get through tonight with her.

The mayor did his best to carry on a coherent conversation with the clueless woman, but it was a losing battle. Tony decided the man had suffered enough and interrupted. "Mr. Mayor, thanks for coming out tonight to support the Christopher Foundation. I'm sure Jason appreciates it."

"Hey, it's a good cause. After hearing his story about how he almost died when he was a kid…well, it touched me. This new charity of his will help a lot of kids and their families."

"You're right about that," Jason said, joining their small circle. "Thanks for coming tonight."

"Thrilled to do it, Jason. I dropped off a check a few minutes ago, and I plan to add it to my list of regular donations."

Tony scanned the room as the trio talked around him. As

fundraisers went, this one was first class. Champagne flowed freely, and the attendees included the highest ranks of Dallas society as well as local celebrities. He had even seen a few Hollywood types who claimed Dallas as home.

So, why was he so freakin' bored?

His gaze traveled over the crowd. There were lots of pretty women all pampered and preening on tuxedo clad arms. There were a few single women, but they, too, closely resembled his "date" for the evening—too thin, too shiny, and too fake for his taste. He preferred his women real, and he was all too aware of how rare those kinds were in these circles.

He resisted the urge to check his watch. It wouldn't kill him to stay another hour or so until the event broke up. Afterward, maybe he'd convince some of the other single guys to accompany him to a bar or a club or somewhere there were women. Real women. He knew there were places like that in Dallas, he just hadn't been here long enough to find one yet.

An elbow jabbed him in the ribs, and he turned his attention back to the group.

"Isn't that right, Tony?" Jason asked.

What? "Um…yeah." He smiled. "That's right."

"See, I told you, Mr. Mayor. This guy is going to make a real difference next season. We're excited to have him in the lineup."

Tony didn't have a clue what they had been talking about. "I'm glad to be here. The Mustangs are a great franchise, and Dallas, what I've seen of it, is a fantastic city."

As he suspected, the comment prompted the mayor into a dissertation on all the finer qualities of his city. Antonio listened with half his brain while he planned his escape with the other half. He eyed the main entrance to the ballroom over the mayor's shoulder. Ninety feet—the distance between bases. He could run it in less than four seconds, walk it in ten.

Someone tugged on his arm. He glanced to his left at the picture perfect face beside him scrunched into a pout. "I'm thirsty." Her blood red, collagen-enhanced lips formed the words meant to either get rid of him or prove to herself she had him where she wanted him. He couldn't have cared less which. It was an opportunity to get away from her for a few minutes.

Christ. What made women think pumping chemicals into

their lips was a good idea? He extricated his arm from her perfect red claws. "I'll get you a drink." No need to ask her what she wanted. She'd been drinking skinny cocktails all night.

He excused himself. If he was lucky, she would find someone else to prop her up for the rest of the evening. He crossed his fingers and threaded his way through the crowd to the bar in the farthest corner where he ordered her trendy drink and a plain soda for himself. He leaned one elbow on the high counter and waited for the bartender to complete the order. A flash of blue near the door caught his eye.

Holy mother of God. Who. Is. That?

His skin tightened and blood rushed south. He straightened, craning his neck to get a better look at the goddess who had just entered the ballroom. Alone.

He'd always thought love at first sight was a myth. Until this moment.

Now, he knew better.

He didn't know what exactly drew him to her. Even from across the crowded ballroom, he could tell her skin was creamy smooth. He silently cursed the fluorescent lighting making it impossible to tell if the glossy mane cascading in soft waves over her shoulders and framing her face in silk was dark brown or black. Either way, it would look perfect fanned across the white sheets on his bed.

If she wore makeup, it was understated, barely there at all. She smiled at someone, and Tony's knees almost buckled. *Damn.* Petal pink lips were such a turn-on. He bet there were a few other places on her luscious body he would find the same delectable color, and he vowed to taste every last one of them.

"Put your tongue back in your mouth." Tanner Haverford, the Mustangs short stop stepped up to the bar, blocking Tony's view. "You look stupid."

Tony stepped to the side and zeroed in on his royal blue target. "Shut up."

She was round in all the right places, and he had no trouble imagining how wonderful her soft curves would feel beneath him. But there was more to his feelings than lust—though that certainly wasn't in doubt. He knew her on some deeper level he didn't pretend to understand. She was his soul mate.

The thought rocked him back on his heels, but he couldn't

take his eyes off her. His woman headed for the silent auction tables set up around the perimeter of the room. He studied the sway of her hips. God, he was a lucky man. He would gladly follow that around for the rest of his life.

She paused at the first table, and after studying the auction item, bent over the table to write her bid on the list.

"Scotch, on the rocks," Tanner said to the bartender then turned to Tony. "Your drinks are ready."

"Take 'em. They're yours."

"What's with you?" His unwanted buddy turned. "Ah…I see."

"No you don't. Don't look at her. She's mine."

Tanner smirked. "Good luck with that."

He whipped his head around. "You know her?" he growled.

"Yeah. You won't get anywhere with her."

His blood boiled. He didn't stop to consider why he felt the way he did. He'd kill the fucker if he had already touched her. "How would you know?"

"Whoa!" He raised his hands in mock surrender. "Down, boy. I'm just saying. You want to tread lightly there. She's the organist at the stadium."

Convenient. Tony took a step in her direction, and was stopped by a firm hand on his elbow. "Hold your horses. Didn't you hear what I said? She's off limits, man."

"I heard you."

Another thought hammered him, and he saw red. "She isn't married, is she?"

"Nope. Single."

Why the hell was she single? Were these Texas men insane? "Why?"

"Maybe because she's—"

"Don't you dare say what I think you're about to," Tony warned.

"I'm not saying anything. I just prefer my women…thinner."

A thought popped into his head—his most brilliant idea ever. He reached for the drinks he'd ordered. "Got your drink?"

"Yeah." Tanner took the glass the bartender set on the counter.

He pulled a twenty from his pocket and stuffed it in the tip jar. "Come on. I have someone you need to meet."

The middle infielder followed him through the crowd.

"What's her name?" Tony asked over his shoulder.

"Clare something or other."

Clare. A real name for a real woman. He liked it.

They reached their destination. Tony pressed the "skinny" martini into what's-her-name's hand. "This is Tanner. Tanner, this is…."

"I know who this is," the second baseman crooned, reaching for the model's free hand.

Tony turned his back on her and bumped shoulders with the man who was unwittingly going to be his savior. "She's all yours," he mumbled. He didn't wait to see if the man was okay with the new arrangement. His teammate had arrived solo tonight, and judging by his reaction to the introduction, he wouldn't be leaving the same way.

With a little luck, he wouldn't be either.

CHAPTER TWO

Clare signed her name to a slip offering a weekend cruise on a private yacht and, with a sigh, moved on to the next one. As she studied the bid item, a custom designed diamond ring from an extremely high-end jeweler, she became aware of a man behind her. He stood close enough she felt heat radiating off his body and the subtle deep tones of his aftershave filled her nostrils. Her body urged her to get closer. She shifted to her opposite foot instead. Out of the corner of her eye, she watched him pick up the pen she'd just set down. He was going to outbid her for the cruise!

Part of her breathed a sigh of relief, but another part wanted to weep as a tiny bit of her fantasy died. Then she noticed the man's hand. Strong. Smooth olive skin dusted with dark hairs. Oh wow! His handwriting was neat as he signed his name. *Tony Ramirez.*

Her breath caught in her lungs, and her heart raced. If there was any man on the planet she wanted to take along on her fantasy cruise, it was Antonio Ramirez! She had come to the fundraiser tonight hoping to get a glimpse of him, perhaps even an introduction if she was lucky. But getting this close to him? This was beyond her wildest imagination. It took her breath away. The Mustangs new center fielder was the sexiest man alive—or so said *People* magazine. And, if the rumors were true….

Her skin flushed with embarrassment at her wayward thoughts. She swallowed hard. He lifted his hand and put it down again over the column for bid amounts.

Besides, no one had any concrete evidence. It was only a rumor, and Major League Baseball excelled at rumors. The sport practically existed on them. Who would be traded and to whom. Who's contract said what. Who was dating whom. Who played *The Game.*

Gossip had it that Antonio not only played *The Game*, but he had helped invent it.

Clare had spent more lonely hours than she would admit contemplating what she would say or do if someone invited her to play, too. Would she say yes? *Hell, yes!*

She'd never stood side-by-side with any of the alleged players, and though she was at this moment, there was no danger he would pay her any notice, much less invite her to play. All her thoughts on the subject had been nothing more than another one of her fantasies.

His fingers were long and, she imagined, rough from playing baseball, but they'd held the pen gracefully. She couldn't help thinking he would handle a woman's body with the same care. The thought sent a wave of heat from her core all the way to her toes.

He'd written a number beneath her meager bid—a ridiculously obscene amount that all but guaranteed he would win the trip.

"If I win, I'll take you with me."

She knew that voice, the distinct accent of a native New Yorker. Her gaze snapped from his perfectly formed hand to his more perfectly formed face. "What?"

"I said…I'll take you with me, Clare Kincaid."

"You know who I am?" *Nu-uh. No.*

"I do now." He moved closer until his hip grazed hers. A tingle ran up and down her side and spread over the rest of her body like a heat rash. "I'm Antonio Ramirez. You can call me Tony."

"Er…."

"You know who I am?" he parroted her earlier comment.

"Er…yes," she breathed. "Of course I do."

"Good. Then this will be easier."

What? What was going to be easier? Her knees shook, and she racked her brain for something to say.

"Are you going to bid on the ring, too?" he asked.

"Um…."

He bumped her hip again, and she stepped to the side. He took her place in front of the ring for auction. "We're going to need one of these," he said as he penned his name and another ridiculously large bid amount.

"Wait." She shook her head. "What are you talking about?"

"We're going to need an engagement ring and wedding bands. If you don't like the ones here, we'll use this for something else. I'd like to see you wear my jewels."

Okay. So, she was prone to fantasies, but this was ridiculous. She closed her eyes and shook her head. When she opened them, he was still there. A sick feeling she was all too familiar with took hold in her stomach. Humiliation.

Bitterness rose in her throat. She'd been here before. It was bad enough the stunning women who hung out at these events used her vulnerabilities to elevate themselves in their own eyes. She could deal with them—had been for years. But did good-looking guys have to use plain women to boost their egos, too? Wasn't being rich, talented, and gorgeous enough for a guy? *That's the trouble with meeting the object of your fantasies. They never live up to the image in your mind.* She swallowed hard, trying to force the bitter pill of yet another ruined fantasy down.

"This isn't funny, Mr. Ramirez." She was proud her voice remained steady when all she really wanted to do was hide somewhere and cry.

"And it isn't meant to be. I intend to marry you, Clare. Do you have a problem with that?"

"Yes, I do…."

He smiled and anger joined humiliation and bitterness in the volatile mixture brewing in her stomach.

"Have a problem with that," she added. *What an ass.*

"Well then, I'll just have to convince you. We'll have lots of time together. I've outbid you on the spa day, the luxury hotel weekend, the private yacht and now the diamond ring. I'll win them all, and we'll enjoy them together."

Why wouldn't her feet move? "Please," she whispered. "Don't."

He continued as if he hadn't heard her. "What else do you want to bid on, *il mio cuore?*"

Ooh. Italian. Her inner woman swooned, and her knees turned to jelly. But her brain didn't. She bet he'd brought plenty of women to their knees with talk like that. *Not me, buddy.* She glanced around to see if anyone might save her. They had the corner of the room to themselves—a situation she had dreamed of for ages, which at the moment, felt like her worst nightmare. She was on her own.

"Look, um…Mr. Ramirez…."

"Tony."

Be cool. Don't let the bully know how much it hurts. Just act normal. Then get the hell out. "Antonio," she sighed. "This is…flattering. But you have to stop."

"Why?"

"Why?" Her voice rose above the din surrounding them, causing a few heads to swivel their way. Clare plastered what she hoped was a smile on her face and lowered her voice to a conversational level. "Because you and I both know this is a game, and I don't want to play anymore."

Of all the fantasies she'd conjured up about this man over the years, she'd never dreamed he could be cruel enough to toy with a woman.

He slipped his arm around her waist and steered her along the display table. Every cell in her body thrilled at his touch while her brain screamed for her to run. But that would turn an already unbearable moment into an embarrassing scene. The last thing she needed was for one of the ballroom bullies to witness an altercation between her and The Sexiest Man Alive. She'd never hear the end of it.

"Come on," he urged. "There are a few other items we should bid on. I saw them earlier, but I didn't bid because there wasn't anyone I wanted to share them with."

Clare walked beside him, her hip rubbing along his as he held her close. She kept her hands clutched in front of her. They stopped at a bid item that offered a ski weekend in Aspen. Keeping her pinned to his side, Antonio bent and added his bid to the bottom line. If she played along, maybe she could salvage some part of the encounter After all, from a distance it probably looked like he was interested in her. He did have his arm around her waist. *Take that, bitches.*

He set the pen down and beamed at her. "Maybe we'll get snowed in."

He bid on two more items that were part of her fantasy package, only the amounts he wrote down were outrageously large. When they reached the end of the tables, he steered her toward one of the many bars scattered around the room.

"Soda for me, and a white wine for my lady," he said.

The bartender glanced her way and winked. A tide of heat rose from her décolletage to her hairline.

"I've got to go," she said, taking a step back.

His hand on the small of her back reeled her in like a fly ball snagged before it cleared the outfield wall. "Don't go. Not yet." He pressed a glass of wine into her hand and picked up his soda. "We haven't had nearly enough time to talk."

They'd had plenty of time, in her opinion. It only took a few seconds to find out Antonio Ramirez was just like every other hunky guy out there. Full of himself. Not that her traitorous body gave a damn. But her brain did. Her opportunity to escape presented itself, and she took it.

"Will you excuse me?" she shoved the wine glass in his direction. "I'm going to the ladies room. I'll be right back." *Right.* She'd be in her car and pulling out of the parking garage before it occurred to him she'd ditched him. *Jerk.*

She turned on her heel and stopped short.

"Clare," her uncle said, automatically bussing her cheek with a kiss.

"Mr. Walker. Good to see you again." She hoped he caught on to her formal greeting. There were times she enjoyed playing the my-uncle-is-the-team-manager card, but mostly it was something she tried to keep quiet. Her present situation was humiliating enough without having her uncle come to her rescue as if she were a helpless damsel in distress.

Bless his heart, he raised an eyebrow at her greeting and, with a smile, turned to the newest member of his team. "Tony, I see you've met our organist."

"Yes, sir. I have. We were just going to go someplace

quieter and get to know each other."

Doyle shifted his gaze to Clare. She shook her head. "Actually, I was just leaving." She stepped around her uncle, putting him between her and Antonio.

Behind her, Antonio called for her to wait up, then her uncle's voice told him to let her go. She made a beeline for the hotel lobby and the bank of elevators that would take her to the underground parking garage. Thank goodness she couldn't afford valet parking, or she would be stuck outside waiting for her car. This was much better. In a few minutes, she'd be safe in her darkened car where no one would see her tears.

"Clare! Wait!" Tony reached for her, but she moved too fast, and he grabbed a handful of air. He took a step to follow, coming up short when Doyle placed a hand on his chest.

"Let her go."

He hurt inside, and it had nothing to do with the palm pressing against his upper body. There was something about the hitch in Clare's voice that speared him in the heart.

He brushed the older man's hand away. Damned if he knew how, but he'd hurt her, and he needed to make it right. "You don't understand."

"I understand that you aren't going after her. And you *are* going to hear me." The team manager's tone warned him he'd better listen—or else.

Clare disappeared through the ballroom doors.

"Say what you have to say then I'm going after her."

"No, you're not. Leave her be, Ramirez."

"I can't do that."

"You can, and you will. I've heard about the kind of games you like to play, and Clare isn't that kind of girl."

Tony went cold inside. So, even the Mustangs management had heard the rumors. No worries. He'd left that behind in New York. "This isn't a game. She's special."

"You have a reputation for being reckless, on and off the field. She isn't your type," Doyle argued.

"She's exactly my type. She's beautiful, and intelligent, and sexy as hell.”

“I'm warning you. Don't drag her into your world, Tony. Stay away from her.”

“With all due respect, sir, I can't do that. Did you hear her? She's upset, and I don't know why. I've got to find her.”

“Didn't you come with some model tonight?”

Shit. Tony scanned the crowded room for his date. She was as tall as most of the men in the room, so she was easy to spot. Only she wasn't. And neither was Tanner.

“She ditched me for Tanner,” he said. *And good riddance.* His publicist wasn't wouldn't be happy, but he'd gladly suffer her wrath in return for his freedom tonight. He silently vowed never to let her goad him into escorting another one of her clients again.

“You still aren't going after Clare.”

Tony sighed and allowed his shoulders to relax. He couldn't afford to piss off the team manager. Multi-million dollar contract or not, the man didn't have to play him if he didn't want to. Refusing to escort sequined toothpicks couldn't possibly hurt his career, but having his ass benched before the season even began most certainly would.

“Okay. You win, but will you do me a favor?”

“Depends on what it is.”

“Call her. Or call someone to check on her. I didn't mean to upset her, and I don't want her to be alone when she feels that way.”

Doyle studied him for the longest time. Tony fought the urge to fidget. Any sign of weakness on his part would confirm the manager's suspicions and condemn him to low-life status in his eyes forever. Somehow, Tony would convince him his intentions were honest and honorable.

“I'd never do anything to hurt her, sir. I know my track record doesn't look good, but I'm asking you to trust me.” He lowered his voice. “I'm through with that lifestyle, Doyle. I know the Mustangs run a spotless operation. Why do you think I wanted to come here? I wanted to start fresh—clean up my reputation.” Tony spit out the half-truth with ease. He had come to Texas in order to put distance between him and his vices, but one look at Clare Kincaid and his brain nearly exploded with images best not examined at too closely. The miles between

Dallas and New York made acting on his less than reputable impulses more difficult, but clearly, the move hadn't extinguished them.

Tony squirmed under Doyle's intense scrutiny.

"I usually don't care who my players are off the field, as long as they stay out of jail and out of the tabloids. I won't cut you any slack, Ramirez. None at all. Your secret club isn't much of a secret among the owners and managers. This is the only warning you'll get from me. If I even suspect you have involved Clare in that mess, you'll spend what's left of your career in the minors."

For a man known for masking his emotions in the dugout, Doyle made no attempt to veil them now. He froze Tony with a death stare before he turned and stalked across the ballroom. Tony breathed a sigh of relief, but he took the warning to heart. That didn't mean he would stay away from Clare.

He couldn't stay away from her. She was his.

CHAPTER THREE

It took two days to find her, but when he entered the small booth housing the stadium's organ, he knew the wait had been worth it. He leaned against the doorframe and admired the view. Bent over the console with her ass in the air, her backside reminded him of a wrapped gift—one his hands itched to unwrap.

She sighed and tucked a strand of sable hair behind her ear. Just that small gesture had his cock aching for her touch. He imagined that sweep of hair brushing against his skin, and his abdominal muscles tightened.

He had a good view of one side of her face. Her cheek was flushed, her jaw tight with frustration. He knew the feeling. For the last two days, he'd tried to find the Mustangs' elusive organist, but most of the people he asked didn't have a clue where to find her, and the ones who did refused to say. But luck was on his side. He'd come to the stadium to meet with HR and get all the employment paperwork in place. Insurance, direct deposit, tax forms–all done. Nothing to do now but find a place to live and wait for Spring Training. And find Clare Kinkaid.

Then luck stepped in and gave him the opportunity he'd been waiting for. Coming out of the Mustangs offices, he'd caught a glimpse of Clare stepping into the elevator. He waited to see which floor she stopped on then followed her.

She mumbled something that sounded suspiciously like a curse and straightened.

"Lose something?"

She let out a squeaky scream and turned. Her blue eyes were wide with alarm, and while one hand rested on the console behind her, the other rested on her chest. A lock of dark hair swirled over her left shoulder and curled seductively around her Mustangs jersey-clad breast.

For just a second, he imagined her standing in his apartment wearing nothing but his jersey. He was instantly hard and shifted to ease the pressure, hoping she wouldn't notice the bulge in his pants.

"Oh, it's *you*." She dropped her hand to her side. "What do you want?"

It wasn't exactly the greeting he had hoped for He took a step inside the cramped booth, and she seemed to shrink away from him. Damn. He'd never get anywhere with her if she continued to treat him as if he was a walking STD.

"This is where you work?" He tore his gaze from the most interesting thing in the room—*her*—and looked around. There wasn't much to see, just an old-fashioned organ and a small control panel. A neatly folded hunk of gray plastic he assumed was a cover sat off to one side. On the other side, a headset hung from one of those stick anywhere plastic hooks adhered to the wall. A plate-glass window afforded a damned fine view of the field.

"Yes, and I'm busy."

So, she had a bossy side. He liked it. He took another step in her direction, and she moved. He peered over the console. "What did you lose?"

"My keys slid off the window ledge. I can see them, but I can't reach them."

Yep. There they were within easy reach of someone with long enough arms. He straightened and turned to her. Maybe he could use this to his advantage. "I can get them, but it's going to cost you."

She crossed her arms across her ample chest and scowled at him. "Seriously? You want me to pay you to get my keys?"

He smiled. "I won't charge much. Have dinner with me."

Her chest heaved with each breath she took. He found it very distracting.

"My eyes are up here." She uncrossed her arms long enough to point toward her face.

Tony obliged, reluctantly. Not that he didn't want to look at her face. She was beautiful, and the warmth coloring her cheeks had him imagining how the color would look on certain other body parts.

"Don't you have things to do?"

"Actually, no. I'm surprisingly free for the next few months." He mimicked her crossed arms stance.

She huffed out a breath that might have included another muffled curse. "Why?"

"Why, what?"

She waved a hand in the air. "Why are you doing this? Why me? Do you get off on humiliating women?"

His blood froze. He bent and retrieved her keys and held them out to her. "I'm sorry if you thought I was in any way making fun of you. I'd never do that to you, or any woman. My mama would box my ears if I did."

She snatched the keys from his palm, folding them into a white-knuckled fist.

"I just want to get to know you, Clare."

"Why?"

"Because." He shrugged. Telling her she was his soul mate and he lusted for her day and night probably wouldn't go over too well, so he settled on a lesser version of the truth. "You're beautiful and sexy, and I don't know anybody in this town. I'd like to have a meal with someone on occasion, and I'd prefer my companion to be easy on the eyes. There's no one on the team who fits that description."

A smile ghosted across her face. "Well, I don't fit it either, but since you got my keys for me, I suppose...."

"Good." He edged his way to the door. "Ready to go?"

Clare covered the keyboard, grabbed the tote she had come for, and glanced around the cramped quarters to see if she had left anything behind she might need over the next few months.

She hadn't forgotten the fundraiser. The humiliation still

stung, but if she let those kinds of instances rule her life, she would never leave the house. Besides, he'd made the effort to find her. Her heart sped up just thinking about what that might mean. Perhaps he was trying to make amends for his behavior.

Or, he could still be toying with her. A man like him couldn't possibly be interested in someone like her. She smirked. Yeah, he would run far and fast if he had any idea the kind of fantasies she harbored about him. But that was all they were, fantasies. Hot, sexy guys like Antonio Ramirez didn't get down and dirty with plain women. Beautiful women threw themselves at him, and there were enough tabloid photos of him with Hollywood starlets and supermodels to support the assumption he enjoyed their company.

"Wait. Why are you here—at the stadium?"

"I had paperwork to do if I want the Mustangs to pay me, and believe me, I want them to pay me."

"Oh. Well…are you done?"

"All done. And even if I wasn't, I'd tell them to go to hell before I'd turn down an opportunity to spend time with you."

His voice was like a sensual caress that made her skin tingle and her lady parts wish a relationship with him could be real. He was new in town, and he probably needed a friend. Her lady parts would just have to settle for what they could get.

She reached for her purse. "Okay then, if you're sure."

He stood aside, and she felt his heat as she scooted past him to the door. "I'm sure. But I wouldn't blame you if you changed your mind. Doyle Walker has already warned me to stay away from you."

She stopped in her tracks, turned. "He did? Really? When?"

"Yes. At the fundraiser. Right after you walked out."

She was going to be sick. Uncle Doyle…what, stood up for her? Tried to protect her? Oh Lord, how embarrassing. And in a way, more humiliating than what Antonio had done. She was a grown woman. She could take care of herself. Well, she hadn't handled the situation at the fundraiser very well, but she had handled it. She didn't need, or want, her uncle interfering in her personal life.

"I'm sorry." What else could she say? God, he must think she was pathetic.

"Don't be. I told him to mind his own business."

"You didn't." Could the situation get any worse?

"Not in so many words, but he isn't going to keep me from seeing you."

"Why?"

"Why what?"

"Why are you here, with me?"

"Because I want to be. Because I can't stop thinking about you. About doing this."

He moved fast. One arm snaked around her waist, the other around her shoulder. He hauled her body tight against his before her brain could process what was going on and formulate a protest. Then his mouth was on hers, stealing her breath, her last thread of sanity, and her pride.

For a moment, it didn't matter she wasn't stick thin or cover girl gorgeous. It didn't matter they were standing in a hallway and absolutely anyone might see them. All she could do was feel. His kiss was everything she had ever dreamed it would be. His lips were hard on hers at first, then softer, coaxing her to let him inside. She opened for him. His tongue stroked hers, rimmed her mouth then plunged deep.

She was lost. No one had ever kissed her like this before. It was carnal. Hot. Seductive. Cream your panties sexy.

Then it was over. His large hand splayed across the back of her head, pressing her forehead into his shoulder. She gasped for breath against his heaving chest.

"Shh," he whispered. "Don't move."

She couldn't move, even if she wanted to—which she didn't. He held her in an iron grip. Blazing heat warmed her front in counterpoint to the cold at her back. When had he backed her against the concrete wall?

His heartbeat—or was it hers?—thudded in her ears. Coming to her senses, she picked out the separate and distinct sound of footsteps. Coming closer. *Oh God.* She was going to get caught making out with Antonio Ramirez in the stadium!

He held her until the footsteps faded away around the corner before his grip eased and he stepped back.

"Who was that?"

"I don't know. Some guy. Maintenance staff, I think."

She pushed against his chest. He didn't budge and inch. "Let me go."

A work-roughened finger beneath her chin urged her to look up. "No. I don't care who sees us, Clare."

"What if he recognized me?"

"So what if he does? Are you embarrassed to be seen with me?"

She shook her head. "No. Heaven's no. Why would you think that? I just don't want you to get in trouble with the team."

"Don't worry about me. There isn't anything anyone can do or say that will keep me away from you. Not after that kiss."

She groaned. Closing her eyes, she let her head fall back. It hit the solid wall behind her with a thud. "Antonio…."

"I like the way you say my name. Everyone calls me Tony, but there's something about the way you say my full name with your molasses thick southern drawl that makes me want to eat you up." His lips nibbled at her jaw then down the exposed column of her neck, leaving a trail of hot, wet brands in their wake.

Her knees shook, and her lady parts all but begged for his attention. As if he'd heard their silent pleas, his hands began to roam. Everywhere he touched—her hips, her waist, her ass, her breasts—flamed with need.

"We can't…."

"You're right," he whispered in her ear and then traced the shell of her ear with the tip of his tongue. "Not here."

CHAPTER FOUR

The restaurant was intimate and expensive. She had to admit the mood-lit, secluded booth provided them with the kind of privacy not available at a lesser price. She couldn't imagine having the kind of conversation they needed to have at some place with napkin holders on the table and high chairs in the aisle.

Antonio ordered wine without looking at the menu. Clare waited until the sommelier moved off to fetch Antonio's selection before she spoke.

"What's going on here, Antonio?"

He rested his forearms on the table and nudged the flickering candle in the center with his index finger. "We're getting to know each other."

Despite the carnal kiss at the stadium, she couldn't shake the feeling he was toying with her feelings. Lord help her if he was because she had gone from closet stalker fan to hopelessly infatuated—and possibly crazy in love—the moment his lips had touched hers. Not that he would ever know. Before her stupid heart got any more involved, she wanted to know what he was up to.

"And why do we need to do get to know each other?"

"Because I don't think I can keep my hands off you, and I want more than just sex." He flashed her a grin that made her pussy clench. "In the interest of full disclosure, I'm hoping there will be plenty of that, too."

The sommelier brought their wine. Antonio went through the approval process like a pro and sent the man away, explaining he preferred to pour it himself.

"I thought he'd never leave," he said as he filled their glasses with the expensive liquid.

"Look, Antonio, I don't understand what's going on. I'm not your type."

"Don't say that. I wouldn't be here with you, and I certainly wouldn't have kissed you like that, if you weren't my type. I knew from the moment I laid eyes on you at the fundraiser I had to have you. That's why I bid on all the things you did. At first, I just wanted to give you the things you liked then I realized everything you bid on was something for couples to do together, and I wanted to do them with you."

"I didn't mean to win any of the items I bid on. It's just what I do at those things." She pulled her wine glass close then pushed it away. Drinking wouldn't make her admission any less painful. "I can't afford any of the stuff they auction at those things, so I pick a theme and bid on items that fit in. Someone always outbids me, but at least I help to escalate the bidding."

"What was the theme for Jason's fundraiser?"

She changed her mind about the alcohol and took a sip of her wine. "Romantic Interlude," she said, half-hoping he wouldn't hear her words.

He smiled. "That fits. I won them all."

"That's nice." *Someone's going to get lucky.*

"Don't look that way, Clare." His voice had a hard edge to it, and she realized she was frowning. "I want you to do them with me. Every last one of them."

Oh.

"We can get to know each other better."

She stared at him. Her mind replayed the list of bid items. Some were innocent enough, but most were cozy, intimate things that could possibly—*would* probably—lead to even more intimate things.

"Will you enjoy them with me?"

She pointed a finger at her chest. "Me?"

"I understand if you don't want to. I promise we can keep it quiet if you don't want people to know you're seeing me."

"No! I mean…I just can't believe you really want to…with *me*."

"Let me prove it to you. Some of the out of town things will require planning, but others we can take advantage of now."

"Like what?" She couldn't believe she was actually considering his proposal.

"There's the spa thing, for one."

The bid item had been donated by a very exclusive local spa, and if she remembered correctly, it included several full-body treatments and a massage to be enjoyed as a couple. That would mean getting naked or mostly naked in the same room with Antonio.

"Um…."

"I could use a massage." His eyebrows danced.

She narrowed her eyes at him. "That's disgusting."

His laughter filled the room. Heads turned. Clare ducked.

"Hush," she hissed.

"I wasn't talking about right now, but I like the way your mind works."

Heat radiated from her cheeks. This would never work. She had to get away from him before she made a bigger fool of herself. She reached for her purse.

"Don't go, Clare. Please." His pleading voice stopped her.

Go, her brain urged.

Stay, her body countered.

"At least have dinner with me. I promise to behave the rest of the evening."

Half of her wanted him to behave while the other half would give anything to have him misbehave—with her. She dropped her purse on the seat beside her.

"I'm sorry. I misunderstood."

"That's okay." He relaxed against the booth, slinging one arm across the back. "If I tell you something, do you promise not to run screaming out of the restaurant?"

"What?"

"Promise not to run?"

She crossed her fingers and toes. "I promise."

"I was thinking the same thing, but I didn't want to say it. When you read my thoughts, I couldn't help but laugh. No one has ever done that before. Read my mind, I mean."

She tried to contain it, but it was a futile exercise. Laughter bubbled up and spilled over, uncontrollable. Tears coursed down her cheeks, and her side ached. She was so in trouble with this guy. There was not a single doubt in her mind. She was hopelessly in love with him. Just like she had known she would be if she ever had the chance to actually meet him.

He ordered for her while she used her napkin to dab at her eyes. Every time she looked his way, she burst out in another bout of laughter. It was absurd, but he'd smile knowingly at her and happiness tinged with wariness welled up and popped out in helpless waves.

"I'm sorry," she said when the waiter left with their order. "Oh, God. I have to get control here."

"No you don't. I feel the same way, Clare. Happy. Scared shitless." His face now was pensive and helped her sober up. "I want you so bad I can't think of anything else, and somehow, I know when I finally have you, a lifetime won't be enough."

She was stone cold sober.

"Spend time with me, Clare."

"I don't get it, Antonio. I'm no one special. I'm an organist. I'm—"

"You're beautiful," he supplied. "When I said I can hardly keep my hands off you, I meant it. I like a woman with curves. Making love to one of those stick thin women is about as much fun as sleeping with a two-by-four."

"Then you weren't making fun of me at the fundraiser?"

"Hell, no! I didn't even realize you thought that until it was too late. I can't tell you how sorry I am I gave you that impression."

"It wasn't your fault. I jumped to the wrong conclusion." Her face flamed under his intense scrutiny.

"But you had reason to believe a man would treat you that way, didn't you?"

Oh, yeah. Lots of reasons. Her teenage years had been nothing but hell—moving from city to city, changing schools, and never being accepted by the popular crowd because she didn't fit into the ultra-skinny mold. And there wasn't anything on the planet more brutal than a woman who hated other women. "I don't want to talk about it. Let's just say you're right and forget about it, okay?"

"I won't forget it, but you don't have to tell me right now. Maybe one day you'll feel like you can talk about it with me. For the record, if I ever find out who made you feel that way, they better stay the hell away, or I'll make them sorry they were born."

CHAPTER FIVE

She had officially lost her mind. That's all there was to it. Why else would she be meeting Antonio downtown to help him look for a place to live?

He needed a friend in Dallas. With her, he could have a woman's companionship and not feel threatened in any way. Despite his protests otherwise over dinner the other night, she couldn't seriously expect a man like Antonio to fall for her, and he knew she knew. In his eyes, she was safe. No play at that base. He'd gone to more trouble than necessary to insure her company until he settled in and made some new friends.

All his seductive talk had been just that—talk.

Clare circled the block, looking for the entrance to the hotel's parking garage. She spied the opening she needed, but a quick glance over her shoulder confirmed she would have to make the block again before she could get into the correct lane to turn in. She mumbled a curse.

Boy, would Antonio be surprised if he knew how unsafe she actually was. Ever since her days at Julliard, she had harbored a crush on him. He'd been a rookie with the Marauders then. She had pulled every familial string she could to get tickets to the games as often as possible. It had been easy to get them when the Mustangs were in town, but her uncle had only been able to do so much the rest of the season. Their connections, plus a lot of scrimping and saving on her part, got her into the stadium a few times each year. All so she could drool over Antonio Ramirez. And dream. Or rather, fantasize. Dreams were for girls. Her fantasies were those of a red-blooded, fully hormonal woman.

It hadn't been until years later she'd overheard a conversation and glimpsed the small, gold charm with the jeweled bases. What Jessica had done to earn it had been shocking, and the bitch delighted in reminding Clare every time she had a chance that Clare wasn't pretty enough to play *The Game*.

She almost hated Antonio for making her think, even for one short afternoon, they could be any more than friends or that she might one day earn a Bases Loaded charm of her own.

Two more trips around the block got her into the parking garage, and a few minutes later, she searched for Antonio in the hotel's expansive lobby. As a sought after free agent, he had pretty much written his own ticket, signing a gazillion million dollar, multi-year contract with the Mustangs. He could easily afford the opulence of a five star hotel while he settled into his new life in Texas.

Scanning the lobby, she felt out of place in jeans and the soft blouse that had been one of her favorites for a number of years. She at least expected to see a few tourists with kids, but everyone wore business suits, men and women alike. She caught sight of a pair of sneaker-clad feet across the room and felt marginally better until the body attached to the feet came into view.

Damn. Antonio strode toward her like a jungle animal that had just spotted dinner. Heads turned when he walked by. The man carried himself with an air of confidence that quietly stated clothes didn't make the man. She would have wagered not a soul in the place noticed what he was wearing.

Her heart did a somersault then lodged itself in her throat.

Confident strides brought him closer. His gaze stripped her bare long before he came to a stop in front of her.

"Babe," was all he said before he wrapped one arm around her waist, commandeered her cranium with the other, and insinuated one thick thigh between her legs. He hauled her up against him, and before her brain could comprehend what was happening, he kissed her.

Lips. Tongue. Teeth. He devoured her right there in the hotel lobby as if he'd snatched an appetizer off a passing plate.

When he finally broke the kiss, they were both gasping for air. Clare disentangled her fingers from his hair—too dazed to consider how they'd become tangled there in the first place.

"I missed you," he said, allowing her a little space, but still holding her close.

"Antonio…." She glanced around the room. A few people stared at them. A few more tried to look like they weren't watching two adults making out in public, but most apparently hadn't found the encounter remarkable at all and had gone on with their business.

"Did I tell you how much I like to hear you say my name?"

"Yes, you did," she said, returning her gaze to his.

He smiled, and her knees turned to jelly.

"Whoa, there." The muscles in his arm tightened against the small of her back, supporting her. "Are you okay?"

She pushed against his chest. "I'm fine. Really."

His fingers dug into the soft flesh at her waist.

"Antonio," she warned.

He loosened his hold on her slightly, and she managed to create an inch or so of space between them.

"I was worried about you earlier. I thought you might have changed your mind about helping me."

She explained her reason for being late and secretly vowed never to be on time if being late would get her kissed like that. "I don't know why you're here. Downtown, I mean. Doesn't the traffic make you crazy?"

"Babe, I'm from New York. This is nothing."

He allowed her a little more distance, and she took advantage, stepping away from him.

She adjusted her purse strap on her shoulder. "Shouldn't we be going?"

"I'd rather take you up to my suite and forget the whole apartment hunting thing."

But he wouldn't. She knew that, even if her heart did do another acrobatic move at the thought of mattress aerobics with him. "You can't live in a hotel forever, Antonio. You have a six-year contract."

"Okay. You convinced me. Let's get this over with." He grabbed her around the waist again, and they walked out hip-to-hip, despite her pleas for him to let her go.

The realtor met them at the first high-rise, where she led them through a penthouse apartment that had recently become available. The place had about as much appeal as an empty cracker box, and Clare said so.

"It's not you, Antonio."

"Why not? It's big." He strode over to the floor to ceiling windows. "There's a view, and the building has security. What's wrong with it?"

What wasn't wrong with it? "It's cold," Clare countered. "Even if you filled the place with warm colors and furnishings, it would still be cold."

He shrugged and asked to see what else the realtor had. Clare shot down two more apartments before they called it quits for the day.

In the cab on the way back to his hotel, Antonio said, "Tell me what kind of place you think I should buy, since I clearly don't have a clue what kind of living space I need."

"Are you mad at me?"

"No, just frustrated. I thought you would like all of those places, but you hated them."

"I did. But if you liked them, then choose one. You're the one who's going to have to live in it. Not me."

He had draped his arm over the back of the seat and allowed it to drop to her shoulder. With little effort, he slid her across the seat toward him. "Describe your perfect house."

"That's easy. It's Georgian. Big, but cozy, with hardwood floors and high ceilings. Fireplaces in all the key rooms, living room, den, dining room, bedrooms. Maybe even one in the kitchen. It has a large yard dotted with hardwood trees that light up like marquees in the fall. It's on a quiet street where kids can ride bicycles. It's old, but not rundown old. It has history, if you know what I mean."

"You've given it a lot of thought."

"Every little girl has a dream house, a dream prince, and a dream wedding."

"And where is this dream house?"

The cab stopped in front of his hotel. A liveried attendant opened her door and waited. "I have no idea, but I can tell you this—it isn't downtown."

"Let me buy you dinner. It's the least I can do for dragging you all over the place today."

Clare stopped in the lobby and turned to him. "I appreciate the offer, Antonio, but no. I need to get home. Things to do."

He walked with her to the parking garage despite her insistence she didn't need an escort. "I know you don't, but humor me. I like spending time with you."

She stopped at her car, fished a set of keys from her purse. He stood by while she unlocked the door. Just before she ducked into the driver's seat, he caught her by the elbow and pulled her against him.

Her mouth gaped in surprise. He swooped in to steal another kiss. It seemed the only way he would get to taste her was to catch her with her defenses down. So far, the plan was working out well. He'd caught her off-guard three times, and every time, she'd tensed then melted against him.

He savored her unique flavor combined with a hint of the coffee the realtor had insisted on purchasing for them. Careful not to let his hands roam places they weren't invited, he kept one on her elbow and carefully slid the other to the base of her skull. The fall of silken hair over the back of his hand conjured thoughts he was sure she would deem inappropriate if she were apprised of them.

Tires screeched, reminding him of where they were. They broke apart.

"I've got to go," she said.

He loved the breathless quality of her voice. She might be holding him at a distance, but she wasn't unaffected. Patience was called for.

He watched her car until it disappeared up the ramp toward the exit. The ache in his groin was something he was getting way too familiar with. It had been an almost constant companion since she walked into that ballroom, and his life.

When he signed the contract with the Mustangs, he hadn't given much thought to where he would live. He'd grown up on

Bases Loaded

Long Island and spent a sizeable chunk of his first Major League signing bonus on his Manhattan apartment. He liked living there—in the heart of the city. And everyone he knew had said his apartment was nice. But then, no one's opinion had mattered but his. Now that he'd met Clare, he wanted a place she would be comfortable with, and that clearly wasn't anything in downtown Dallas.

He took the elevator to the thirty-fourth floor and entered his suite. He tossed his keys on the nearest hard surface and raided the mini bar. After the roller coaster of the last few hours, he needed a good stiff drink.

It hadn't occurred to him Clare wouldn't like a downtown apartment. In fact, he had done a lot of picturing the two of them together, but his imagination had only gone as far as the bedroom. And for the life of him, he couldn't recall a single detail of the room except it had a big bed and they used every inch of its surface. He'd never gotten past that in his Clare-and-Tony-together thoughts. It didn't matter to him where they lived, but it mattered to her. He needed to look deeper.

What had she said about the three places they had looked at? *It looks cold. This one has no soul. It's okay, but I just don't see you living here. This is a pop hit, and you're more of a classic.*

No one had ever compared him to a classic. No one but Clare. He couldn't explain what the comment meant to him, but he did know he wanted to do everything in his power to live up to the man she thought him to be.

He closed his eyes, remembering Clare standing in the middle of the first apartment they had seen. She had nailed it. The place was cold and lifeless, and even though she was as hot as they came, her vibrant heat hadn't touched the austerity of the room. Now that he had stepped away, he could see what she saw. She would hate his Manhattan apartment. It was all glass and chrome and cold stone floors—all the things Clare said were not him, and he knew for certain weren't her style.

Maybe he would put it on the market, furniture and all. That way he could start over completely in Dallas. He'd find a place that suited both him and Clare.

He mulled that over for a few minutes. Yeah, it was time to make changes in his life. He hadn't lied to Doyle Walker. He *had* actively sought out the Mustangs when his contract with the

Marauders expired. He loved New York, but he'd always liked it when the Marauders played in Dallas. There was something about the city that appealed to him. It could be the slower lifestyle or the more hospitable climate. Or maybe he'd sensed Clare was near.

He needed to leave more than New York behind. It was time to relinquish his spot in Bases Loaded to someone else. The club existed in the shadows of the Major League. The brainchild of some players with giant egos and even bigger libidos, it wasn't for everyone. Most of the membership hailed from East Coast teams, but thanks to trades, there were members on just about every team. As far as he knew, he was the only one on the Mustangs, but perhaps not the first to wear the red and blue uniform.

Sworn to secrecy, the women who played the game successfully earned a clit piercing along with a gem and diamond studded charm. He hated that every time he took Clare in his arms, he thought about how beautiful she would look running the bases.

Clare would probably club him over the head if he suggested she any such thing. She wasn't the kind of woman to do something like that, and he damned sure wasn't going to corrupt her by suggesting she play. He would not project his depravity on her.

But that didn't keep him from imagining how the tiny charm would look dangling from her clit.

Shit.

He shifted to relieve the pressure behind his fly. If this kept up, his cock would have a permanent indentation of his zipper along the length of it.

He *would not* invite Clare to run the bases. He wasn't even going to tell her about the club. Thankfully, the tattoo on his ass was easily explained away as a tribute to his baseball playing days. She need never know the truth of it, even if he did manage to get close enough for her to see his butt. Maybe when they were tottering around the nursing home together in about fifty years, he would tell her what it really meant. Perhaps they could laugh about it then.

He snagged a soda from the mini-bar and set his laptop on the desk near the window. He logged onto the real estate website and plugged *Georgian* and *big yard* into the search engine.

Clare slipped into her comfy sweats and huddled under the throw she kept on the sofa. She wasn't really cold, but after spending the afternoon with Antonio, she wanted to hide from the world. What had come over her? What kind of alien had taken possession of her brain to make her blurt out her house fantasy?

He must think she was totally insane. And really, she'd opened her mouth and shot down every apartment they had looked at—all because she had some fantastical image of the man in her head. Maybe he liked all those ultra-modern designs. He probably did. That's why the realtor had to show them all those places. They'd been what he had asked to see. He'd probably be the proud owner of one of those apartments right now if he hadn't asked her along.

She pulled the fuzzy throw over her head and groaned.

Well. That was that. He wouldn't call again. He probably ran up to his suite and called the realtor as soon as he saw Clare's taillights leave the garage. It wasn't any of her business if he wasted his money on a place that was all wrong for him. It wasn't like she would ever see it anyway.

She groaned again and popped her head out from under her makeshift tent. Her obsessing over Antonio needed to stop. Ever since the fundraiser, all she did was fantasize about him in between bouts of hating him for making her feel so many different emotions.

The red-blooded woman in her wanted to believe he found her attractive, but the insecure girl in her had more doubts than the Mustangs had wins last season. Still…he had kissed her three times. Was that considered first base? It certainly was in her book, especially the way Antonio kissed.

If she never had a moment alone with the man again, she could live off the memories of those kisses and everything she'd felt when he held her in his arms. She had never experienced anything as exhilarating, as arousing. His body was hard all over, and she had sensed his strength. It was as if he knew he could hurt her and took care not to. Maybe that accounted for the odd sense of safety she felt when she was with him. Maybe that was why she'd told him about her auction fantasies and her perfect house fantasy.

Thank God, he hadn't asked her about her perfect man fantasy because she probably would have blurted out that *he* was the perfect man she fantasized about.

Okay, so she did believe him when he'd said he liked her body. Maybe a little. Both times he kissed her, he had held her close enough to notice his arousal. Maybe he *was* attracted to her. It wasn't out of the realm of possibility. She wasn't a total dog. She had been in a few relationships, and a couple of those resulted in trips to the bedroom. But none had lasted long after Mr. Wrong had gotten what he wanted from her. After Mr. Wrong number two, another professor at the local college where she taught music theory, she had decided platonic relationships were the way to go. She couldn't get her heart handed to her on a platter if she kept her clothes on. Removing her clothes stripped more than her body, it stripped her soul bare, and the only thing worse than finding out a man didn't want her body was finding out he didn't want her soul either.

Not that Antonio was going to call again, but she'd do well to stay at home if he did. She'd already shown him too much of herself, inside and out.

CHAPTER SIX

Clare parked her car in front of the exclusive spa. Indecision was her middle name today. She almost didn't get out of bed. Then she almost called Antonio to cancel. Then she almost didn't dress for the occasion. Then she almost didn't leave the house. On the drive across town, she almost turned around and went back home. Twice.

The place oozed opulence—even from the outside. She ran a hand over the black slacks she had finally decided on. Not that it mattered what she wore. If she went inside, she wouldn't be wearing them for long. This auction item was for a couples massage which meant being naked in the same room with Antonio Ramirez with nothing but a sheet to hide behind.

Her skin tingled just thinking about it. This was the stuff of her fantasies, but now the reality of it was on the other side of those massive carved wood doors, everything looked a whole lot different. She chewed her bottom lip and stared at the doors, trying to work up the nerve to get out of the car.

One step at a time. She closed her eyes and held the steering wheel in a death grip. A knock sounded on the window beside her, and her heart leapt into overdrive. She let out a squeak that should have been a scream but didn't quite make it.

Oh, shit. Antonio. With one hand braced on the top of her car, he leaned down to peer through the window at her. Her hand trembled as she fingered the button to lower the glass.

"Hi," he said.

"Hi." She mustered what she hoped was a smile.

"Right on time. I like that." He reached for the door handle and tugged, but the automatic lock was still engaged.

"Sorry." Clare powered the window back up and removed the key from the ignition. The number of possible escape scenarios had just dwindled to zero unless she concocted a sudden illness. It wouldn't be much of a stretch. Her stomach felt like gangs of butterflies were having a turf war inside, and imagining Antonio naked beneath a sheet had warmed her skin enough to perhaps convince an EMT she had a raging fever.

She reached for her purse with one hand and pushed the unlock button with the other. Antonio held the door open for her, stepping back so she could exit the car.

"Were you waiting for me?" he asked.

"Uh…. No. I mean…."

"You were deciding if you were going to go inside."

No point in denying it. He'd caught her. "Yes."

She slumped against the car. He stood less than a foot from her, close enough she could smell his aftershave. Masculinity shimmered off him like some kind of testosterone aura. It made it darned hard to think. "I…this…."

He closed the distance between them, pinning her back against the car door. His hands came to rest on her hips, holding her in a soft caress. "We'll have separate tables. No touching. No peeking. I promise."

His smile was genuine and disarming. She opened her mouth to speak, but he held up his hand, cutting off her protest.

"Just let me lie beside you for an hour or so. That's all I ask." *For now* hung in the air like a flashing neon sign.

"You won't look?"

"I'll make a deal with you. I won't peek unless you do. That puts it entirely in your hands. If you peek at me, I get a peek at you. If you don't, I don't. Think you can handle that?"

No. Not at all. She was absolutely dying to see every naked inch of Antonio, and if truth be told, she had spent considerable time in the last few days imagining ways to accomplish it without him knowing. If the rumors were true, he had a certain tattoo somewhere on his body, and today's massage was most likely the only opportunity she would ever have to see it—if it really existed.

"How will you know if I sneak a peek?" As soon as the question left her lips, she recognized it for the admission it was.

His fingers dug into her hips, and a sound resembling a growl rumbled in his chest. "I'll know, Clare. Trust me, I'm aware of every move you make."

She didn't know what to say to that statement, so she kept quiet.

"Is it a deal?" he asked.

"I won't peek," she said. *Liar.*

He wrapped an arm around her waist, pulled her to his side, and ushered her toward the doors of doom.

Since this was a couples session, and the staff assumed she and Antonio were a couple in the most intimate sense of the word—why else would they have booked such a session? She eyed the cozy suite that would be theirs for the next hour and a half. A fire flickered in the gas fireplace, casting a golden glow over the dimly lit room. If she hadn't driven to the spa herself, she might have thought she'd been spirited away to an opulent mountain retreat. Two massage tables, draped in snow-white linens, occupied half the room. The other half held a plush seating group, inviting the room's occupants to linger. A bottle of champagne chilling in a crystal ice bucket flanked by gold-rimmed flutes sat on the coffee table.

"You'll find everything you need over there," the spa attendant said, gesturing toward the massage tables. "Feel free to use the terrycloth robes. Or not. It's up to you. When you're ready, ring the bell—" She indicated a call button within reach of one of the tables. "—and your attendants will join you."

Antonio thanked the woman, shutting the door behind her. He turned to Clare. "What do you think?"

"It's even more beautiful than I imagined."

He wrapped his arms around her from behind, nestling her snug against his hard body. His chin rested against her temple. The intimacy of the gesture warmed her. For a split-second, she allowed herself to imagine he wanted her the way she wanted him.

"I'm glad you like it," he said.

"I've never had a massage," she confessed.

"Then you're in for a treat, though I have to admit I'm already jealous of whoever gets to put their hands on you." His lips brushed the shell of her ear, sending a tingle all the way to her toes. "I wish it was going to be me."

God, she wished it was, too, but it wasn't going to happen. She cringed inside, imagining his disappointment if he ever saw her naked. He might claim to like curves, but one look at her body and he'd be shopping for two-by-four's again. What did it matter if he had the tattoo? It wasn't like he would ever…with *her*.

She gave herself a mental shake and tried to get the conversation back on track. "So, what do we do now?"

Extricating herself from his embrace, she sat on the plush couch and ran her hand over the luxurious upholstery.

"Champagne?" he said. "Then I'll let you go first in the changing room. You can get situated while I get out of my clothes. How does that sound?"

"Fine."

As he handed the glass to her, their fingers brushed. The instant heat transfer shot through her body like a flash fire. She brought the flute to her lips and sipped. The crisp, cold liquid on her tongue was a shock to her system.

She took another fortifying sip. Cold courage. Straight from a bottle. Resisting the urge to drain her glass, she placed it carefully on the table.

"Something wrong?"

"No. I'm not used to drinking in the middle of the day, that's all."

"Me either, but if ever there was an event that called for champagne, this is it."

The alcohol already fuzzed her brain. She knit her brows in confusion.

Antonio smiled over the rim of his glass. "You. Me. Naked together. That's cause for celebration in my book."

Her entire body heated with a blush. Before the liquid courage wore off, she stood. "I'll get changed now." She edged past him to the dressing room door. "Remember your promise."

He saluted her with his flute. "No peeking. I promise." The

twinkle in his eyes and the tilt of his lips told her it was a hollow promise, though she had no intention of allowing him a chance to break it.

With an extra tug at the knotted belt on her terrycloth robe, Clare stepped out of the changing room. Antonio stood. Wide-eyed, his gaze raked her from head to toe, stopping at the triangle of exposed skin on her chest. He licked his lips, and his nostrils flared like a predator scenting its prey. Instinctively, she grabbed the lapels of her robe and clutched them tight, but it was too late. The fire blazing in his eyes sparked an answering inferno low in her belly, and for a brief moment, she forgot her physical shortcomings. She felt beautiful. Desired.

Her body hummed, and her toes curled in the plush carpet in a classic fight or flight response. The fight would be epic if she ever found the nerve to let him get close enough.

"Your turn," she said, forcing her feet to move toward the massage tables. Every step felt as if she fought an invisible force field, pulling her back into his space. Only her knowledge that having sex with her one time would be enough for him kept her going.

"I'll be right back," he said.

Anchored by nerves, she remained still, following his movements with her hearing alone. There was the distinct click of crystal on wood then the hard jolt of the changing room door cutting off a muffled curse. She looked over her shoulder to make sure he was gone before loosening the tie at her waist and wrapping a folded sheet around her body.

She felt awkward lying on the massage table like a beached whale, but it was too late to turn back. She'd swam into these waters, and she would see it through—no matter what. Behind her, a door opened. Tiny pinpricks of heat traveled from the soles of her feet to the top of her head. She held herself perfectly still, hardly daring to breathe as Antonio crossed the room.

He did his best to entice her to peek—wiggling and flopping around, cursing as he did so. He was known on the baseball field for pushing the limits, so she should have expected this type of behavior. She bit her lip to keep from smiling and kept her face buried in the oval cutout in the table. Patience would win this game. If she pretended disinterest, he would eventually drop his guard, allowing her the chance to check out portions of his body without him knowing. It was a shame the rumors didn't specify where exactly the tattoo would be—if it existed at all.

He summoned the attendants who arrived on quiet feet and set to work.

Antonio groaned and moaned and talked. All. The. Freaking. Time.

"Ahh, that feels good."

"Yeah, right there. Oh, man."

"What kind of oil is that? It smells good." When his masseuse named the product, Antonio said, "Clare, honey, we've got to get some of this stuff." Then he groaned again.

Why couldn't he just drift off to sleep or something, so she could look all she wanted?

After a while, she tuned him out and concentrated on the hands gliding across her skin. The attendants had introduced themselves when they came in. The woman, Serena, was there for Antonio. Clare's attendant was a guy named Raul, who, it turned out, had the hands of a god. At first, she'd been self-conscious about having a strange man touch her, but between Antonio's incessant noise and the way Raul systematically reduced her muscles to putty, she quickly forgot all about being naked in a room with three other people.

Two of those people were professionals and had been paid handsomely to keep their opinions to themselves. Antonio, however, couldn't and wouldn't keep his mouth shut.

"Feeling good, Clare?" he asked right after Raul coaxed a soft moan out of her by working some kind of magic on the small of her back.

"Mmm…."

"It sounds like you are."

"Go away, Antonio."

His laugh sounded like he was short on air. "That good, huh?"

"Shh. Raul has magic hands."

The sound that came from the other table wasn't laughter. It sounded more like Serena was strangling Antonio with a towel. A flash of lightning shot through Clare. Antonio didn't like hearing about her massage. Maybe he was jealous.

Bases Loaded

"Do that again, Raul." She tested her theory, purring the words. "It feels *so* good."

Another strangled sound came from the other table, along with a lot of shifting around.

She actually enjoyed herself. Teasing Antonio was fun.

Raul pulled the sheet up to her armpits and asked her to roll onto her back. Who knew it took so many muscle groups just to turn over? She moaned.

Antonio growled.

Raul went to work on her arms, stretching them above her head, pulling and kneading until she couldn't have lifted a slip of paper if her life depended on it. Then he moved to her legs, rolling her calf muscles, moving up slowly to her thighs. It was Heaven.

He tugged on her right thigh, and she realized he needed better access to the inside of her legs. "Open for me," he said.

It happened fast. One second, Raul's talented fingers were liquefying her leg muscles, and the next—they were not. Her eyes flew open.

Serena gasped and backed into a rolling cart. Bottles and pots of cream crashed to the floor. Clare sat up, clutching the sheet to her breasts.

Across the room, Antonio pinned Raul to the wall with one hand at his neck while his other hand held a sheet at his waist. The white fabric hung between the two men, presumably covering Antonio's junk, but left his oiled back and ass exposed.

And there it was. A neatly penned baseball diamond graced his left buttock. Each base was filled with a different color, and below home plate were the words "Bases Loaded." Just exactly like the tiny charm Jessica had worn on her clit.

Bases Loaded is real. The club wasn't an urban legend, after all.

Her head spun, remembering what Jessica said she had done to earn the charm. *Oh, Lord.*

She swallowed hard, imagining herself at the center of all that masculine attention. She only vaguely understood how it could even be possible, but her body hungered for the experience.

Antonio's voice cut through her lust-fogged brain. "Keep your hands off her."

The masseur's face was purple, but he gasped out his agreement while he clutched at Antonio's wrist. "I won't touch her. I swear!"

"Antonio!" Clare yelled. "Let him go!" She swung her feet off the table and wrapped the sheet around her body, toga-style.

Raul's feet hit the floor. He shot an apologetic look at Clare and ran out of the room as if the hounds of hell were after him. Antonio turned. From the look on his face, Raul had been wise to escape while he could. Her partner was seriously pissed. His oiled chest rose and fell with each short, rapid breath. Anger made his olive complexion even darker, and something wild dwelled in the depth of his eyes.

His gaze landed on her—swept her from head to toe in carnal assessment. Her nipples tightened and heat gathered in her abdomen. It was mating time at the OK Corral, and she was the hobbled mare. Her knees rattled. She opened her mouth to warn him off, but a squeak from her right drew his attention away. He shot a look at Serena who appeared ready to faint. Huddled between the two massage tables, she clutched a towel to her throat as if that would protect her in some way.

"Leave us alone," he growled.

Serena glanced her way.

Clare nodded at the frightened masseuse. "Go ahead. I'll be fine." *I hope.*

She'd never witnessed a violent act up close and personal before, but behind the violence in Antonio's actions lurked something even more frightening. Lust. No one had ever looked at her with the same intensity she'd seen in his eyes when she'd ordered him to let Raul go.

The woman wasted no time worrying about Clare's well being. She scooted sideways past Antonio and fled the scene.

"What was that all about?" Clare asked as soon as the door clicked shut.

"Are you kidding me?" Antonio raked his hair back from his face with the same hand he'd used to control Raul. "He was *touching* you."

His chest heaved with exertion. Despite the sheet he still held over his groin, his nakedness made it hard for her to think straight.

"Yes, he was. He had been for the last forty minutes or so.

It may have been my first massage, but I know touching is part of the process."

Antonio blinked. "Yeah, well, he had no business telling you to...to.... It wasn't *that* kind of massage."

"He was massaging my legs." Which she suddenly realized were about to collapse. She reached for her robe and turned her back to him. "My legs were too close together." *That's what happens when you have fat thighs.* She slipped the borrowed garment on then allowed the sheet to drop to the floor. She tied the belt at her waist and made it to the loveseat against the far wall just as her knees gave way.

Antonio chose that moment to drop the sheet covering his crotch and reached for his robe. She allowed herself to check out the rest of him as he shrugged the terrycloth over his shoulders, pulled the front closed, and belted it in the most unselfconscious manner she'd ever seen. He was clearly comfortable in his body, and why wouldn't he be? He was beautiful—all hard, sculpted muscle from his broad shoulders to his slim hips and long legs. An athlete's body. Toned and honed to play the demanding outfielder's job.

Her gaze swept over the defined ridges of his abs and locked on his erect penis. Her mouth went dry.

"No one touches what's mine." His voice snapped her back to reality.

"Yours?" *Me?*

Antonio refilled their champagne glasses. She automatically took the one he thrust in her direction, being careful to avoid touching him.

He drained his glass and refilled it. "Mine, Clare."

It was easy to see the Italian blood he'd inherited from his mother when he was agitated. He stood like a Roman god, his feet braced apart, his spine straight. His eyes were fiery shards of obsidian. "I thought I could do this, but I can't. I want you, Clare. Now. Today. Tomorrow. Forever. No more massages. I fuckin' can't stand the thought of another man's hands on you."

So much for the Bases Loaded fantasy.

"And it's okay if another woman touches you?" she asked in an effort to mask her disappointment.

"That's different," he reasoned.

"I don't see how. You were doing an awful lot of moaning

and groaning over there. What exactly was Serena massaging?"

He stared at her. She'd gone too far. A man like Antonio wouldn't tolerate a woman being jealous where he was concerned.

"You're jealous." It wasn't a question.

"Maybe."

His sensual lips curved into a broad smile. "You are." He nodded and sipped his champagne. "I like it."

"What?" she gasped.

"I like it. No one's ever been jealous on my behalf before."

Clare set her glass down before she spilled it. "I wasn't jealous. I was pointing out that you seemed to be having a lot of fun over there."

A frown replaced his smile. "I was trying to distract you, so you could relax and enjoy the massage. Then you did, and it was all I could do to keep from leaping from my table to yours. Those sounds you make when it feels good…you were killing me, Clare. Raul had no business saying those words to you. I don't care what you think he was trying to accomplish. The man was hitting on you. That was the last straw."

"He wasn't—"

"He was hitting on you. Believe me, I know." His tone allowed no argument. He paced away then back again. "Look, I understand you don't think men find you attractive, but you couldn't be more wrong. Men lust after women like you."

"Oh yeah, that's why I have more dates than I can handle. I have so many I have to turn most of them away, or I'd never get to stay at home and wash my hair."

"You equate being attractive with having dates. That's where you're wrong. They don't ask you out because they know it would be the end of the road for them. No more sowing wild oats and all that shit. They'd be goners, and they know it. That's why they don't ask you out. But, you see, that's where I'm different. I told you I was scared shitless, but not because I think you're my forever, but because I'm afraid someone else might get to you before me."

She grabbed the champagne she'd abandoned and drained the glass.

"I want to spend time with you. I want to get to know you, and I want you to get to know me, too. And, fuck yeah, I'm going to be jealous and possessive. And as soon as you'll let me, I'm going to claim what's mine."

A knock sounded on the door. Antonio arched an eyebrow at her. She clutched the lapels of her robe tighter and nodded.

"Come in," he called out.

CHAPTER SEVEN

A man wearing a business suit complete with an understated tie cautiously opened the door. Stepping inside, he shut the door behind him.

"Sir, Miss." He nodded at them. "I'm Nathan James. This is my establishment. I'm so very sorry for what happened here." He shook his head and made a face as if he'd tasted something vile. "Raul has never done anything like that before. We've never had a complaint against him, and he's been in my employ for several years. Nevertheless, once is all it takes. He no longer works here. Please, accept my profound apologies."

"That was quick," Antonio said.

"Serena told me what Raul said to your...."

"Wife," Antonio supplied.

He shot her a look that said no argument would be tolerated. She decided to let it slide. Under the circumstances she'd rather they believe she was Antonio's wife than his...whatever.

"What he said to your wife," Mr. James continued. "Unacceptable. He clearly found your wife's charms irresistible, but that is no excuse. He didn't conduct himself in a professional manner, and anything less will not be tolerated in my place of business."

"I appreciate your position and your swift action regarding the matter. If you'll give us a few minutes to shower and dress," Antonio said, dismissing the business owner.

"Take your time. The suite is yours as long as you require it." Then he was gone, and she was alone with a smug looking Antonio.

"I told you he was hitting on you."

"That's absurd."

"You think so?" He parted his robe, allowing his cock to spring free. He wrapped his fist around it and stroked. "This is what you do to me, Clare. I want you every minute of every day. I think of you when I close my eyes at night and I wake up dreaming of sinking into you."

"Really?"

He sounded so sincere, and with the evidence plainly in front of her, she could almost believe it was true.

He tucked his erection under the flap of his robe in the same unselfconscious way he had earlier, as if his arousal was something he'd learned to live with. He reached for her hand. "Come here." One firm tug and she was on her feet following him across the room. "Let me show you what I see when I look at you."

He pushed the changing room door wide, so they were face-to-face with the full-length mirror on the back. There were two things she hated in this world—cameras and mirrors. They could be counted on to shatter any illusions one held about themselves, and the last thing she wanted to do was confront her ample shortcomings with The Sexiest Man Alive. Eyes lied. Reflections did not.

His strong arms bracketed her waist, anchoring her back to his front. The thick ridge of his arousal pressed against the small of her back. She tugged at his forearms in a futile effort to dislodge herself. He held her tighter and moved his lips against her ear.

"Look in the mirror, Clare."

Reluctantly, she raised her gaze. Her heart fluttered at the picture they made together. She looked almost small cradled against his much larger frame. Her ivory skin appeared pale in contrast to his darker bronze tones.

"You're breathtaking." His hand came up to trace the lines of her face. "You have the features of an angel." His thumb swept over her mouth, leaving a trail of fire. "Your lips would tempt a saint to sin. And your eyes…they're windows to your soul." His gaze met hers in the mirror. "Everything you feel shows in them. Right now, you're wary but excited. Aroused, perhaps."

"I'm not." Even she didn't believe her breathless lie.

"Ah, but you are." His fingers closed around her jaw then slid down to span her neck. "Your pulse is racing, and your eyes are dilated. You want me to touch you. Don't even try to tell me otherwise."

She wouldn't, couldn't.

"However, I will stop if you want me to. Say the word, Clare, and I'll let you go." He held her still for the space of a moment. "No protest?"

She shook her head because she was positive no sound would come out if she tried to speak.

"Good, then I'm going to touch you, look at you. I'm going to show you why I, and every other man on the planet, would want to be with you."

His hand at her throat slipped lower, past her clavicle, dipping into the V of her robe, coming to a stop just above the swell of her breasts. Sensations rippled across her skin, and her nipples tightened in anticipation of his touch. She grew lightheaded. Her body recognized the problem, and her lungs involuntarily filled. Her heart raced in response, sending oxygen rich blood to her brain.

A scrap of sanity wedged into her consciousness. Then he took her left breast in his hand, and she couldn't think of anything other than the sexiest man on the planet was touching *her*. It had to be a dream.

His fingers massaged the soft mound. He pinched her nipple, and a bolt of lightning shot straight to her womb.

No dream. Shocking reality.

"Let me see you." His warm breath caressed her ear.

She reached for the tie at her waist, but before she could loosen the simple knot, his fingers closed over hers, guiding her hands to her sides.

"No. Keep your hands right here until I tell you to move."

Clare watched in the mirror as he grasped the collar of her robe and gently peeled the garment over her shoulders, exposing her breasts to his heated gaze. Her nipples pebbled, and her breasts grew heavy.

He stood behind her, his hands on the bunched fabric at her elbows. "My God, Clare. You are…." He shook his head. "Beautiful. *Magnifica. Glorioso.*"

The blended romantic languages that were his heritage strummed at her heartstrings.

"The words aren't enough, bella."

She glanced at the reflection of her breasts then up to his face. His lips were parted, his eyes dilated and fixed on her chest. A fire burned in the dark orbs, tempting her to believe.

"They're just breasts," she asserted. *Maybe a little above average in size, but nothing special.*

"No." He shook his head then reached around her to cup each one in the palm of his hands. Heat seared through the delicate skin. He held her breasts as if they were precious possessions. "They're femininity. They're a symbol of womanhood. They're a wonder of nature—a God-given gift meant to entice and nurture."

She had never felt as cherished as she did in that moment. This gorgeous specimen of a man thought *she* was beautiful.

"Put your hands where mine are," he instructed, guiding them into place. "One day soon, I hope you'll offer your breasts to me, but for now, just hold them. I like to see them in your hands."

Holding her breasts felt awkward until she caught a glimpse of Antonio's rapt expression in the mirror. She'd hold them all day, every day, if he would continue to look at her with desire in his eyes. His hands fell to the tie at her waist, and his fingers slowly and expertly worked the knot loose. Her robe fell open, revealing her worst features. She closed her eyes. She couldn't bear to see the look of disgust on his face when he saw her round belly and plump thighs.

He splayed his hands across her abdomen then moved lower, trailing fire everywhere he touched.

"Open your eyes, Clare."

She shook her head and bit her lower lip. His thumbs brushed her mound, and his fingers rested on her upper thighs.

"Okay then. Let me tell you what I see."

She wanted to run, to tear herself out of his arms, and yank her robe closed. She wanted desperately to hide from Antonio, from the world, from herself. For a moment, she had believed she was beautiful, but he was asking too much of her. Hot tears formed behind her eyelids. The way he held her, his arms trapping her elbows where she had no choice but to cradle her own breasts, made it impossible to wipe the tears away. They slid from the corners of her eyes, and she added shame to her growing list of humiliations. Knowing he was a member of Bases Loaded seemed trivial now. No way would he and his friends want a cow like her.

"Please, let me go," she begged.

"Not until you open your eyes and hear me out."

"I can't," she whimpered.

His hands stroked her belly. "You can, and you will."

He continued to caress her. His roughened hands abraded her soft skin and made her weak with wanting him. His heat surrounded her like a warm blanket, enticing her to give in to his demands.

"I've never seen such beauty," he crooned, his voice stroking, arousing, as surely as his hands. "You're everything a woman is meant to be."

His hands skimmed her hips, down to her thighs, and up over her mound. "I'm just a mortal man, and your body calls to mine. You're Eve. A woman built for a man. Built to pleasure a man, to bear his children."

His fingers slipped between her feminine folds and stole the last shreds of her self-respect.

"Please," she begged, but for what, she didn't know. For more? Or for him to let her go?

"You have the body of a Madonna, and there isn't a man in the world who doesn't want to have that in his bed." His fingers played with her clit. He pressed his lips to her bare shoulder and plunged his middle finger inside her.

Her eyes popped open. The scene in the mirror made her knees buckle.

Antonio supported her effortlessly. He rocked his hips

against her buttocks making the hard ridge of his erection impossible to ignore. "Feel what you do to me, and to every red-blooded male who sees you. You're a desirable woman, Clare, and I want you more than I've ever wanted any woman."

She believed him, if only for that moment in time, because it suited her to. He nudged her feet farther apart and inserted a second finger into her slick channel.

"Let me give you pleasure," he pleaded unnecessarily.

She was past rational thought, past the ability to refuse him anything no matter what the cost later on. What he was doing to her went beyond every fantasy she had ever had about being with him, and there was no way she would end it now. She spread her legs and rocked against his palm.

"That's it, babe. Take what you want. Let it happen."

A third finger stretched her. She groaned and let her head fall against his shoulder in surrender. He pressed his lips to her neck, scraped his teeth across the vein pulsing there, and she shattered. Unintelligible sounds escaped her throat. Antonio murmured incomprehensible things in her ear while her body convulsed and poured liquid love over his hand. And through it all, he held her in the shelter of his arm wrapped around her waist, cloaking her with his heat and strength.

She slowly became aware of her surroundings and that his hand cupped her now, gently massaging the tender flesh between her legs. Embarrassment washed over her like a blazing sunset. She grabbed at his arms, trying to dislodge them only to have him tighten his grip.

"No. Let me hold you a minute longer, Clare."

She didn't dare look in the mirror, choosing to keep her eyes tightly shut, acquiescing to his demand because she had no choice. Her weak struggles were nothing compared to his strength.

"I'm truly humbled, bella. Thank you for letting me see you this way."

They stood there, silent but for their labored breathing, until her knees ceased to tremble and her skin became chilled. He eased the robe onto her shoulders and deftly retied the sash at her waist before letting his hands come to rest on her hips.

Braver now that she was covered, she raised her gaze once again to the mirror. He peered over her shoulder.

"I don't want you to doubt your beauty ever again," he said. "I wanted you the first moment I laid eyes on you, and I'm going to have you."

"Antonio…."

"Shh. No more protests. We'll take it slow. We won't do anything you don't want to do." He turned her to face him. "Say you'll spend time with me. Say you'll give us a chance."

He tugged her closer, and she shuffled her feet to stand between his. When his arms closed around her, she pressed her cheek to his chest. His heartbeat thumped out a steady, reassuring rhythm. Her hands came up to embrace him as naturally as if they did it every day. She took her first deep breath since Antonio appeared at her car window earlier in the day. Beneath his understated woodsy cologne, he smelled of what she supposed was pure testosterone. Saying no to him wasn't an option.

"Okay."

CHAPTER EIGHT

Two days had passed since their spa date, and Clare hadn't heard a word from Antonio until a few minutes ago. Why wouldn't he just leave her alone? She'd shown him more of herself, literally and figuratively, than she had any other man—ever. She'd shown him enough to send him running back to New York, she thought.

But he hadn't run. He was on his way up to her office. *Probably to say goodbye. Well, goodbye, yourself, Antonio Ramirez. Go find yourself a skinny-assed actress to play the part of your wife. I'm through playing your games.*

She shoved random clutter into her file drawer and silenced the metronome tick-tocking away on her desk. She never should have answered the call, but when his name appeared on the caller ID, she had practically gone into cardiac arrest. She'd been starved for the sound of his voice. Couldn't get the feel of his hands on her out of her head. Couldn't breathe without missing his scent.

She had just crammed the latest set of ungraded test papers into her briefcase when he filled her doorway. One look at him and she realized she wanted nothing more than to play every game in the book with him. If only he would ask.

Leaning against the jamb, his arms crossed over his chest and one knee bent, he looked like a billboard for sex. *Want sex? Call-800-Antonio.* Warmth flooded her system, and she swallowed hard.

"You done, babe?"

She nodded, not trusting her voice.

He straightened and took a step inside, closing the door behind him. He folded his hands behind his back and leaned his shoulders on the door. No one wore a T-shirt like Antonio Ramirez. The fabric wasn't tight, but it clung to his hard chest and abs. He shifted slightly, drawing her attention lower. Tight jeans left no doubt as to his state of arousal.

"I tried to stay away. I tried to tell myself you needed time, that I could wait to have you, but I was lying to myself." One hand moved to the doorknob. "I want you. Right here. Right now." His index finger and thumb closed over the lock mechanism. "If you feel the same way, say yes, and I'll lock the door."

Oh, God. Oh, God. Oh, God. Did she feel the same? Hell, yes! Her body throbbed with want and need.

Her mind raced through practicalities and details. *Here? What if a student comes by? The hell with office hours. Underwear? Not sexy, but decent.* She'd shaved and trimmed this morning—thank God. It was now or never. How many times would she get an offer like this? Never again, she was sure.

She clenched her hands into fists in her lap and squared her shoulders. So what if he only wanted a fuck buddy until he found someone more to his liking in Dallas? She'd have to be insane to turn down an opportunity like this.

"Yes," she said.

Before she finished the single syllable, he set the lock and pushed away from the door.

Her heart leapt into her throat. This had to be a dream. Maybe she'd nodded off and her subconscious was having a field day. She dug her fingernails into her palms until the pain told her she was awake.

His legs made short work of her small office. Her feet shuffled, spinning her chair to face him as he rounded her desk. Antonio leaned over and placed his hands on the arms of her chair, boxing her in and surrounding her with his now familiar scent. Desire pulsed through her system.

"Don't move," he said, sinking to his knees in front of her. He parted her legs and filled the space with his body. A shaft of late afternoon light crowned his head, burnishing his blue-black hair with gold highlights. "How much time do we have?"

Her brain scrambled for an answer. "Um…. My office hours are almost over, so…as long as we want?"

His smile almost melted her panties. "Oh, babe, you don't know how happy I am to hear that."

He cupped her knees then slid beneath her skirt, up to where her underwear banded her thighs. Clare stared at the bunched fabric covering his hands. *So close.*

"These have to go." His thumbs brushed cotton, found the elastic at the top, and tugged. Somehow, he lifted her and slipped the conservative garment to mid-thigh without her help. Then they landed on top of her desk in a twisted heap, and he was right back between her knees, only this time his fingers teased the short curls beneath her skirt.

"Your skin is silk. I could touch you all day, Clare, but I need to see you. The other day, at the spa…I can't get it out of my mind. Can I see you like that again?"

"Yes." A slight nod accompanied the whispered word.

"Unbutton your blouse for me, babe." His thumbs pressed between her legs then gently pulled, opening the top of her slit. If he could see through the skirt fabric, he would see her clit peeking out, begging for attention.

She lifted trembling hands to the top button on her blouse. Dazed, she did as he said. One by one, the buttons slid free. Cool air rushed in and caused her heated torso to break out in goose bumps. When she reached the last button above the skirt's waistband, he said, "Pull it open for me. Let me see."

His hands were still beneath her skirt, lazily toying with her folds, her clit, driving her insane while his gaze roamed every inch of exposed skin above. Her clit pulsed and throbbed.

"Now the bra. Push it up. We'll unhook it later."

She worked the fabric upward so her freed breasts were framed by her bra on the top, her open blouse on the sides and the waistband of her skirt below. Cool air hit her nipples, and they tightened into hard points. Heat crept from her chest to her face. She closed her eyes and bit her bottom lip while her hands gripped the chair arms as if she were about to be launched into space.

Lord, what was she doing? She'd had her share of horny professor fantasies, but never anything that came close to this. Antonio had trapped her within his force field, almost had her believing the things he said to her.

"You are so fucking beautiful, babe."

Pretty little lies.

Moving quickly, he took her right breast in his mouth, swirling the nipple with his tongue, suckling hard. She arched her back, encouraging him to take all he wanted. She held onto the chair in a death grip while he lavished attention on one breast, then the other. He seemed to know just what to do to make her lose her mind. She was wet, drenched between her legs. His fingers found her, plunged deep, retreated, and plunged again.

She writhed against his hand, sliding her ass across the seat toward him until she was about to fall off the edge. He groaned, sending a shiver of pure carnal lust from her breast to her pussy.

She ached for him. Needed more than fingers and a solo orgasm. She didn't think twice. She begged.

"Please."

He released her breast with an audible pop at the same time he withdrew his fingers leaving her empty and beyond desperate. Before she could muster a protest, he stood, lifting her as if she were a feather.

"Got to have you," he said.

Supporting her with one hand, he shoved her chair out of the way and lowered her to the floor.

God, the man could move fast. *Home plate to first base in three point nine seconds.* He stood, stripped off his jeans and boots, yanked his shirt over his head, and dropped to his knees between her splayed legs, wearing nothing but his socks and a pair of white cotton briefs. He worked her skirt up to her waist and sat back on his heels.

"I'm speechless," he said. "Tell me you want this."

He was speechless? He had a body every woman dreamed of—all hard planes and tight skin over defined muscles. Flat, dark nipples punctuated powerful pecs. His ribcage, wide at his chest, tapered to a slim waist and hips that would fit perfectly between her legs. She'd never wanted anything or anyone more in her life. He made her feel reckless and wanton, and the desire in his eyes made her feel beautiful. If he never looked at her that way again she would take this moment and cherish it forever.

"You better have a condom." She'd have to kill him if he didn't. Where that bit of sanity came from, she didn't know.

He reached for his jeans, fished a foil packet out of his pocket, and shoved his underwear down his thighs. His erection sprang free. Her mouth watered. He rolled the sheath on with the ease of a man who had plenty of experience and not an ounce of self-consciousness.

The moment of sanity was gone.

Clare lifted her hips in invitation.

She wanted him inside her.

Now.

His hands slipped beneath her thighs, lifting and spreading her wide open. Then he was there, pushing into her, stretching her, filling her. The angle allowed her to watch his cock disappear inside her, one thick, pulsing inch at a time. She forgot to breathe until he gave one final push and seated himself fully.

She arched her neck and drew in a deep breath. He lowered her ass to the floor, bracing above her, his forearms on either side of her head. His heat enveloped her and his weight anchored her to the solid reality of his presence. His gaze met hers, and her heart lodged in her throat. Fingers combed through her hair, fanning it out around her in a move so tender it almost broke her heart.

"God, babe. I…you…ah, shit! I've got to move." His voice was tight, revealing the energy he expended to take it slow.

She didn't want slow. She wanted hard and fast, and wild. She wanted *him*. But she couldn't say that, wouldn't wish this experience away so quickly. But if he didn't move soon, she would die.

"Do it, Antonio. Oh, God, do it."

Sex had never been like this. Ever. The man had super human control. He flexed his hips, eased out of her as if it was the last thing he wanted to do. Then he plunged back in, hard, the way she craved. She shifted her gaze to the ugly underside of her desk, counted fossilized wads of gum in an effort to keep from coming. It was too soon. Once he had his fat girl fuck, it would be all over, so she darned sure wasn't going to come after only a few strokes.

"I don't know how much longer I can hold out, babe."

Disappointment seared like a firebrand in her chest. She wanted to beg him to make it last, but one look at his face, and she couldn't stop her own release. Pinpricks of heat radiated out from her womb all the way to her toes and fingertips. Her body tensed then the rocket ship she'd been on since he stepped into her office exploded off the launch pad, taking her into an alternate universe full of streaking stars and exploding planets.

Antonio trapped her cries, swallowing them with a kiss that demanded she surrender everything. As if she had a choice.

She drifted back to earth in a haze. Tiny aftershocks rocked her pussy, reminding her of his solid presence still inside her.

"You slay me." He buried his face in the crook of her neck and, propped on his forearms, thrust hard into her.

This was the power she craved, had sensed he'd reined in, but with her, like this, he let go of the reins. It felt wonderful, primitive, exciting. Each stroke caused her ass to scoot on the carpet until her head bumped the caster on her desk chair.

He hissed through clenched teeth then cursed. "Ah, sweet, Jesus!"

He ground into her in short, hard thrusts, his cock pulsing with life. Clare dug her fingers into his ass cheeks and held on. If she could make him stay inside her even a few more seconds….

He collapsed on top of her, sucking in gulps of air. She didn't even care every breath he took smashed her body between his and the floor. So what if she had a few broken ribs? It was a small price to pay.

Holy shit. He was in trouble.

Tony tried to roll to his right, but there was no room between Clare and the desk. Taking care to bring her with him, he rolled to the other side. His back came to a stop up against the cold metal of a filing cabinet. His dick throbbed, still inside her.

After an orgasm that felt like his guts had been ripped out, he shouldn't be thinking about doing it again, but he was. He felt like a fucking superman. His heart raced like he'd downed a five-hour energy drink, and instead of getting soft, he was rising to the occasion—again.

He held her close, loving the feel of her skin against his. A man could get high on her natural scent mingled with the heady musk of sex. He glanced at the goddess lying on the floor next to him and silently cursed himself for an idiot.

He hadn't even bothered to take her clothes off. He was a world-class shit, coming into her office and taking her to the floor without so much as a sweet word. He'd make it up to her soon. Clearly, he wasn't going to get her out of his system—ever—so there would be plenty of time for sweet words and romance later. Right now, he had to have her, and he didn't give a rat's ass there wasn't a bed or so much as a soft surface in sight.

"We've got to get your clothes all the way off next time," he said.

"Next time?"

Was that surprise in her voice, or was she trying to be subtle about telling him there wouldn't be a next time? Good God, no. He rocked his hips against her. "Like, as soon as I can put on another condom, next time."

He held his breath, waiting for her answer.

"You want to do it again? Now?"

"Hell, yes." He rocked harder, so she couldn't mistake his state of arousal. "If you're okay with that. I'll take it slower, I promise."

"I thought…you would be done. Over it."

Damn. Was it that bad for her? He'd never had complaints before, but then again he wasn't in the habit of barging into women's offices and practically demanding sex either. It was a first for him, but she had seemed as eager as he was in the beginning. He needed to set her straight.

He reluctantly pulled out of her and sat up. While he peeled off and disposed of the spent condom, he said, "I'm far from done, and as for *over it*, I don't have a clue what you mean by that." He reached for his jeans and found the condom he kept in his wallet for emergencies. If this wasn't a five-alarm, call up the Reserves emergency, he didn't know what was. He rolled the condom on while he talked. "Babe, I want to be over you, under you, in you. Anything but *out* of you." He reached for her. "Here, let me help you out of those clothes then I think maybe we'll try the desk this time. My legs might hold out long enough to do it standing up."

He helped her to her feet. "Ever done it on a desk before?"

"Uh…no." She eyed the surface in question. "Really, Antonio, you don't have to do this."

She made no protest when he slid her blouse off her shoulders and tossed it on her chair. "You are so wrong about that. Not only do I *have* to do this, I *want* to do this." He flicked the back closure on her bra then spun her around to face him, yanking the garment off in the process. "I don't know what's going on in that pretty head of yours, but I can assure you, I need to be inside you in the next five seconds or I'm going to explode."

He pulled her close, and when she opened her mouth, probably to spout out some more nonsense, he covered it with his. Blood rushed south, making him painfully aroused. Kissing had never been like this before—exciting and *promising*. In fact, he rarely kissed the women he bedded, but he could kiss Clare all day long and never get enough of her taste. That was a conundrum he would have to sort out later. His first order of business was getting her skirt off.

It took some groping, but he found the zipper. More fancy handwork and the fastener slid down, allowing the skirt to fall to the floor. He broke the kiss and stepped back to get a better look at what he had unwrapped.

He gripped her waist and lifted her to sit on the desk. "I need you so damned bad." He stepped between her splayed legs, forcing them farther apart. "Tell me this is what you want, too, Clare. Tell me you want me."

She reached between them and wrapped her hand around his throbbing dick. *Dear God.* He was going to die, right here, right now. He sucked in a harsh breath and tightened every muscle in his body in an effort to keep from shoving her back and slamming into her, or at the very least from collapsing at her feet.

"I want you, Antonio."

He slid her ass, desk blotter and all, to the edge of the desk. "Guide me in."

Their heads bumped as they both bent to watch his cock slide in. His heart skipped a beat. Heaven. He had died and gone to Heaven. Nothing on Earth could feel so good, and Christ Almighty, nothing could be more beautiful than this woman. His dick slowly disappeared inside her. She gave a little gasp when his pubic bone met her clit.

"Okay?" he asked.

"Mmm."

She leaned back, placing her hands flat on the desk behind her. Her head fell between her shoulders, allowing him an unfettered view from her upturned chin all the way to her womanhood. Her breasts were twin mounds of erotic fantasy he was dying to explore thoroughly. He couldn't resist. He touched them, flattening them with his palms. The sound that escaped her lips came from deep inside and told him she liked what he was doing. Her nipples poked his palms. Rolling them between his thumbs and forefingers, he wrenched another strangled sound from her.

He bent and tasted her, sucking hard on one distended bud, keeping the other occupied with his fingers until she writhed beneath him, offering him everything and begging for more.

"I'm going to move now."

"Mmm."

Returning his hands to her hips to hold her steady, he pulled almost all the way out and slid back in as slow as his out of control libido would allow. A half-gasp, half-moan escaped her lips.

"Harder."

The word, directed at the ceiling, was more of a growl, but the request suited his needs. He pulled back again and this time, the slide back in was faster. Her breasts bobbed with the force of their bodies meeting.

Suddenly, Clare sat up. Her arms came around his neck, and she looked him straight in the eye. "Harder," she said. "I need it fast and hard, Antonio."

Who was this woman? He'd promised her slow and sweet, thinking that was what she needed, but looking into her eyes, he could see she meant what she said. He'd be damned if he wasn't the man to give her what she wanted.

"Hang on."

He slid out, flexed his hips, and drove into her hard. The metronome on the corner of her desk swung into action.

Tick. Tock. Tick. Tock.

Her head fell back again, her silken hair brushing the backs of his hands at her waist. The moan/groan that escaped her lips was unmistakable. He repeated the process, and her hands fell from his neck. She slipped to her back on the desk, wrapped her legs around his waist, and raised her arms over her head in complete surrender.

"Faster."

Hell, yeah! He dug his fingers into her hips and gave her what she asked for. Each hard thrust elicited a guttural response from her throat fueling his need even more. Her breasts bounced and jiggled. The metronome kept time. The roller coaster had come completely off the rails. He couldn't stop the wild ride even if the plunge at the end meant sure death.

"Sooo good," she moaned. She moved one hand to her clit and worked the small nub with her fingers. "Oh, God, Antonio."

Shit. He couldn't take his eyes off her hand, the way she touched herself, taking what she wanted, needed. "Babe. That's so fuckin' hot!"

He wouldn't last much longer, and he prayed she wouldn't either. It was a crapshoot as to which would go first, his legs or his cock. He prayed both would last long enough for her to find pleasure.

"Come for me."

He felt it begin—the way her body went rigid, the way her breath caught then exploded out of her on a long, drawn out, primal utterance. Her pussy clenched around his cock in an age-old rhythm that made him want to howl at the moon. He continued to plunge into her, savoring the tight fist drawing his manhood from him.

His climax began as a fireball in the small of his back then like an exploding sunspot, shot to his groin, down his legs, and out to the tips of his ears. His cock rivaled granite on the hardness scale. His release, when it came, was liquid fire. He pressed his palms flat on the desk and ground into her in short, powerful thrusts until his body ceased to spasm.

Heaven.

Clare moaned, and her legs fell away from his waist. *Christ.* He needed to take care of her. He opened his eyes. Her body was flushed with passion, her chest still heaving with exertion. Her hair fanned out over the desk, her head lolled to one side. There was a smile on her lips. God, he'd just fucked an angel.

"Tell me about Bases Loaded," she said.

Hell.

CHAPTER NINE

Tick. Tock.

Little hammers in his brain counted off the seconds to self-destruct.

What was that saying? The best defense is a good offense? *Please, God, let it be true.*

"You really want me to explain baseball to you? Right now?" He poured every ounce of incredulity he could muster into his response and waited. For the love of all that was holy, his dick still throbbed inside her. And he was supposed to think?

Clare used her elbows to prop up, looked at him with a smirk that said she wasn't the idiot he hoped she was at that moment, and said, "No. That isn't what I meant, and you know it. I want to know about the secret club you belong to."

Well, shit. There is no God.

"I don't have any idea what you're talking about," he hedged. He flexed his hips and his dick slid free. He peeled the slick condom off and tossed it into the wastebasket beside her desk. "You might want to take your own trash out today."

She glanced at the waste receptacle, and her face turned crimson, but only for a moment. She sat upright and looked him in the eye. "I saw the tattoo on your ass, Antonio."

Distraction and misdirection, the only tricks at his disposal, weren't going to work. Not with a woman as intelligent as Clare. Time for outright lying. "I play baseball for a living. What else would I have tattooed on my ass besides a baseball diamond?"

She raised her heels to the edge of the desk, exposing her glistening pussy to his view. He completely lost track of their conversation. Blood rushed south, and his cock responded to the stimulus. She kicked him in the stomach.

"Huh?"

"I *said*, open the drawer."

"Okay, okay." He stepped back and slid the center drawer open. He stared at the small, jeweled charm laying right there for anyone to see, and his erection withered instantly.

There were only a handful of those charms in existence, and she owned one.

It wasn't hers, he was certain of that. So…where did she get it? Did she know what it represented? If he lied to her now, would he ever see her again? If he told her the truth, would he ever see her again?

It was a cluster-fuck of epic proportions, and he was caught in the middle with no acceptable way out.

"What do you need out of here?"

"Don't be an idiot, Antonio." She scooted back on the desk and reached between her legs to retrieve the damning charm from her drawer. She used her heel to kick the drawer shut then dropped her thighs to the desktop.

"Tell me about Bases Loaded."

"It's a baseball term that means there's a man on all three bases." He couldn't take his eyes off the piece of jewelry lying in the palm of her hand. A ray of failing light shone through the window behind her desk and winked off the diamond chip representing home plate.

"We aren't talking about those square white things on a baseball field, are we?"

He couldn't speak past the lump of dread in his throat. He shook his head. Lying wouldn't work. She clearly knew more than she should already.

"That's what I thought." She curled her fingers inward and the damning charm disappeared inside her fist. Rocking side to side, she scooted to the edge of the desk and hopped off, forcing him to take another step back. She reached for her skirt and stepped into it. Tony followed her lead, sorting through their discarded clothes, passing hers to her and putting his back on. The small, overly warm room smelled of sex. The metronome on the corner of her desk had been set in motion sometime during their encounter. The steady clicking measured the human silence, broken only by the whisper of clothing and zippers. Muted voices and footsteps sounded in the hallway. Neither one of them had been especially reserved. Chances were someone had heard them. Clare might have some explaining to do.

How in hell he was going to explain Bases Loaded he didn't have a clue, but he needed to come up with something fast. Clare was buttoning her blouse, and she still had the charm clenched in her fist.

"Where did you get that?"

"The charm?" She arched an eyebrow at him then turned to straighten the things on her desk. She stopped the arm of the metronome with her index finger, silencing it. "I found it in an antique mall in Plano. I contacted the owner of the booth to see if she could tell me where she acquired it, but she couldn't remember. She said it was in a box of costume jewelry she picked up somewhere—probably at Canton Trade Days."

"What the hell is a Canton Trade Day?" He raised a hand to stop her from speaking. "Never mind. It doesn't matter. You obviously thought there was more to it than being an interesting piece of jewelry. So, why don't you tell me why you bought it?"

Clare leaned against her desk and crossed her arms over her midsection. "Sit down, Antonio. I want to tell you a story. Then you're going to tell me one, too."

Running sounded better, but that wasn't an option, so he sat in her desk chair and looked up at her. "I'm listening."

"I was at a fundraiser. One of those events like the one where we met. Lots of people were invited. Players past and present. Anyone who might have a few dollars to contribute to the cause. It boggles my mind why they always invite me, but they do, so I go. Anyway, I was in a stall in the ladies room and a group of women came in. I think they'd had too much champagne because their conversation was loud and inappropriate for…well, anywhere. I could see them through the crack around the stall door. I was just about to leave the stall when one of them hopped up on the counter and spread her legs. She wasn't wearing panties, but she *was* wearing one of these."

She opened her fist, and the charm winked in the harsh fluorescent overhead lights.

Shit.

"I was intrigued, so I kept quiet and listened. Needless to say, the explanation as to how she had *earned* it was informative. She was quite proud of it."

Clare nudged the tiny charm with the index finger of her other hand. "So…when I saw this one in the antique mall, I instantly knew what it was. I bought it, thinking if I was going to have one, that was the only way I would get it. Earning one wasn't an option."

"Damn right it's not an option." He placed a hand on her thigh and slid it beneath her skirt. "No one touches you but me."

If her metronome had still been going, it would have kept time with the one word mantra playing on an endless loop in his brain. *Liar. Liar. Liar.* He did want her all to himself, but damn it, he couldn't stop thinking about how lovely she would be—

He derailed that train of thought and tried to focus on what she was saying.

"I have to admit, at first I thought I was just something you wanted to check off your bucket list. Fuck a fatty. Some guys do. But after what we just did, I'm beginning to believe you really might find me attractive. But I'm a realist. I'm not the kind of woman men invite to do the things that woman described. I just want to know if what she said was true. So spill, Antonio. Tell me what she did to earn her charm."

He'd deal with the fact she thought she was fat another time. At the moment, he needed to get her mind off that charm. Once she knew the particulars, no way would she want to earn one.

"Fuck." He stood and paced the two steps to the bookcase against the far wall. He turned to face Clare. "She got fucked. A lot."

"How much is a lot?"

"The charm is only awarded for home runs. If they quit before, they get nothing."

"Go on," she said.

"It's the same as in baseball. You've got to have a man on all three bases at the same time. It's three men and one woman. Do I have to tell you what the bases are?"

"No. I think I can figure that out on my own."

"Okay then. The woman has to…well, the men…take turns on all the bases. If they all come, in all three bases, she's hit a home run, and she gets the charm."

She pursed those wicked lips that could drive him insane. While she thought about what he'd said, he imagined how those lips would look wrapped around his cock and almost missed her next question.

"Timeframe? A few days?"

"Huh? Oh, one night."

"Oh." A crease appeared between her eyebrows.

"Look, Clare…none of this matters because I'm through with the club, and you aren't going anywhere near it."

"How did the woman I saw get the charm…*there?*"

Tony grew hard remembering, imagining doing the same to Clare. "The charms are custom made in advance. The jewels on first and third represent the team colors of the guy who invited her. Second and home plate are diamonds. If she earns the charm, there's this doctor, a former girlfriend of one of the original club members. We meet at her office after hours, and she does the clit piercing."

She dangled the charm between her thumb and forefinger. "How many women have one of these?"

He speared his fingers through his hair. "How the fuck would I know?" he shouted, instantly hating himself for letting her get to him. He took a deep breath and let it out. He tried again. "I know of maybe a dozen. But it could be ten times that, for all I know."

"How many players are part of the club?"

"I don't know exactly. There are a few on each team, I think. People get traded, retire, get married. You know how it is."

"How many women have you invited to run the bases?"

"None."

She arched an eyebrow. "Seriously?"

"That's the truth, Clare." He'd never wanted to, until he met Clare.

"How many times have you played the game?"

"Fuck! I don't know. More than I can count."

"Did they all earn the charm?"

"No. It's not an easy thing to do."

She sighed. "I'm sure it's not." She opened her desk drawer and dropped the charm back into the small, curved indentation meant to hold paperclips. "I know if I earned one, it certainly wouldn't end up in a flea market or an antique store."

"Why in God's name would you want one?"

Clare shrugged. "I don't know. Maybe because it would mean three hunks found me attractive enough to do that with? But I'm sure that's never going to happen."

What the hell? He closed the distance between them and clasped her elbows in his hands. "Look at me, Clare." He waited until her gaze met his. "I don't know what else I can do to make you believe you're desirable. Hell, you're the most desirable woman I've ever seen. I've wanted you from the first moment I saw you at Holder's fundraiser, and I've wanted you every minute since. It makes me crazy to even think about another man looking at you and wanting you, but I know they do." *Yet, I can't stop imagining you on your knees, impaled....*

"Antonio," she protested. "You're in the tabloids and on the news all the time with skinny models and actresses."

"You. Are. Not. Fat. You aren't even close to being fat. You have curves. Women are supposed to have curves. Having sex with a stick thin woman is about as much fun as I imagine fucking a knothole in a piece of lumber would be." He held up his right index finger. "Once, Clare. I did it once, and swore I'd never do it again."

"But—"

"My publicist sets those dates up for me. It's all for publicity. They're her clients, too. They're seen with a baseball player, and we get our picture in the papers. TMZ talks about us. She gets modeling gigs, and I get endorsement contracts. That's all it is."

"Well, I can't compete with that."

"You aren't competing with anyone or anything. There's only you."

She dropped her gaze to the toes of their shoes.

"After what we did today, you still think I'm lying? Christ, Clare. What do I have to do to convince you you're a beautiful woman?"

"Invite me to Bases Loaded."

He backed away, coming to a stop when his heel hit the bookcase. He raised both palms in defense. "Oh no." He shook his head. "No way. No. Fucking. Way."

Her eyes shot daggers at him. "Why not?"

"Haven't you been listening? First off, you don't need other men—" He choked on the word. "—touching you in order to feel beautiful. I'm telling you, you're beautiful. A knock-out. And I fuckin' don't want other men so much as looking at you, much less…*fucking you from here to Kingdom Come.*" He closed his eyes and let his shoulders slump against the row of books behind him. *Tony, you're a lying, perverted ass.* "Ah, Clare, you're killing me here."

"Your friends wouldn't want me. That's why you won't invite me."

His eyes snapped open. He growled. Damn it. How could he make her believe him? "That. Is. Not. True. I won't invite you because they would be all over you like fucking horny rabbits. If I put your name up, there would be a fight over the two other spots on the team. And, if I let you do this, I'd have to kill two of my friends afterwards. Scratch that. I'd kill them before, just to keep them from seeing you naked."

"I want to do it."

He squeezed his eyes shut again and counted to ten. *God damn it all to hell. How could he make her understand when every word out of his mouth was a fuckin' lie?* He forced his eyes open. For her sake and his he needed to put a stop to this nonsense.

"Trust me, you don't want to do this. It's three men." He held up three fingers. "*Three*, Clare. At the same time. Three times in one night. Do the math. That's a lot of fucking. I've seen women who never made it through the first session, much less all three. It's a physical as well as a mental challenge."

That seemed to shut her up. At last.

"Have you ever been with more than one man at a time?" he said.

"Are you crazy? No!"

"Then you have no idea what you're asking for." If only he didn't. He might be able to live with himself.

She folded her arms across her midsection again. Maybe, just maybe, he was getting through to her. Since God didn't seem to be listening to him today, he sent a new-age plea out into the universe. *Please. Let her understand and forget about this.*

She pulled her desk chair back where it belonged and sank into it. Her expression told him he had won, but it gave him no pleasure because if he won on this issue, he'd lost on the other.

"If that's the way you want it. You better go now. I've got tests to grade." She leaned to the side, and when she straightened, she dumped a stack of papers on top of her desk. "Shut the door behind you, please."

He crossed to the door, unlocked it, turned the knob, and paused. "Clare." Her name came out as a plea. He didn't want their relationship to end this way. He didn't want it to end at all.

She didn't look up. "Thanks for coming by, Antonio. It was fun while it lasted."

While it lasted. As in, it was over.

He opened the door. "I'll be back." He closed the door behind him, took a step, and leaned one shoulder and his head against the wall. *Shit.* He sounded like fucking Swarzenegger. "I'll be baaack!" He'd come here simply wanting to take her to dinner then maybe make out a little somewhere before he took her back to his hotel room and got down to business. But one look at her sitting behind her desk, all prim and proper, and he'd gone stone hard and lost his mind.

He knew he should have taken it slow with her. Maybe if he had, she would have forgotten all about that damned charm. No way was she running the bases. No way in hell.

CHAPTER TEN

Clare folded her arms on her desk and dropped her forehead on top of them. The skin on the back of her neck tingled. The sensation morphed into a shiver and ran down her spine all the way to her toes, leaving her cold inside. Lord, what had she been thinking? She had never exposed herself, body and soul to another human being, much less a man like Antonio. He probably thought she was insane.

Her stomach cramped. What had possessed her to ask him to invite her to participate in his secret club's activities? That alone proved her insanity. At least he confirmed the existence of Bases Loaded. Jessica hadn't lied.

She was proud of herself for coming up with the story about overhearing the anonymous woman in the restroom. The last thing she needed was Antonio feeling sorry for her for allowing a vicious bitch to bully her at every opportunity. She'd seen Jessica's pierced clit and endured the torture of hearing how only the most beautiful women were invited to earn a charm. The incident had happened over a year ago, and Clare still made sure she knew where Jessica was before she entered a restroom. Being locked inside once and forced to listen to the witch and her coven spew venom at her was enough.

Bases Loaded

Now that she knew what Jessica had done to earn the charm…. The knowledge went a long way to dispelling the chill creeping over her body. Holy smoley! And here she'd thought Jessica had been unnecessarily graphic, when in fact she hadn't given many details at all.

Antonio had told her all those things to scare her off, and Clare had to admit she'd been shocked at first. But since she'd had a chance to think about it, she was more determined than ever to gain an invitation.

She'd never done anything close to daring. Hell, until today, her only other sexual experiences had been in a bed, and one time on the sofa in her boyfriend's apartment. She hadn't enjoyed it much for worrying his roommate might walk in at any moment. And now she was considering doing it with three men, three times in one night?

She sat up and rubbed her eyes. When her vision cleared, she opened the center drawer and took out the charm. It was beautiful—a work of art that had once belonged to a beautiful, desirable woman. First and third bases were green and yellow, respectively. The Hornets?

No one had to tell her the only women who had these were beautiful. Men might indulge in a pity fuck every now and then, but to do something like what went on in one of those sessions, the woman would have to be a beauty. Something she was not.

She dropped the charm back into the drawer and slammed it shut. She could fantasize all she wanted, but the fantasy wasn't going to become reality. Antonio had said no, and he meant what he said. She would probably never see him again except from high above the field in her little booth. Today had been an aberration. He had probably arrived at her office horny and short on available women—thus the office sex. It wouldn't happen again.

Tears streamed down her cheeks, splashing on the test she'd been staring at instead of grading.

Goddamn.

Antonio sat behind the wheel of his car parked outside Clare's office and scrubbed his hands over his face. She couldn't be serious. He remembered the look on her face when she'd kicked him out of her office.

Yeah. She meant it.

There was no way he would invite Clare Kincaid to run the bases. An image formed unbidden in his mind—Clare naked, that look of ecstasy he'd just recently seen on her face put there by the three men surrounding her. Touching her. Fucking her.

Shit.

"Not going to happen," he mumbled to himself. No matter how hot the image in his brain he wasn't going to share her with anyone.

He put the key ignition and sat back, glaring out the window at the early Fall landscape. Brown leaves clung to lifeless limbs, jostled occasionally by a warm breeze. The grass was still green but, in a few weeks, would probably turn brittle and brown. Time was on his side, he figured. He had the entire off-season to make her forget about the club, and all the auction items he'd won—*if* could convince her to see him again.

He already missed her, and he'd only left her a few minutes ago. He should give her time to miss him before he tried to reason with her.

The hell with that.

Locking his car once again, he headed back into the building. He wouldn't be pushed around on the subject of Bases Loaded. His answer was no. It was always going to be no, and her stubborn, irrational attitude wouldn't stop him from having her again. Somehow, he would convince her to let the subject drop. And one of these days, he'd stop dreaming night and day of her sweet body stretched and filled.

Taking the stairs instead of the elevator gave him a few extra minutes to wipe his brain clean of inappropriate images. She was his future, his forever. Thinking about her in the middle of a cluster-fuck wasn't appropriate.

It's all her fault for bringing up the damn club in the first place.

Pausing on a landing to catch his breath, he leaned against the cool cinderblock wall and squeezed his eyes shut. No matter how much he wanted to place the blame somewhere else, he couldn't. That image, and a few other equally inappropriate ones, had been with him almost from the moment he'd met her.

But he wasn't going to make them a reality. A guy didn't do that kind of thing with the woman he wanted to be the mother of his children.

She isn't going to goad me into letting her run the bases.

Resolve firmly in place, he pushed away from the wall and continued down the hall.

He stopped outside her closed office door and took a deep breath. Letting it out, he ran through the same mental exercise he used when he stepped up to the plate. *Breathe. In. Out. Focus. Stay calm.* This wasn't the first time he'd faced an angry opponent, but the outcome had never mattered as much either. He didn't know what he would do if she threw him out again. Something deep inside told him she was The One, and he wasn't inclined to disagree.

When he had been deep inside her, she *felt* like The One. No one had ever felt that good, that right before. He'd never given much thought to finding The One, but he never imagined she would need convincing. How was it he could feel the connection and she didn't? *Christ!* He'd made love to her, twice, and all she wanted from him was an invitation to a cluster-fuck.

Tony leaned his shoulders against the opposite wall and stared at her door. He wasn't an idiot, but he knew love wasn't supposed to be this way. Maybe he was kidding himself. Maybe he should just get back in his car and drive the fuck away. Leave her be. Forget about Clare Kincaid. Forget about the way his heart felt like it poured out through his dick when he was inside her.

Fuck that.

She was his.

Not bothering to knock, he opened her door. His heart sank to his toes.

"Ah, hell, babe." He closed the door behind him. "Don't cry."

"I...I can't help it." She swiped her damp cheek with trembling fingers.

He crossed the room and gathered her in his arms before he took his next breath. Lifting her out of her chair, he sat in her place. She cuddled into his lap like a broken doll. He ignored his hardening cock and swept her hair back from her face. "I'm sorry, sweetheart. I didn't mean to make you cry."

"I know," she said with a sniff.

"Is this because I was an ass and we fucked in your office?"

"No." A fresh tear leaked from one eye.

"Is it because I won't invite you to run the bases?"

She hiccupped. "Yes."

He closed his eyes, fighting for control. Shouting at her again wasn't going to cut it. He held her until the red behind his eyelids faded to a dull gray. "Make me understand why you want to do it. I've never understood why a woman would want to."

She sucked in a shaky breath. "You wouldn't understand."

"I know I don't, babe. Please. Just tell me why it means so much to you. Make me understand."

She shook her head and squirmed in his lap. His cock swelled. God, he really was an ass to want a crying woman.

"I can't."

"Yes, you can." He gave her a little squeeze. "I'm not letting you go until you do."

He heard her goddamned metronome in his head, tick-tocking away the minutes of his life. He glanced at the corner of his desk. It silently mocked him. *Shit.* Would he always have the thing in his head now when he made love to her, directing the tempo of his thrusts, counting off the short panting breaths she took when she came?

"All the women who do it are beautiful, aren't they?"

He thought of the women he personally knew had run the bases. "Yes, I guess you could say that."

"I want to feel beautiful. If I had three men desiring me, doing those things to me, I think I would feel beautiful then."

"You are beautiful, Clare."

"I hear you say it, Antonio, and I think you must believe it—at least a little bit, or you wouldn't have done what you did today with me."

He stroked her arm with one hand while the other itched to squeeze the delicious bit of hip it caressed. "I do believe it. What I don't understand is why you don't believe it."

"I know it doesn't make any sense, but you know the woman I told you about? The one who had the charm?"

"Do I know her? As in, know who she is?"

"No. But I guess it's possible you do know her that way. I meant, do you remember me telling you about her?"

Not likely he'd ever forget. "I remember." Damned idiot woman showing off her cunt in a public bathroom. Who would do something like that?

"I made that story up, about overhearing the conversation. The truth is, she cornered me in the restroom. Had one of her friends lock the door and stand guard so I couldn't get out."

Bitch. Tony had a sudden urge to kill someone. "Why would she do something like that?"

"Because she's a mean person, I guess."

"What really happened in the restroom?"

"She showed me the charm, like I said. She wanted me to get a good look, because no one would ever want to fuck a woman like me. She said baseball players only wanted beautiful women."

There were so many things wrong with that statement he didn't know where to begin. If he ever found the woman who'd said those things to Clare, he would tell her just how ugly she really was. Beauty might be skin deep, but ugly went all the way down to the bone.

"I'm so sorry. Don't you see? She might be beautiful on the outside, but she's rotten to the core on the inside."

"A part of me understands that, but another part of me recognizes what she said as truth. I know I'm not model material, but I think if I could earn one of those charms, it would prove she was wrong."

"You aren't giving me much credit. I told you how beautiful you are. I even showed you at the spa. I thought you understood then." He tried to keep the frustration out of his voice but failed miserably.

"I did. I mean, I believed you at the time, but then I got home and reality sank in."

"The things I said at the spa were real. The things I said today were real."

"I know you meant them at the time."

"I meant them then, and I mean them now." He nuzzled the top of her head with his chin. "Tell me…why would it be any different if three men told you the same things at the same time. It would only be one time. I don't understand. Why would that be any more believable than hearing it from me?"

"I don't know. It just would."

There wasn't a shred of logic in her thinking. Therefore, any further argument on the subject wasn't going to do any good. Her mind was made up—had been even before she met him. He continued to hold her, enjoying the feel of her in his arms while he contemplated his next move.

Bases Loaded was not an option. Somehow, he would have to think of another way to convince her she was beautiful, so she would drop her insane idea on her own.

He leaned down and placed a gentle kiss on her forehead. "Give me a chance to change your mind. I have all those auction items, and I've got a little over three months before Spring Training starts. Do them with me, Clare."

"Okay. I'll help you use all the items you won at the auction under one condition."

"What's that?" he asked.

"That you at least consider inviting me to Bases Loaded."

He stared at the ceiling for a moment then looked at her. "Okay. I'll consider inviting you to Bases Loaded if you do all the bid items with me." He pointed his index finger at her and narrowed his eyes. "I mean all of them. And, we're going to do them as a couple. That means you'll sleep in my bed, with me, on the trips."

He'd given in to her demands too quickly, which sent more red flags waving in her mind than the Mustangs had pennants. He held her gaze, unwavering. Baseball players. The good ones had the best poker faces, and he was one of the best.

He has no intention of offering me an invitation to run the bases. Well, we'll see about that. The only trick would be guarding her heart while she changed his mind. It was already going to be difficult to walk away from him when he grew tired of her. If she fell any harder for him, the damage would be irreparable.

Despite the risk, it was a challenge she couldn't resist.

"I can do that," she said.

"We'll have sex. With each other," he added. "And we'll act like a normal couple in public. Kissing. Touching. The whole ball of wax. Do you understand what I'm saying?"

"Yes, I think I do. You want me to act like I'm your girlfriend."

"Not act, Clare. You *are* my girlfriend. I'll call you with arrangements for the weekend on the yacht."

He left, slamming the office door behind him. Clare folded her arms around her middle and dropped her forehead to her desk.

She couldn't stop shaking. Where had she found the nerve to talk to him in such a way? She'd never stood up to any man before, but there was something about Antonio that made her forget who she really was and behave like the woman she wanted to be. His parting words echoed through her brain. "You *are* my girlfriend."

Oh. My. God.

An enormous bouquet of red roses greeted her the next morning from the center of her desk. Her heart skipped a beat. *Antonio.* She was just slipping the accompanying note out of the plastic pick holder when someone knocked on her door.

"Come in."

Her fellow professor, and good friend, Laura, stuck her head in. "Someone has been holding out on me."

"Come on in. I take it you let the delivery person into my office?" They had exchanged office keys long ago in case of an emergency. Flowers weren't really an emergency, but they were gorgeous, so she wasn't going to make an issue of it.

"I hope you didn't mind."

"Not at all. And I haven't been holding out on you."

Laura sat in the guest chair facing Clare's desk. "So, who are they from?"

Clare peeked at the card. Not that she needed to. There was only one person on the planet she knew who would send such an extravagant gift.

"It must be someone really special," her friend said. "There must be three dozen roses there."

"They're from a friend," Clare hedged.

"I wish I had a friend like that," Laura sniffed. "You aren't going to tell me, are you?"

"No. Really, it's just someone I met recently. He's just being nice."

"Well, if you don't want him, I'll take him."

Clare moved the arrangement to a corner and sat behind her desk. She slid the card into the center drawer on top of the charm. "I didn't say I don't want him. It's…complicated."

"It must be more complicated than a Mozart symphony to warrant that many blooms."

Clare sighed. "It is. Believe me, you don't want to know."

"That's where you're wrong, girlfriend. I want to know everything down to the smallest detail. How did you meet him? What does he look like? Is he a good kisser? Is he good in bed? Is he husband material?"

Girlfriend. There was that word again—only it meant something entirely different when Laura said it. "I met him at Jason Holder's fundraiser last weekend, and he's more gorgeous than a hothouse full of roses. The rest I either don't know or I'm not telling."

"Lots of different people go to fundraisers, but most of them are rich. That would explain how he could afford the roses. Those things aren't cheap, you know?"

Yeah, she knew. But Antonio could afford them. No problem.

"You already know everyone on the team, so it must have been some Dallas socialite or a politician, maybe."

Thank goodness, her fellow music professor didn't follow sports, or she would know the Mustangs had acquired several new players after the playoffs. But her lack of knowledge played to Clare's advantage. "Maybe," she encouraged.

Laura nodded. "Okay, so you aren't going to tell me." She sat up and leaned over the desk to look Clare in the eye. "At least tell me what he did that requires such an elaborate apology."

"It's not an apology. He wants me to go out with him. That's all." *On a yacht. For an entire weekend.*

"And you don't want to go.".

"I already told him I would. This—" She indicated the bouquet with a sweep of her hand. "—is just overkill."

The other woman sat back and fanned her face. "I wish I had a man who sent me flowers for no good reason. I'd settle for a bunch of daisies."

It was sweet and unnecessary—which made it all that much

sweeter.

"Where's he taking you?"

"I'm not sure. He didn't say." That much at least was the truth. The private yacht was docked somewhere along the gulf coast of Texas, but she had no idea as to where.

Laura stood. "Well, I'm glad you have a date. It's been way too long since you've had one."

"Not that long," Clare protested.

"Months, sugar." She moved toward the door. "It's been at least six months."

As her well-meaning sidekick stepped out into the hall, Clare called after her. "Thanks for letting the delivery guy in."

"No problem." She eyed the giant bouquet. "I'll take my fee in details later on."

Clare smiled as her friend closed the door with a final wave goodbye. She sat for a moment, waiting, just in case she decided to come back. When she was sure she was alone, she opened the drawer and picked up Antonio's note.

She recognized his handwriting from the silent auction bids. It was strong, but there was a flair to it that spoke of his passionate side. She sighed. He definitely had a passionate side. She could attest to that.

She slipped the card from the envelope. Her skin burned red-hot as she read the short note.

I'll pick you up on Friday. Your place. 4pm. It's a clothing optional weekend. He had signed it simply, *A.*

A clothing optional weekend. Oh boy.

CHAPTER ELEVEN

She'd been on a chartered flight once, but it was nothing like the executive jet Antonio had arranged to take them to Galveston where they would board the yacht. As they got closer to the coast, the butterflies in her stomach turned into seagulls. It was all she could do to keep her legs still and her hands from shaking.

"Thanks for coming," he said for the hundredth time since she'd stepped into the limo he'd hired to take them to the airport. "I can't wait to have you all to myself for forty-eight hours."

"I've never been on yacht before."

"I've been on a few. This one is bigger than the others I've been on. The owner said they've taken it to Europe several times."

"Where are we going?"

"Just out into the Gulf. I told the captain to sail around in circles and not to expect to see much of us."

The meaning behind his words sent the flock of birds in her stomach into a tizzy. She had imagined doing all kinds of things with Antonio this weekend, but she hadn't taken into account they wouldn't be alone on the boat. "It's just us and the captain?"

"There's a cook, a steward, and a mechanical guy, too."

"Oh." She turned her face to the window, so he wouldn't see the look of horror that was probably there.

"They're used to this sort of thing," he said, accurately reading her discomfort. "They'll be discreet."

She supposed coming from someone who wanted an invitation to have three men fuck her at the same time, her shyness seemed out of place. But the idea of strangers eavesdropping on private moments was different. "They'll know."

He shrugged. "I'm sure they'll suspect, but they won't *know*. Unless you want them to."

A flush of embarrassment crept over her face. She shook her head. "No. I don't think so."

"You don't think, or you don't want?" His voice was low, seductive, as he called her out on her evasion. "Would you like the possibility of having an audience?"

She shook her head again but with less conviction than before. For the first time in her life, she began to believe someone might find her attractive, and with that amazing realization came a new desire to explore her sexuality.

"Clare." He leaned over and captured her hand in his. "I'm looking forward to making love to you all weekend long. I certainly wouldn't pass up the chance to make love under the stars or on the open deck with the sun warming your skin. If you want to be adventurous, all you have to do is say so, and I'll ask the crew to stay below."

Adventurous. She turned the word over in her mind. She wanted to run the bases with three guys at once, but, truth be told, she didn't know if she had the nerve to actually do it. Perhaps all she really wanted was to be asked. Knowing someone thought her attractive enough to issue an invitation might be enough. But if she took baby steps toward the goal, she could prove to herself and Antonio she was ready to play his kind of games. Then there would be one less reason for him to deny her.

Taking a deep breath, she made up her mind to cultivate her adventurous side. Heck. She'd already had sex in her office. That counted, didn't it?

"I think I'd like to be daring," she said.

He squeezed her hand. His smile was brilliant. "We'll see. I want you to enjoy this weekend as much as I intend to."

The moment the wheels touched down on the runway until they set foot on the deck of the yacht, Antonio kept her hand in his, their fingers intertwined just like she imagined their bodies would be soon. She wasn't sure if the gesture was meant to comfort or to ensure she didn't run. It did both, she decided as she gazed longingly from the aft deck toward the rapidly disappearing dock.

So far, everyone had been wonderfully attentive, assuring them both of their wish to be of service, performing their duties then quietly disappearing.

They'd settled onto chaise lounges in the sun. Sheltered from the wind, and thanks to a Fall heat wave, the air temperature was just right for lounging.

He brushed his thumb over the back of her hand. "As soon as we have something to eat, I'm going to take you to our cabin and have dessert."

There was a wicked tone to his voice that left no doubt as to what he considered dessert. She stared straight ahead, acknowledging his comment by returning the thumb caress. Her body warmed from the inside out, imagining what she hoped he had in mind.

They watched the sun disappear below the horizon in a blaze of jewel-toned colors. Dinner was served al fresco on a white-draped table illuminated by candlelight and a blanket of stars. The servings were generous, and she ate like she'd been told it was the last meal she would ever have, despite her earlier nerves.

"This is delicious," she said, reaching for another warm roll.

"The sea air always makes me hungry," he said. "I could never be in the Navy. I'd eat until I couldn't get through the hatches."

"Good thing you took up baseball."

"I suppose so. I never would have met you if I had taken another route."

"I doubt that would have been a great loss."

She sensed a change in the atmosphere and glanced up at

her dinner companion. Candlelight flickered off the hard lines of his face. His dark eyes seemed to absorb more light than they gave off.

"What do I have to do to convince you, Clare Kincaid, that you're a game changer for me?"

His earnest admission stole her breath. She wanted to believe him. "I'm a conquest for you. Nothing more. I understand that, and I accept it."

"No. You don't. You don't understand anything." He folded his napkin and placed it on the table. He sat back in his chair and let out a long breath. "Look, I don't want to argue with you. I know what I know, and I'll eventually convince you, too. In the meantime, can we just enjoy each other's company?"

She rose and walked to the railing. Wrapping her arms around herself, she gazed up at the full moon. What he was asking wasn't unreasonable. She *had* agreed to his terms, which meant she'd agreed to sleep with him. It wasn't as if they hadn't already done it. But this was different than the time in her office.

That had been spontaneous combustion.

Tonight was a planned seduction with all the time in the world to see it through.

Be adventurous. Take what he's offering for as long as it lasts.

Antonio joined her, enfolding her in his arms from behind, startling her.

"Shh. It's just me, sweetheart," he whispered in her ear.

"Antonio…."

"You look so lovely in the moonlight." His lips left a trail of heat along the length of her neck to her collarbone. "Relax. Let me love you."

She leaned back letting him take her weight. He was solid and heat radiated off him, so it was easy to imagine the star-splashed black sky as a blanket cloaking them from the world. When his fingers slid along her arms to capture her hands, guiding them to the rail, she made no protest.

"Hold on," he said.

She gripped the polished wood, grateful for its unyielding presence. His hands moved to the buttons on the front of her summer blouse, and as he worked the fasteners free, warm air caressed her exposed skin. When the garment hung open, he cupped her midriff between callused palms and let his fingers explore from the band of her bra to the waistband of her shorts.

Clare closed her eyes, allowing her to focus all her senses on enjoying the feel of his work-roughened hands touching her.

"So soft." His voice was anything but. The shell of her ear tingled where his lips brushed then nibbled. She pressed her mouth tight to keep from groaning out loud at the erotic sensation. He nibbled again, this time taking the lobe between his teeth, biting lightly then soothing the prick of pain with his tongue. A sound escaped then. A moan? A groan? Whatever it was called, she felt sure it'd been loud enough to summon Merfolk from the sea.

Antonio's silent mirth rumbled around in his chest pressed to her back. Smiling, he pressed a kiss to the side of her neck.

Damn man. It wasn't fair what he could do to her with so little effort.

Covering her breast with one hand, the other inched below her waistband, stroking, sending tendrils of want and need to her pussy.

Giving her no time to protest, he'd upped the seduction to a whole new level.

She flexed her hips in a vain attempt to coax his fingers toward the swollen flesh between her legs, but he wouldn't be goaded into speeding things up. In answer, he pulled his hand from her shorts.

"Let's get this off." He brushed her hair over one shoulder and placed a kiss on the nape of her neck while he worked her blouse over her shoulders.

She tried to shrug it back in place. "We can't...."

"We can. I told the staff to go below for the night." He divested her of her top and bra before placing her hands back on the rail. "Don't move."

Her nipples puckered in the warm night air. She quickly scanned the ink-black ocean for signs of life. They were alone with the vast sparkling blanket and the moonlight. She was half-naked and all alone with Antonio. An errant breeze teased a loose tendril of hair, adding to the wild and decadent feelings rushing through her.

Behind her, he adjusted his stance, fusing his front to her back. He'd removed his shirt so they were skin to skin.

"God, you feel so good," he said, his cheek pressed against

her temple He growled out the words, his chest vibrating against her back sending a shiver of awareness all the way to her toes.

His hands once again learned the shape of her shoulders, her ribcage, her breasts. "I love your breasts." He handled them reverently, testing their weight before brushing his thumbs across her nipples, making them grow impossibly harder.

He dipped his head low and rolled each aching nub between his thumbs and forefingers. "Beautiful," he breathed, planting an open-mouthed kiss on her shoulder. He gave her nipples a sharp tug and released them.

Clare gasped at the sudden jolt of pain, but the gasp turned to a groan when his hands moved to her ribs to stroke and caress.

"I'll be back to them, sweetheart. I promise." His fingers made short work of the front closure on her shorts, and before she could formulate a protest, he pushed them and her panties over her hips. She braced her feet apart for balance on the swaying deck and the garments lodged just above her knees. His hands smoothed over her backside like a blind man committing a piece of art to memory.

"You have a magnificent ass." He gave both cheeks a firm squeeze. "Time for dessert."

He moved, his hands skimming down her thighs. Clare looked over her shoulder and caught sight of the top of his head sinking low...lower. *Oh God!*

"Got a good grip on the rail, sweetheart?"

She flexed her fingers and gripped the wood tight enough to leave indentations. "Y-yes."

"Good." His palms caressed one ankle—lifted it. Her shorts and panties slid down. Antonio removed them from the leg he held aloft before gently guiding her foot to the deck. As her leg descended, his lips worked their way up from her ankle to her very naked ass.

She had only a moment to absorb the fact she was stark-naked outdoors in a place where others might see her. What most concerned her was Antonio was on his knees, which meant he had to be...eye-level with.... Clare bit her lower lip to keep from voicing her misgivings.

"Luscious," he breathed, or at least she thought that's what he said before his tongue swept across her left cheek. He followed the taste with his teeth, nipping her skin.

Clare yelped and jerked her hips. Firm hands held her fast.

"Easy," he said. "Did I hurt you?"

"N-no. You surprised me, that's all."

"Good, then you won't mind if I do it again?" Clearly, he didn't expect an answer since he gave her no time to respond before he did it again, this time soothing the bite with his tongue. "Ah, Clare…you don't know how that turns me on."

Clare dug her fingers into the railing while Antonio amused himself placing small bites across one cheek then the other. Her heart raced. No man had ever lavished so much attention on her bottom before. He said it turned him on, but Lord, it did the same to her. If he didn't move on soon, her pussy would drip all over the deck.

"More. Spread your legs for me," he said, applying pressure to the inside of her thighs.

She shifted her feet.

"Sweet Heaven."

He fixed his mouth to her pussy. Blinding pleasure overrode any qualms she might have had about her public nakedness.

"Oh!" Her nails dug into the railing. She clenched her teeth and shut her eyes.

His hands gripped her bottom, holding her open for his merciless tongue. And Lord, did he know what to do with his tongue. He kept her off balance, lapping at her slit with the flat of his tongue then dancing over her clit and plunging inside her. He employed the use of lips and teeth liberally until her fingers ached with the attempt to hold onto reality, and her knees trembled.

He wrapped his strong arms around her thighs, anticipating her collapse, and held her steady. She'd long since given up trying to stifle the cries his attentions drew out of her body. If they summoned all the mythical creatures of the sea, so be it. She was one of them tonight.

The darkened ocean and sky enveloped them. The warm salt breeze lifted the ends of her hair and teased at the curves of her body. How decadent she must look. A sea nymph draped over the railing, her hair wafting in the breeze, a god on his knees, worshiping her very core.

Her heart beat a primal rhythm that matched the hushed breaking of waves against the hull of the boat.

She spiraled out of control. Each stroke of his tongue, every flick across her clit, drove her closer to the unknown. There was a dangerous abyss out there. She couldn't see it, but she could feel herself inching that way.

She couldn't remain still. Her hips moved in contretemps to the rhythm he'd established. Antonio seamlessly adapted to her movements, using her contribution to his advantage.

It seemed as if even the slight movement of the ship had joined in the quest to drive her past the edge of sanity, rocking in perfect time with her hips and Antonio's mouth. It was too much. She couldn't fight it, didn't want to. The mysterious tightening began in her clit and spread to her abdomen. Another swipe of his tongue. Another dance inside her, and out to shuffle with her clit….

The tight coil unwound, exploding into a shower of stars behind her tightly closed eyelids. An incoherent cry escaped her lips and was swallowed up by the vast emptiness surrounding them. Antonio's mouth wrung every last spasm from her before he sighed and pressed his cheek to her inner thigh. He kissed each trembling thigh and slowly stood, cradling her with his strength.

She fell into his embrace, snaking her arms around his waist and pressing her face against the satin heat of his skin. Beneath her cheek, his heart thumped like a caged animal wanting out.

"I'll never get enough of you." The words rumbled in his chest before they broke free on a groan.

"That was…." She shook her head, unable to come up with adequate words.

"Incredible?"

"Better."

"I know what you mean, sweetheart. It was for me, too." His hands swept lazy circles on her back.

"But you…."

"No, I didn't." He placed a finger beneath her chin and tilted her face up. Their gazes locked. "I want to be inside you, Clare. Now." To emphasize his point, he rocked his hips against her belly making his state of arousal abundantly clear.

"Yes."

The word had barely left her lips before he scooped her into his arms. His lips covered hers in a kiss every bit as carnal as the ones he'd placed between her legs. Their tongues dueled, Clare experiencing for the first time her own taste on a man's lips. She groaned and wrapped her hands around the back of his head in a futile effort to control the kiss. Antonio parried back, devouring her mouth, taking, demanding her surrender.

She relaxed her hold and let her fingers wander through his hair. He eased back.

"Here or the cabin?" he asked.

"Here. Under the stars."

Antonio looked around. After a moment of indecision, he headed in the direction of the double chaise, and deposited her on it. He dug in his back pocket and retrieved his wallet. After removing a condom from it, he tossed the wallet to the deck and shucked the rest of his clothes. Clare sat up. Moonlight framed his body. His erection jutted toward true North. Before he could open the small foil package, she took it from him.

"Not yet." She scooted to the edge of the chaise and closed her hand around his shaft. "I want to taste you."

Holy mother of God.

Tony watched his cock disappear past her ruby lips. She stole his equilibrium, and he was afraid he was going to come down her throat or fall on his ass. Either was possible and both were imminent. He braced his feet farther apart to absorb the roll of the boat and bracketed her head in his hands. God, her mouth was hot, and that thing she did with her tongue…it was…was….

"Clare," he hissed through gritted teeth. "I'm…." *Too far gone. Fucked.*

He dug his fingers into her scalp, but she continued sucking him down the road to perdition. His balls drew up tight.

He should stop her. He wanted to fuck her into oblivion, but Christ Almighty, her mouth…. Her lips formed a perfect O, framing his dick. He watched, fascinated. Her cheeks hollowed out each time she sucked him in and holy hell….

Her tiny hand tightened around the base of his cock. She sucked harder, took almost his whole dick into her mouth.

Bases Loaded

Fuck!

She gazed up at him, and he could have sworn she smiled. Her mouth gave one more hard pull, and he lost it. Lightening shot from the small of his back, radiating to his extremities as if he'd backed into a high-power line. His cock got as hard as a Louisville Slugger and felt twice as big.

Too late.

"Can't. Stop." He was on a runaway train, speeding down the mountain with no brakes, and nothing but an epic crash in his future. No woman's mouth had ever felt so good. No *woman* had ever felt so good.

His fingers twisted in her hair and dug into her scalp. He clenched his ass cheeks, flexed his hips, and drove his cock to the back of her throat.

Fuck. Shit.

Fire shot from his cock in spurts of pleasure so intense he thought his head might explode. He had no control over any part of his body, least of all his cock. The circuits connecting his brain and his tongue malfunctioned, and a garbled string of expletives tumbled from his mouth with each gut-wrenching spasm.

When he came to his senses, he stumbled backward. He wanted to blame it on the roll of the boat but knew it was all Clare's fault.

He collapsed on the chaise, dragging her down beside him. She snuggled against him like an innocent kitten. He could practically hear her purring. "Christ, woman. You killed me."

She rose to one elbow and looked down at him. "I'm sorry."

"Don't ever be sorry for blowing my head off. Not that way." She placed her hand in the center of his chest, leaned over, and kissed his nipple.

Every cell in his body shot to attention. "Holy hell." He rolled her to her back and covered her. "Give me a minute, would you?"

She smiled playfully, and he kissed her.

"You aren't sorry at all, are you?" he asked.

"Uh-uh."

His cock surged between them. "Witch."

After the blowjob she'd just given him, he shouldn't be

breathing much less horny and hard. He wasn't a stranger to fucking all night, but he did have his limits. It usually took him longer than a few heartbeats to recover, but with Clare, it seemed as if he was always ready. All she had to do was look at him, and he was hard.

"God. I need you again." He ground his erection into her stomach.

She brushed a lock of hair off his forehead. Her lips curved up slightly. "I need you, too."

She spread her legs, and he willingly slipped into her welcoming shelter. He reached for the condom he'd dropped earlier. She made a grab for it, too, but he got to it first.

"Nope." He shook his head, peeling the packet open. "You aren't going to distract me again. I'm going to fuck you like you deserve to be fucked."

She lay back and arched an eyebrow at him. "And how do I deserve to be fucked?"

"Fast and hard," he said, sheathing himself. "We'll do long and slow later."

He knelt between her legs, wrapped his arms beneath her thighs, and lifted her ass. He positioned his cock at her entrance. "Hang on, sweetheart."

She raised her arms over her head and clutched the edge of the cushion. Antonio thrust into her, burying his cock to the hilt. She gasped at the abrupt intrusion but rolled her hips to take him even deeper.

"Vixen," he said, sliding out to repeat the thrust.

She was hot and wet, and she had an unnerving way of stealing his brains and ripping his soul from him. No other woman had ever claimed so much of him before. She'd bewitched him from the moment he laid eyes on her.

"Antonio." His name rent the air, a plea from her lips.

"Anything you want, babe."

"I want...I need...."

"Touch yourself," he rasped.

He almost choked on his own spit when she placed the fingers of one hand on her clit and rubbed. He maintained the rhythm of his thrusts, but just barely. There seemed to be no end to the ways this woman could distract him.

Spurred on by her self-stimulation, it was only a matter of

minutes before he felt the tension in her thighs. Lord, she was a sight to watch when she came. Every muscle in her body grew taut for a fraction of a second, then like a rubber band snapping under too much pressure, she succumbed. Her hips bucked in short erratic bursts, her inner muscles clamped his dick in soft waves. After a few moments, her body went lax, spilling across the cushion like hot wax melting in the sun. Her fingers slipped from her clit to feather across her stomach. Her chest rose and fell.

"Antonio," she said on a soft moan.

He let her hips fall to the chaise and came over her. Sated, she was soft and pliant beneath him. She opened herself to him and he took what he wanted, pounding into her until that lightning ball of pleasure he'd come to expect with her claimed him.

CHAPTER TWELVE

He'd ordered breakfast brought to their cabin so they needn't dress just yet. Tony stared at her bathrobe-clad form across the array of breakfast foods on the table between them. She'd pulled her hair into a high ponytail that swished from side to side with every move she made. Consequently, he'd forgotten all about eating breakfast. All he could think about was wrapping that hank of hair around his fist, pulling her chin up, ramming his cock inside her from behind, and riding her like a prized mare.

An image formed in his brain, and he couldn't have dislodged it with a riding crop.

That sweet mouth of hers would open wide only to be filled with cock, silencing her pants and groans. He'd switch to her ass and lower her pussy onto another cock. God, she would be beautiful taking all of them in at once.

Shit. He should not be thinking of her running the bases. Wasn't going to happen, even if the only way out of the club was to invite a woman and have her complete the game. He'd stay an inactive member until he died before he would expose Clare to that kind of debauchery. She was too pure, too real for that kind of kink. Maybe their weekend together would convince her she didn't need anyone but him.

He'd taken her hard last night then made love to her slow and easy before sunrise. If he was any kind of a gentleman, he would let her rest today so they could do it all over again in the evening. He felt like a kid with a new toy. He wanted to play with it all the time. At this rate, he'd wear it out before the weekend was over, and that wouldn't do. If he played his cards right, he'd have a lifetime to enjoy her body.

"Antonio?" Her voice cut through his lust-fogged thoughts.

"Hmm?" He reached for his coffee.

"Earth to Antonio." She waved a hand across his line of vision. "Are you listening to me?"

"Sure," he lied. He sipped the bitter brew that had grown cold while he mentally romped in the stable with his filly and his stud friends.

"I asked if you liked what I did to you last night?"

She took a bite of biscuit smeared with jelly. Her pink tongue darted out to capture a wayward glop of purple goo. Blood rushed south so fast he could feel his brain cells dying. No problem, his auxiliary brain sprang into action.

"Uh…." *Eloquent, genius. Focus.*

"I'd never done it before. Never wanted to, but when I saw you standing there, and I'd just tasted myself on your lips…well…."

He swallowed a generous gulp of cold acid, hoping his body would send some blood north so he could decipher the code she was speaking. Last night. Never done it. Tasted herself.

"You'd never done what?" His voice sounded like an acid-erosion victim, but he mentally patted himself on the back for successfully stringing together an entire sentence. That wasn't easy when his only functioning brain would fit in his fist.

"You know…." She blushed, speared half a strawberry with a fork, and brought the succulent morsel to her lips. She chewed and swallowed. "Done a man with my mouth."

His balls were so hot and tight they felt like someone was holding hot charcoal briquettes to his groin. Lord, she was going to be the death of him.

He coughed into his fist and shifted his lower half. His cock throbbed. He snagged his water goblet, briefly considered pouring it over his lap to put out the fire, but decided it was useless to throw water on a nuclear meltdown. Instead, he lifted the glass to his lips and drained it.

"Did I do it right?"

Holy hell. "Any more right and I'd be dead," he answered truthfully. *And damned grateful for the send off.*

She blushed again, crumpled her napkin, and placed it on the table. "I want to do it again."

Lust momentarily blinded him and stole his voice. He clamped his mouth shut to keep from drooling like an idiot.

"Would you mind?"

His cock pulsed out its own answer. *Please. Please. Please*

"Come here," he said, scooting his chair back from the table.

Clare walked around the table. He motioned her between his knees and parted the thick terrycloth robe he'd donned this morning. His cock was locked and loaded. A pearly drop crowned the tip. *Probably my brains leaking out.*

With one hand, he carefully adjusted his balls, reaching for her wrist with the other.

She allowed him to guide her, sank to her knees between his thighs. He caught the gleam of wicked delight in her eyes as her tongue darted out to wet her lips. *Witch.*

"Babe, you can suck my cock anytime you want." He wrapped one hand around her nape and pulled her head into his lap. Holding his dick in his other hand, he pressed the head against her lips. Clare obediently opened and took him in. Paralyzing pleasure gripped his entire body, and for a few moments, all he could do was fist his fingers in her hair and fight off the wave of darkness threatening to take him under.

His hips rose off the chair thrusting his cock to the back of her throat. She faltered, looked up at him with questioning eyes. He felt like a shit. She was giving him something precious beyond words, and he couldn't control himself long enough to accept the gift.

"Sorry. You're doing good, babe. Don't stop." He stroked her concave cheek. Her eyelids dropped, and she pulled him down into the depths of insanity. He wrapped her ponytail around his fist, gripped the chair arm with his other hand, and hung on for the ride.

Bases Loaded

It took every ounce of self-control he possessed to keep his ass pressed into the seat cushion when instinct told him to move, to take charge, and fuck her hard. He loved fucking pussy and ass, but Heaven help him, Clare's mouth stole his sanity.

Her tongue swirled around the head, the rough texture against his most sensitive flesh almost sent him into orbit. She took him deep, licking his length, making him blind with lust and the need to come down her throat.

"Can't…. Going to come."

She grabbed his balls, rolled them in her palm then tugged.

"Fuckin' Christ!" His entire body tensed. He let go of the chair arm and used both hands to hold her head steady. He came down her throat in hard, jerky movements that wrenched his soul.

She sat back on her heels and wiped her mouth on the sleeve of her robe. Her beauty stunned him, but her lack of confidence broke his heart. Behind her sweet smile lurked the brittle vulnerability she tried so hard to mask.

Tony peeled his fingers off the arm of the chair and untangled the others from the silk rope of her hair. He needed a minute to catch his breath. His heart hammered against his ribcage, and his dick lay against his stomach like an overcooked cannoli. His balls felt like they'd just been sprung from prison. *Free at last, boys.*

With a little rest, the equipment would be operable again. Thank God. Now, if he could jump-start his brain.

Clare stroked the inside of his thighs. "Antonio?"

"What?"

"Was that good?"

He chuckled. She had no idea. "Babe, good doesn't come close to describing what you can do with your mouth. You could bring world leaders to their knees. Your mouth might be the answer to world peace."

"Am I good enough to run the bases?"

Zing. Electrodes zapped his brain into hyper-drive. His head came up off the back of the chair like it had been launched from a rocket. Forbidden images flared against his cranium, taunting him.

"What? You aren't still thinking about that, are you? Because we've been over that subject. You know my answer."

She ran her hands up and down his thighs. He'd yet to try to cover himself, figuring the energy was better used elsewhere. Clare leaned in and placed a kiss in the small indentation where his sternum gave way to his ribcage. He jerked upright. He brought his knees together, forcing her to scoot backwards. She sighed when he whipped his robe closed and cinched the belt at his waist. Some conversations required clothes, and this was one of them. Thank God she'd never taken her robe off. The pure white terrycloth covering her helped remind him he was dealing with Clare. An innocent. Mostly.

Hell. He raked his hands through his hair and stood, putting distance between them so he could think. Stopping with his bare toes over the threshold of the balcony door, he filled his lungs with fresh sea air.

"I know, but I was just wondering...you know. Was that good enough?"

He faced her. "It doesn't matter. You aren't going to run the bases."

"Why not?"

"Because." He gripped his head with both hands to keep his skull from exploding.

"You said you would think about it if I agreed to—"

"I know what I said." He dropped his hands, clenching them into fists at his side. "I've thought about it, and the answer is no. N. O. There's no way in hell I'm going to let you suck another man's cock." He shook his head. "No way."

"Are you saying I'm not good enough?"

"Babe, what did I just say? You're the best, and even if it would bring about world peace, I wouldn't share that mouth of yours with anyone."

She narrowed her eyes at him. "You're just saying those things so I'll quit asking about Bases Loaded."

"What is it with you and that club?" he shouted.

"Shh!"

He reined in his anger enough to lower his voice, but couldn't squelch it entirely. "I don't understand. Think about it. Do you really want another guy's dick in your mouth...or anywhere else for that matter?"

"Yes. I do," she stated, fisting her hands on her hips.

"No, you don't. You think you do, but trust me, it's not

anything like what you're thinking. Maybe it's fun and exciting the first time, but then…." He shook his head. "Then you have to do it two more times. With strangers, Clare."

"They wouldn't have to be strangers. Why couldn't I meet them before? Maybe I have met them. I know a lot of baseball players."

Godamnit. "That's not how it works. You don't get to shop for your team, and believe me, if you had met any members of the club, you would have had an invitation already, and we wouldn't be having this insane conversation."

"Then why won't you invite me?"

Why wouldn't he? He was painfully aware of his own hypocrisy on the subject, but he'd made up his mind. He was going to keep Clare all to himself, and at the same time keep her from seeing the dark side of his personality. She just thought she understood, had built the whole thing up in her mind into something it wasn't.

Knowing full well she would jump all over it, he offered up the only reason he could think of. "Because!"

"Keep your voice down," she warned. She glared at him with steely determination. "Why?"

"Because I'm trying my damndest to get out of the club," he confessed.

"And how do you go about getting out of Bases Loaded?"

Tony turned to look out at the sea. A few steps would bring him to the balcony railing. He could throw himself overboard and end this insanity now. Or he could tell her.

"Well?" she asked.

God, save us from determined women. "The only way out for good is for one of your invites to earn the charm. Then you can resign from the club."

"Then invite me. It's a win-win for both of us."

"No." He shook his head. He needed to make her see his side, and he damned sure didn't understand why she was hell-bent on playing the game. "What if you ran the bases and that wasn't enough…what's the word I'm looking for?"

"Validation," she supplied.

"What if it's not enough *validation* for you? What then? Am I supposed to arrange for more men to fuck you until you finally see what I see?"

"You're just being crude now, Antonio." She crossed her arms over her middle. "I want to run the bases once. Nothing more."

He stared at her with the same look he used to intimidate on the field. She shifted her feet, but didn't cave.

"I don't believe this," he said. "I don't believe we're having this conversation."

"Believe it. I know what I want, and I'm not going to forget. You say all the right things to me, but refusing to invite me to run the bases makes a liar out of you. If I was pretty enough…." She sighed and waved her arms around. "Or good enough, you wouldn't think twice about the invitation."

"That's bullshit. I won't invite you because you're mine. I. Don't. Share. What's. Mine," he growled. His inner conscience picked up a now familiar chant echoing around his empty skull. *Liar. Liar. Liar.*

"I'm not yours."

He took a step toward her. "Mine."

She took a step back and shook her head. "This is ridiculous. I'm a fling to you. A diversion until you get settled in Dallas. You and I both know it."

"Don't put words in my mouth." He advanced on her again.

"I'm not your type," she argued.

"I haven't been out with a woman I considered my type since high school. Unfortunately, Mary Catherine Rinaldi's type played football. She got knocked up by the quarterback and married him the day after graduation. I really thought she was the one, but I was seventeen. What did I know?"

"See. That's what I'm saying. You don't really want me anymore than you wanted Mary what's-her-name. People like me don't hook up long-term with athletes. We're nice for a night, or a weekend, or to help out when you need someone to look at apartments with you. But we aren't the kind of women you want sitting in the stands when the cameras pan around looking for wives and girlfriends."

"Are you saying all I want is a trophy to occupy a seat behind the dugout so the commentators will have a reason to mention my name?"

She nodded. "Yes. That's exactly what I'm saying."

"That's absurd, and how shallow would it make me if it were true?"

"I've been around professional baseball all my life." She waved off his objection. "Players' wives are gorgeous."

"There you go, selling yourself short again. I'd love to see you sitting in my seats, and even if you weren't the most beautiful woman I've ever seen, which you are, it wouldn't matter one bit. As long as I think you're beautiful, what does it matter what anyone else thinks?"

"Tell that to your publicist."

"I don't give a good goddamned what my publicist thinks. If I did, I would have married one of the matchstick models she's paired me with for the last few years." He let out an exasperated sigh and sat on the end of the bed. "I want you, and only you. I don't want to share you with anyone, least of all my perverted friends."

"You think *I'm* perverted because I want to run the bases?"

"No, I don't. Maybe perverted isn't the right word for the guys in the club. I didn't think of myself that way when I participated, so it isn't fair to label them that way. Look, Clare…I think you have the wrong idea about the guys…or what motivates them. Men…well, it doesn't take much to excite us."

She tapped her foot. "Oh?"

"Would you quit that?"

"Quit what?"

"Jumping to conclusions. I'm not talking about my reaction to you, that's different. I'm talking about men in general and the guys in the club in particular. You're under the impression only a beautiful woman will excite these guys to the point of running the bases, but let me tell you, most of them have never seen an unattractive woman in their lives. Pick any woman off the street, big, little, round or flat as a board, have her strip naked in front of them, and they'd be off and running—so to speak. So even if you ran the bases, you wouldn't necessarily be getting the…what was it, again?"

"Validation," she repeated.

"The validation you're looking for."

"So, let me see…You admit, since you're a member of the club, you'll fuck any woman who sheds her clothes for you. I took off my clothes, therefore, I might conclude you couldn't help yourself. You fucked me. *Nice.*"

"Damn it. You're doing it again, putting words in my mouth. I did not say that."

"What part did I get wrong?"

He scrubbed a hand across his face. "If I remember correctly, and believe me, I'll never forget that day in your office, you had your clothes on. Mostly."

"Yeah, well—"

"Let's get back to the subject. You want an invite to Bases Loaded, and I'm not going to give you one. Subject closed. Now, can we get back to enjoying our weekend?"

"No. Not until you agree to think about the invitation. I mean, really think about it. I understand where you're coming from on this, but you have to see my side of it, too. I need to do this. I need to prove something to myself. I'm not saying it will change the way I feel about my body, but it will put me on equal footing with the kind of women I wish I could be. And, if I earn the charm, you could get out of the club. It's a win for both of us."

He shook his head. "Leave me out of this. I can remain on the membership roster until I quit playing ball. There aren't any participation requirements. This is about you. You are the most stubborn woman I have ever met, bar none. You're talking about outward beauty, Clare." He held up a hand to stay her protest. "I've already told you how beautiful I think you are, so let's talk about inner beauty. You have all those women beat in that category. You'll never be on equal footing with them. They'll always be beneath you. I don't know why you can't see it."

CHAPTER THIRTEEN

Fish. Fucking fish.

Tony was so angry, every time he closed his eyes he saw fishing lures with tiny gold charms hanging from them. What was supposed to have been a weekend-long private orgy turned into a fucking fishing trip, and he had the slimy carcasses to prove it. He lifted the borrowed cooler into the trunk of the limo waiting for them at the airport.

"Do you like fish?" he asked the driver.

"Sure."

"I'll give you a hundred bucks to take that—" He pointed to the cooler. "—off my hands." He pulled out his wallet, selected a bill, and pressed it into the driver's hand.

"What about the cooler?"

"Keep it." He'd spring for a new one. If he never smelled another fish, it would be too soon.

After their spat on the first morning aboard the yacht, Clare hadn't spoken a word to him or let him touch her. Purely out of spite, he'd asked the cabin steward if there was any fishing equipment, and once it was located, set to fishing as if he loved the sport. Clare spent the day sunbathing nearby, all that exposed skin driving him slowly insane.

He slid into the backseat. The love of his life was scrunched in the opposite corner, as far from him as possible, literally and figuratively, and he had no idea how to reach her.

"Clare."

She gazed out the side window. Any one of those damned fish in the cooler would have been more welcoming. Tony settled on his side of the seat and mirrored her posture. Somehow, in the two days they'd been gone, the Dallas landscape had grown as bleak as the prospects of a veteran Minor League player, and suited his mood to a T. As the miles ticked by, he thought about his predicament. He was in love with the most impossible woman in the world, and she wasn't speaking to him.

It didn't matter what she thought running the bases would do for her, and no matter how many nights he lay awake imagining her naked in the arms of three men, he would not give in. To either fantasy.

His involvement in the club had been non-existent for months now, and he wanted to keep it that way. In a few years, most of the active members would have moved on and the new ones wouldn't ever know about his membership. It wasn't like they called roll.

Besides, he only had a few good seasons left in him anyway, and his membership would terminate naturally when he retired from baseball. He didn't need Clare to get him out of a commitment he never should have made in the first place.

"This is ridiculous. How long are you going to keep up the silent treatment?" he asked.

"How long is it going to take for you to give me what I want?"

"I'm not going to change my mind."

"Then we have nothing to talk about."

That's what you think, babe.

Clare slumped into her desk chair. She hadn't heard from Antonio in five days, not since the limo dropped her at her apartment following their weekend trip to Galveston. After the way he'd reacted to the two blowjobs she'd given him, she'd thought for sure he would change his mind and invite her to run the bases. But no.

She closed her eyes and let the memory take form. She licked her lips, remembering his unique taste, the feel of his cock in her mouth. It hadn't taken long to figure out where and how to stroke with her tongue to make his thighs tremble. Oh, what fun that had been!

He might be big, strong, tough Tony Ramirez on the field, but she'd reduced him to a helpless, quivering weakling with her mouth. She could still hear the strangled moans coming from his throat when he came. Her fingers curled, remembering how impossibly hard he'd became just before the internal spasms began.

Her sense of power had grown with each hot spurt of semen down her throat. Antonio was a strong man, but when she took his cock in her mouth, she dominated him. He might have thought he was in control, but she knew better. He had been completely at her mercy, and he had loved every minute of it. She was sure of it. So why was he being so stubborn about the invitation?

Because you're not pretty enough.

Because you're ordinary. There's not a glamorous bone in your body.

Five days. If she needed proof she wasn't the kind of woman a man like Antonio wanted long-term, she had it. He'd protested her analysis of the situation, but the silence of her telephone proved her theory. She'd given herself to him for a weekend, well, half a weekend, and he was through with her. The next time she saw him he would be with another model or actress, she was sure of it.

Athletes were predictable, and Antonio fit the mold perfectly. They'd take good sex anywhere they could get it, as long as it was behind closed doors. But in public, they kept up appearances. It didn't matter how skilled she was, he couldn't ask his friends to fuck an ugly duckling even if it would get him out of the club he claimed to despise.

She sighed and reached for the next test in the never-ending pile yet to be graded. Antonio Ramirez could go to hell.

The phone rang an hour later, startling her.

"Cripes." She tossed her pen down, glared at the streak of

red across the paper she'd been grading, and reached for the handset. "Clare Kincaid."

"I hope I'm not disturbing you."

She eyed the stack of yet ungraded tests. She'd made a serious dent in it. "Not at all, Uncle Doyle. I needed a break." She rubbed her eyes. "What's up?"

"Cathy has the flu."

"Oh no!" If Doyle was her favorite uncle, his wife, Cathy, was her favorite aunt. "What can I do to help? Do you need me to stay with her? Or I could make some chicken soup."

"No, but thanks. I've got that covered. But I need a date for the Press Association dinner tomorrow night. Cathy can't go, and I don't want to go alone. Those things are boring enough without having a pretty woman beside me."

She smiled at the compliment. "Pouring it on a little thick, aren't you?"

"Not at all," he protested. "Say you'll go. Please. Maybe you could develop a headache right after dessert, and I'd be obliged to take you home."

Clare propped her elbows on the desk, held the receiver to her ear with one hand, and pinched the bridge of her nose with the other. The annual P.A. dinner. It didn't get more stuffed shirt than that.

"I haven't got a thing to wear, Uncle Doyle."

"Buy something. Hell, go to one of those spa places tomorrow and have the works. On me. Stop by the house and pick up my credit card this evening. It's the least I can do for the favor you'd be doing me."

She fingered the ungraded tests. She had at least another hour of grading. Not exactly the most exciting way to spend a Friday night.

"Come on, Clare," he pleaded. "You work too hard. Enjoy life a little. Come get my credit card, pamper yourself then I'll take you out for a free meal and free booze."

She laughed. "You forgot the free boring conversation, and free boring speeches."

"Did I mention free booze?"

She smiled at his playful tone. "You did." Her shoulders drooped. "Okay. I'll go, but I wouldn't do this for anyone but you."

"Thank you!" His relief came through the phone line loud and clear. "I'm serious about the headache thing. Say the word, and we're out of there."

She could feel one coming on already. "I'll keep that in mind."

When she stopped by to pick up the credit card, Doyle answered the door. He handed over the plastic. "That's Cathy's. She said no one would question you if her name was on it, but they might if mine was. Oh, and one second." He reached for something on the hall table. "Cathy said to give you this."

She took the business card he held out. "She has appointments tomorrow for her hair and nails. She said you might as well use them since you're going in her place. They're expecting you, and it's all paid for."

Clare turned the card over and read the appointment times listed. "Thanks."

"Don't thank me. You're doing me a big favor. I'd rather dig holes in solid rock with my fingernails than go to this thing, but it's part of the job. Having a pretty woman with me makes it somewhat bearable."

She fished her wallet out of her purse, stowed the two cards, and tucked her wallet back in place. "You can cut out the flattery. I already said I would go with you."

"It's not flattery if it's true," he said. "Now scoot. The mall is still open. Go see how much you can charge on that card before they close."

She turned and headed to her car. "Be careful what you ask for," she said over her shoulder.

The dress she picked out would have made her credit card weep, but Cathy's didn't even whimper when the clerk rang up the sale. She hadn't intended to purchase anything so expensive, but when the salesperson asked about the occasion, she insisted Clare would be out of place with anything less than a formal gown.

After a day of pampering on Saturday, Clare stepped into the gown and eyed the finished product. The midnight blue dress hugged her curves, and the tiny crystals scattered across it winked liked stars. With the crystal-studded headband, the faux diamond bracelet at her wrist, and the flecks of glitter in her nail polish, she sparkled from head to toe. On the advice of the makeup artist at the salon, she added a swipe of red to her lips. There. She'd never looked better. Too bad it would be wasted on a date with her uncle.

Tony fidgeted in his seat. Beside him, the woman his publicist had fixed him up with this time looked more like a mannequin than a human being. Jeff Holder's twin brother, Jason, was receiving an award tonight, but Jeff and Megan's baby had come down with a fever. Jason had called, asking if he could fill in at the last minute to round out their table. Tony had argued against it, but Jason reminded him how important it was to make nice with the local press, and he'd caved. A call to his publicist, who was ecstatic about the invitation, and here he sat next to a plastic person and wished to hell the evening was over instead of just beginning.

It wouldn't be so bad if Clare had been beside him. He could endure just about anything as long as he had her to talk to. He still hadn't figured out a way to smooth things over with her, or he would have nixed this arranged date and called her— not that she would have answered his call.

Fucking caller I.D.

Who ever thought that was a good idea?

Well, it was what it was. The booze was free, and he'd already had his photo taken several times—something that would make his publicist swoon and maybe entice her to pursue a few more endorsement contracts on his behalf.

Ignoring his date, Tony turned to the man who had invited him and lifted his champagne glass. "To the man of the hour."

Jason raised his glass in acknowledgement. "Thanks, but I owe you one. These dinners can make you wish you were never born."

Tony sipped from his champagne flute and returned it to the table. He nodded at the two empty seats across the round banquet table. "Who are the lucky no-shows?"

"Not lucky and not no-shows." Jason pointed toward the door. "Doyle and his date are here. His wife has the flu. I almost envy Cathy."

Tony's gaze swept in the direction of Jason's pointing finger. A couple stood framed in the entryway, scanning the room. His body snapped to attention. Blood rushed to his groin, leaving him lightheaded and unable to breathe.

Clare.

Having spotted their assigned table, the couple wove through the ballroom, stopping to speak to acquaintances. Clare remained by Doyle's side, smiling, shaking hands. Her mouth moved.

Christ almighty! He couldn't tell what she said, but his dick remembered those lips and strained for an intimate meeting.

She'd done something with her hair, tried to tame it, but a few tendrils had escaped the up-do to frame her face like silk ribbons and tease the tops of her shoulders. She'd wrapped her body in the night sky, complete with stars that winked on and off when she moved. The dress left her arms and shoulders bare, long expanses of sun-kissed ivory begged for a man to taste them. His mouth watered, ready to oblige.

Doyle lingered, and Clare moved on. A woman at a nearby table waved to her. She stopped, and the bright smile she'd worn since her arrival dimmed to cool-white.

Tony tensed. The woman looked pleasant enough, but he could tell by her body language it was all she could do to maintain her polite façade. Doyle rejoined her, placed his hand on her elbow. She said something then allowed Doyle to usher her to her seat.

What the hell just happened? Every protective cell in his body screamed for him to find out who the witch was who'd taken the joy out of her evening and make sure she never spewed her poison in Clare's direction again.

He stood as the couple approached.

"Doyle," he said. His gaze shifted to the woman beside him. "Miss Kincaid."

The older man pulled out her chair before taking the seat beside her.

"Tony," he said. "I didn't know you were going to be here."

"Or I wouldn't have brought Clare," was unspoken. Tony chose to ignore it as he had the manager's warning the night he met her.

"Jeff and Megan had a change of plans," Jason explained.

"I conned Tony before he had a chance to check it out. I knew no one else on the team would agree to fill in." Everyone laughed, with the exception of the woman he loved.

Head bent, she unfolded her napkin and draped it over her lap. The smile that had lit her face when she'd first arrived was nowhere in sight now. Tony wanted to kick something or someone.

Doyle grinned and nodded. "The Mustangs version of hazing. Trick the new guy into going to the most boring dinner of the year." He inclined his head toward the man of the hour. "No offense intended, Jason."

"None taken," he assured.

"I was happy to help," Tony said. *Even happier that you brought Clare.* "I just hope Jeff's baby is all right."

"She'll be fine," Carrie, Jason's wife said to the table at large. "Megan said she thought Amy was teething, but with the flu going around, she didn't want to take any chances." She turned to the newcomers. "Clare, it's so good to see you. You look marvelous tonight."

She accepted the compliment with ease, and the conversation around the table turned to the recent flu outbreak and plans for the upcoming holiday season.

Tony couldn't take his eyes off her. He'd spent the last week wrestling with memories and inappropriate thoughts and dreams starring her. Images of her on the deck of the boat, wearing nothing but the night sky haunted him, and here she was, sitting across from him, draped in midnight blue velvet and stars. Soft lighting in the room cast her in moonlight.

If he didn't know better, he would have thought she'd worn the dress with the express purpose of driving him insane. He felt like the deck was shifting under him. But who was he kidding? He hadn't been on solid ground since the first time he saw her. She'd walked into the ballroom a few weeks ago and he'd been drunk on lust and love ever since.

The conversation swirled around him. Her voice was the only one he heard. "Everyone knows someone who has it."

"I hope so, too."

"I'd love to go shopping. When?"

"No, I have a class on Wednesday. Would Thursday work?"

"It's a date."

"Will you excuse me?" She scooted her chair back.

Tony was halfway out of his chair when Doyle's voice cut through the fog in his brain.

"Tony, what are you doing for Thanksgiving? Visiting relatives in New York?"

He lowered his butt back to the seat. His gaze never wavered from Clare's swaying backside weaving through the ballroom. *Mine.* She disappeared through the door, and he turned his attention back to the man who could make or break his career. He couldn't afford to alienate him.

"No, sir. I have some business to take care of here, so I'm afraid there won't be enough time to make the trip."

"We're having a big gathering, mostly family and a few friends. You should join us."

"Thanks. I would enjoy that." He pushed his chair back again. "If you'll excuse me."

Making his way to the exit, he ignored several shout outs to get him to stop and talk. Reaching the door, he stepped out and saw her across the lobby. "Clare!"

She stopped in front of the ladies room, turned, and waited for him to catch up. She glanced around. "Where's your walking stick?"

It took him a second to figure out what she was talking about then it registered and he laughed. "You mean What's-her-name. She's back at the table. I wanted to talk to you."

"You don't know her name?"

He shook his head. "No. It's something like Pia, Pea. It doesn't matter. She doesn't know who I am either. I needed someone on short notice to occupy a seat. My publicist found her." The hurt in her eyes made his heart ache. He looked at his toes. "I should have called you, but...."

"No." Her voice held a finality that broke his heart and confirmed his earlier thoughts. She wouldn't have picked up the phone, but at least she would know he had tried. Shit. He'd swung and missed again.

"What did you want to talk to me about?"

"How are you? I've missed you."

"I'm fine."

"You look more than fine. You're stunning tonight." He

caught a whiff of her perfume, floral with a hint of something sensual that reminded him of moonlight on her skin and made his fingers itch to touch her.

"Thank you. Now, if you'll excuse me." She turned, flattened her palm on the ladies room door.

"Who was that woman? The one you stopped to talk to on the way in tonight?"

Her shoulders tensed for a second then, as if she made a conscious effort to relax them, they dropped back into place.

"Is she the one you told me about? The one with the charm?"

"There's nothing charming about her." She pushed the door open and disappeared inside.

Tony waited, staring at the door until she reappeared. She stopped when she saw him. Stunning didn't come close to describing the way she looked, but on closer inspection, her eyes hinted at weariness.

"What do you want, Antonio?" She folded her arms across her middle and glared at him as if he were a pesky child.

"Are you okay? You look tired."

"Remind me to stay out of ladies restrooms. Before I went in I was stunning."

He smiled. At least she still had a sense of humor. "You're still stunning. I wasn't criticizing, just observing."

"I have a headache," she admitted.

"Let me take you home."

"No. Doyle will take me home as soon as the awards are over."

"Then let me escort you back in."

"That isn't necessary. I'm perfectly capable of walking on my own."

He'd never had to work so hard to get close to a woman in his life. Enough was enough. He took her hand, wrapped her fingers over his forearm. "I never said you weren't." Steering her toward the ballroom, he said, "Let me do this for you."

Pausing inside the door, he let his eyes adjust to the dim lighting before threading their way through the tables. He made sure to follow the same route she'd taken when she arrived. He slipped his arm down and around her waist, pulling her snug against his hip. She squirmed, but he tightened his grip, and she had little choice but to wrap her arm around his waist as well.

"Trust me," he whispered in her ear. "And whatever you do, don't hit me."

Before she could ask what the hell he meant, he dipped his head and nipped her on the neck. She gasped, and he swung her around so they were face to face. Her arms automatically came up to drape around his neck. *Perfect.*

Hands on her hips, he walked her backward through the crowded room. "I could just eat you up." He made sure his voice carried at just the right moment.

"Antonio," she hissed.

"Shh," he nuzzled her neck. Damn, he could get drunk on her scent. "Babe, let's go somewhere we can be alone."

He held her close, gazed into her eyes, imploring her to go along.

"Clare. Darling." The woman's voice held a hint of malice that set Tony's teeth on edge.

Clare tensed from head to toe. He held her gaze.

"Come with me," he begged, infusing the plea with as much sexual innuendo as he could muster.

She nodded. "I'd like that, Tony. My place or yours?"

He grinned. *Tony.* She never called him that. She understood the game he was playing. *Good girl.*

"Come on," he turned her, laced their fingers together, and tugged her toward their table. "Let's get your things and say our goodbye's."

CHAPTER FOURTEEN

"Doyle." She tapped her uncle on the shoulder to get his attention. "I have a headache. Antonio is going to give me a ride home."

Her uncle stood. "I can take you."

"No. Stay. We can't all abandon Jason on his special night." She turned to the award winner. "Forgive me. I really wish I could stay…."

"Think nothing of it," Jason said with a smile. "I'd be out of here, too, if I thought I could get away with it."

Clare made her apologies around the table. While they'd been in the lobby, Antonio's date had abandoned him for a sit-com celebrity at another table. Antonio informed her he was leaving, and she waved him away.

He returned, wrapped his arm around Clare's waist.

Doyle kissed her on the cheek. "Thanks for coming tonight. I hope you feel better soon."

"I will. Enjoy your evening."

"Tony, thanks for taking Clare home. I'll be in touch about Thanksgiving."

She opened her mouth to ask what he meant, but Antonio

ushered her away before she uttered the first word.

"Later," he whispered near her ear. "Smile."

Clare plastered on her best smile. Heads turned as they passed, and she sensed the scrutiny of dozens of pairs of eyes watching them leave together. When they passed Jessica' s table, Antonio tightened his hold on her and said loud enough for half the ballroom to hear, "I can't wait to get you home."

Her face flushed with heat. *Oh Lord.* What did he think he was doing?

"Clare, oh, Clare!" Jessica's voice rose over the background music, sounding like a crazed fan trying to get the attention of a rock star.

"Ignore her," Antonio said. "And smile." His hand on the small of her back dipped lower and took liberties with her left cheek. Being eye-level with everyone they passed, the move would have been hard to miss.

She smiled all the way to the elevator and, once inside, loosened the lid on her temper. "Thanksgiving? Are you kidding me?"

He punched the button for the parking garage. "Doyle invited me to spend Thanksgiving at his house."

This could not be happening. What had her uncle been thinking? "Aren't you going to New York to see your family?"

"Not for Thanksgiving. I'll make the trip closer to Christmas when I'll have more time." The doors swooshed open, and he stuck his arm out to hold them open for her.

She stomped out of the elevator and turned left, putting distance between them before she exploded in tears. How was she ever going to forget about Antonio if he kept popping up in her life? All week she'd battled memories of time spent with him. She couldn't set foot in her office without remembering the day he'd come to see her. It had become impossible to work at her desk without memories rushing in, taking over her thoughts. Midweek, she'd posted a note on the door, directing students to find her in the library during office hours.

The move hadn't quite done the trick. Thoughts of Antonio decreased from constant to barely every three minutes. She had hoped tonight would provide enough distraction to take her mind off the insufferable man, but noooo. He had to show up at the Press Association dinner, too. And now he would be at their family Thanksgiving dinner? Not that he knew she was family. She went to great pains to keep her relationship to team management quiet. The last thing she needed was reporters hunting her up in hopes of getting inside information.

She stopped, looked around at the expanse of vehicles, and realized she had no freakin' idea where she was going. "Where's your car?"

Silence.

She turned. Antonio stood in front of the elevators. He pointed in the opposite direction.

Well, shit.

She stalked back to where she'd begun. He smirked and headed toward the back of the garage. Clare closed her eyes and prayed for patience. He was driving her insane. She took a deep breath, let it out, and followed him.

He slid behind the wheel of a brand new SUV and waited until she'd buckled her seatbelt before he started the engine.

"I'm not going to New York for Thanksgiving," he said, pulling out of the garage. "I have things to do here, and with the short holiday and the probability of bad weather interfering with travel plans, I thought I'd skip this one. Doyle was only being nice."

It was nice, and just like her uncle to open his home to a lonely single guy during the holidays. She huffed out a noncommittal breath.

"I take it you plan to be there, too?"

"I was thinking about it."

She saw him nod out of the corner of her eye. "I'll decline the invitation if you want me to."

How small would that make her seem? "No. It's a big house."

"You really want to be like that woman?"

The change of subject caught her off guard, and she snapped her head around to look at him. "Huh?"

"The woman who earned the charm. You really want to be like *her*?"

"Jessica. Do you know her?"

He shook his head. "Never saw her before in my life. Can't say I want to see her again, either."

She turned her gaze back to the mostly empty downtown streets. For some reason, she was ridiculously happy Antonio hadn't been one of the Bases Loaded members who'd bestowed the coveted charm on Jessica. She didn't think she could bear it if he had been. The idea of him being with that witch made her sick to her stomach. Anyone but Jessica.

"You're better than her, Clare, and more beautiful."

She had no comeback, so the comment hung in the air between them until he stopped the SUV in front of her apartment complex.

"Back to the silent treatment?"

"We've got nothing more to discuss," she said, reaching for the door latch.

"Hold on a minute." He opened his door and came around to her side to help her out of the car.

She headed up the walk toward her apartment, and he fell in step beside her. She put the key in the lock and turned the knob.

"Clare…."

"Go away." She stepped inside, turned to shut the door, and bumped into a wall of muscle.

Antonio had followed her inside. He closed the door and leaned against it. "We need to talk."

"I wasn't lying. I do have a headache." The convenient excuse was a reality, thanks to seeing Jessica. The woman always played nice until she lured her prey close enough to pounce. When would she learn to stay on her toes at the kind of functions the witch attended? Jessica's comment about the age of her date had seemed innocent enough, but knowing the witch's methods, she understood there would be more sharp barbs later—when she got her alone.

She hated she couldn't respond the way she wanted to, but announcing she was doing her uncle a favor in the middle of a ballroom full of sports reporters would have done more damage to her peace of mind than enduring whatever Jessica had in mind for her in the future. So, she'd accepted the thinly veiled insult with as much dignity as possible and tried not to let it ruin her evening.

Then she'd come face-to-face with Antonio.

She set her purse on the small table behind the door and

tossed her keys beside it. "I'm going to take something for my headache and get out of this dress. When I come back, I expect you to be gone."

He wasn't going to leave, but that knowledge didn't keep her from straining her ears listening for the sound of her front door opening and closing. No such luck. She downed a couple of painkillers and after carefully hanging her new dress in the closet, donned her favorite sweatpants and an oversized Mustangs shirt, butter-soft from thousands of washings. To complete her look, she put on fuzzy, bunny rabbit slippers. A glance at her reflection in the full-length mirror on the back of her closet door confirmed her intention. "Nothing sexy or inviting about this look," she murmured.

She peeked around the corner. He had made himself at home on her sofa, and even though she hadn't exactly invited him in, it wasn't every day a drop-dead gorgeous, tuxedo-clad male graced her home. She took a moment to admire the view and wrestle her body under control. Her head pounded in tandem with her heartbeat, and damned if her heart wasn't beating like a tribal drum. She was so hot for him it was a wonder smoke signals weren't coming from her ears.

A soda can sat on the coffee table in front of him, and he had found the remote. Short snippets of sound confirmed his channel surfing. Other than the tuxedo thing, and the fact he had the appearance of a god, he was an ordinary guy. He lifted the soda and brought it to his lips.

She stepped into the room and time stood still. Antonio froze in the process of sipping his drink. He gazed at her over the top of the drink. Her knees trembled under his scrutiny, and suddenly the armor she'd donned seemed more like the fabled emperor's clothes. It was as if he could see right through them.

He set the can on the table and unfolded from the sofa without taking his eyes off her. He sidestepped around the coffee table and closed the distance between them in two steps. Her bunny slippers were glued to the floor as if mesmerized by the approach of the big bad wolf and helpless to get away.

He stopped in front of her.

"Still have a headache?"

She nodded, unwilling to trust her voice.

He reached for her hand. His touch was gentle and like

tinder to the fire smoldering inside her. He brushed his thumb over the back of her hand and sparks flew.

"Come here," he said. "Let me make it go away." His voice was low, seductive, hypnotic. How else had she ended up on the sofa with her bottom within the V of his thighs? The thick ridge of his erection pressed against her hip, sending flames of desire licking up her side like a forest fire climbing the trunk of a tree.

"Relax." He wrapped one arm around her shoulders and tucked her up against him.

The soft fabric of his jacket was cool against her cheek. She inhaled deeply and felt drunk on his scent.

"Did you think this getup would send me running?" He held her close with one hand while the other stroked along her leg from hip to bunny slipper.

"It isn't working, is it?"

"Nope." He flicked a bunny ear. "Those are the sexiest slippers I've ever seen. You know what they say about rabbits, right?"

She'd made a tactical error, obviously.

"And the way these sweatpants mold to your curves." He helped them along, tracing the outline of her leg beneath the worn fabric. "And this shirt? You couldn't have seduced me better with lace and see-through fabric."

His hand slid beneath the hem of her shirt. "And I don't need x-ray vision to know you aren't wearing anything under it."

His hand found bare skin then burned its way up to cover her breast. She melted into a puddle of sensitized goo under his expert touch.

"So soft." He massaged the mass with the grace of a baker preparing a delicate pastry. His gentle handling brought tears to her closed eyes. "Your breasts are beautiful. Just touching them makes me feel like a man. It's humbling." He rested his cheek against the top of her head. "You don't know what you do to me."

He didn't know what he did to *her*. Or perhaps he did because he certainly knew *what* to do to her. Every touch, every caress tugged on her heartstrings, tangling her up in a knot of want and longing and need. Her assessment days ago that she was nothing more than a passing fancy for him didn't hold up against his continued interest in being with her.

Maybe, if she wished hard enough, her dreams would come true. Maybe he could love her the way she loved him—with every fiber of her being, with everything she was and ever would be.

He brushed a thumb over one nipple until it grew hard and tight and made her ache for more. She pressed her thighs together to ease the throbbing there.

"How's your headache?"

"Better." Almost gone, she realized.

"Do you trust me?"

He might be a rat about other things, but he'd proven many times over she could trust him with her body. She nodded her answer, praying he would fill all her empty places.

His hand abandoned her breast and burrowed past the waistband of her sweats. "Let me take care of you," he crooned. His fingers crept lower, parted her cleft, and found the secret button that made her thighs fall open. "That's it, babe."

His fingers explored further, finding the embarrassing evidence of her need.

"You're so wet for me. I love the way your body does that." He closed his palm over her sex. "Can you tell? Your lips plump up and you get all juicy like a ripe peach. It drives me insane wanting you, wanting to shove my cock inside you."

She groaned and clutched at his lapel, crumpling the expensive fabric in her grip. No wonder he'd won four Golden Glove awards, the man had magic fingers. They stroked and played and teased at her tender flesh while his words strummed every raw nerve ending in her brain and the tangled strings of her heart.

Unable to remain still, she writhed against his hand, demanding more. Her silent plea did not go unheeded.

Antonio pressed the heel of his hand against her mound, applying firm but gentle pressure that helped alleviate some of her need but only increased it in other places.

"Please," she whispered into his collar. "Please, Antonio."

Two digits rimmed her vaginal opening. "Shh." He spread her natural moisture over her aching flesh. "I'll always take care of you."

One long, callused finger entered her. She cried out, and her pussy clamped around the digit. Her hips rose, taking all she could inside her.

"Beautiful," he rasped against the top of her head. "So fucking beautiful."

Another finger joined the first. Her heels slid against the sofa until they met the solid rock of his thighs. Her knees fell open in surrender. A slow moan escaped her lips.

"That's it. Let me give you this."

He kept up the pressure with the heel of his hand and pushed a third finger inside her. Clare lost the ability to think. He massaged her pussy, inside and out, twisting her up into a tight knot of need so acute she screwed her eyes shut against the pain. She clawed her way up his chest until her breasts were squeezed between them, and her face was buried in the crook of his neck. Winding her arms around his head, she clung to him.

"Clare, sweetheart." His words were a caress, the arm at her back a band of steel. "Take it. Now."

He twisted the knot tighter then with one plunging tug, jerked the end of the string holding her together. She fell from the precipice with only his arm around her to break her fall.

His shirt collar absorbed her tears but couldn't contain her sobs. He slowly extricated his hand from her pants and cradled the back of her head while she cried out a week's worth of anger, loneliness, and frustration.

"Shh. I've got you, babe."

More than you know. A week without him, without his touch had been torture. He might understand her body, but he didn't understand her. She sniffed and peeled her upper body from his.

"I'm sorry." She swiped at her cheeks with her fingertips, keeping her eyes downcast. She couldn't bear to look at him, or she would burst into tears again. She patted his shoulder. "I ruined your tux."

He shrugged. "No problem. I have another one."

Of course he did. What was she thinking? This was Antonio freakin' Ramirez. He made a gazillion dollars a year.

She couldn't figure out a graceful way to remove herself from his lap, so she pushed against his shoulders, scooted her butt over one hard thigh, and turned her back to him. There. That was better. She sat cross-legged and buried her face in her hands.

"Clare?" His hand swept over her back in big circles. "Talk

to me."

"No."

Circle. Circle. Circle. "How's your headache?"

She took mental inventory of her physical self. Her headache was gone, drat the man, but the rest of her body felt as if she'd just run a marathon. "Gone."

Circle. Circle. Circle. "I missed you."

She tried to breathe deep but hiccupped instead. *Dignity, Clare. Find some dignity.* "I missed you, too."

Circle. Circle. Circle. "You should go to bed, get some rest."

She nodded and unfolded one leg. Before she could unfold the other one, Antonio stood and scooped her into his arms.

"Let me down."

"No. Just let me do this for you. For once, let me take care of you."

It felt so good to be in his arms, she squashed all further argument and let him carry her to the bedroom. He set her on her feet next to the bed, drew the covers back, waiting patiently while she slid between them. He tucked the covers around her, letting his hands linger over her curves as if he needed to touch her again so he wouldn't forget.

She couldn't remember anyone ever treating her with such gentleness, and the thought brought on a fresh bout of tears.

"What now?" he asked, perching on the edge of the mattress.

"It's just…."

She couldn't tell him. It was so much more than tonight. It was everything and nothing at the same time. Her love for him. The way he made her feel inside. The insecurities that lurked so deep inside her not even making love with Antonio could banish them. The loneliness she would feel when he was gone, not just tonight but every night for the rest of her life, because he *would* leave her.

The pad of his thumb scratched her cheek as he gathered her tears. "Trust me, and I'll make it my life's work to make sure you never cry again."

Deep lines etched between his brows and she hated what her lack of control had done to him. He was too beautiful to worry.

"Please." She forced the word past lips swollen from

crying. "I'll be fine. I just need to be alone for a while."

He combed her hair back from her forehead with his fingers, and his lips tipped up in a smile that said he didn't understand but he *understood.*

"Okay, love. I'll go. But just so you know, tonight was special." He planted a kiss on her forehead. Feathered a few more over her eyelids, her cheekbones, her chin. "I could spend a lifetime making you come and never get tired of seeing you take your pleasure from me."

He cupped her cheek in one gentle palm and leaned in to place a tender kiss on her lips. She craved so much more, but he'd given her too much already.

He stopped in the doorway and turned. He looked like a GQ model framed in her bedroom doorway, wearing his rumpled tuxedo. Fully clothed and tucked under layers of bedclothes, she felt naked and exposed. He flicked the light switch, plunging the room into darkness. Light from the hallway turned him into a James Bond movie silhouette.

"Sweet dreams," he said. Then he was gone.

She listened for the sound of the front door opening and closing before she curled into a ball and let the tears fall.

CHAPTER FIFTEEN

He drove too fast on the way back to his hotel. Crisp November air rushing through the open car windows did nothing to cool the nuclear reactor his body became the minute Clare walked out in her don't-fuck-with-me sleeping gear. Women had no idea what that kind of get-up did to a man. Sure, the barely there concoctions they bought to drive a man crazy with lust were nice, in an "I'm easy" sort of way.

When a woman wore one of those outfits, a man knew he was going to get some. He wasn't even going to have to work for it. It was sort of like waking up on Christmas morning to find none of your presents were wrapped. Sure, they had ribbons and bows on them, but the mystery, the suspense, the anticipation of tearing the wrapping away to find the surprise inside was gone. Kaput.

Not that he didn't appreciate a fancy gift on occasion, but Clare's outfit tonight? Damn.

She might as well have waved a red flag in front of a raging bull. It was a dare, a challenge issued. Seeing her in those makeshift pajamas almost did him in. She was damned sexy without even trying.

But she'd been trying all right. Trying to discourage his

interest. She had no way of knowing her strategy was flawed. Women back in the day knew the score. The only way they could get by in the world was to get married, so they wore dresses that covered everything except an enticing glimpse of tits. Men were so hard up to see what the women had under all their voluminous skirts, even glimpsing a bit of ankle would give a guy ideas. He would marry the woman just so he could unwrap the package.

Women today could learn a few things from their predecessors.

When he and Clare were married, he would buy her a closet full of pajamas—flannel ones with buttons down the front so he could have the pleasure of taking them off of her every single night. He'd unwrap her one button at a time, tasting each inch of skin, lavishing attention on her breasts until she begged him to do more. Then he'd flip her over onto her stomach, dip his fingers past her pajama pants waistband, and yank them down. He'd sink his teeth into her ass a few times to let her know who was in charge. Then….

Christ! Where was an ice storm when you needed one?

He couldn't remember ever wanting a woman as badly as he had wanted Clare in those bunny slippers. Hell, his need hadn't wavered one bit—his dick was still hard enough to drive rivets through steel. But he wouldn't trade a fuck with a dozen willing women for the evening he'd just spent pleasuring Clare. She'd needed some TLC, and he'd given it to her. That was enough.

He lifted his hand to his face and sniffed. Heaven scented his fingers. He rubbed his thumb over the pads of his first three fingers, recalling the feel of her tight channel. His fingers curled in, stroked his palm. Man, she fit so perfectly in his hand. He could still feel her clit grinding against his palm, her soft, bare pussy weeping for his touch.

Shit. He exited the freeway and came to a stop for the red light at the end of the ramp. He had no idea why she'd cried afterwards. He'd never made a woman cry before, and he didn't have a clue what to say or do for her. Maybe he should have stayed with her.

The light turned green, and he accelerated through the intersection. Damn, her tears twisted up his gut.

Clare wasn't like other women he knew. She was intelligent and strong. Her breakdown meant something—he just didn't know what. But he was damned sure going to find out.

He made his way to his hotel, dropped his new SUV with the valet, and made a beeline to his suite. Standing in the shower, letting the cold water work its magic, he contemplated his next move. Thanksgiving was coming up. He'd find some way to get her alone so he could talk to her, show her the surprise he'd bought for her.

Another bouquet of red roses atop her desk greeted Clare the next morning. She dropped her briefcase on the floor and pulled her chair from the kneehole. She smiled at the small stuffed toy tucked into the bouquet. Pink bunny ears flopped over the card it held in its furry paws.

"Who are they from?" Laura stepped into the office. "Same guy as before?"

Clare nodded. "Same guy."

"Wow. Must be getting serious." Her friend put her nose to the bouquet, closed her eyes, and inhaled. "What's with the rabbit?"

"I don't know." She carefully removed the bunny. What had happened the night before between her and Antonio was somehow too private to discuss with anyone else. The feelings he'd stirred up in her were too new, and she needed to hold them close a while longer. At least until she understood them better. "Maybe the florist was out of teddy bears."

Laura shrugged and plopped into a visitor's chair. "So, who is this guy?"

Clare sat, opened the drawer where she kept miscellaneous stuff, and dropped the stuffed animal inside. "Antonio Ramirez," she said, carefully tucking floppy ears down so they wouldn't get stuck when she closed the drawer.

"Baseball player?"

She sighed. "Yep. One of the best." *At all sorts of things.*

Her friend studied the flowers. Clare rocked back in her chair and closed her eyes. Blessed silence descended on the room.

"You aren't just talking about baseball, are you?"

She sat up. "No. He's amazing."

"And he sends flowers the day after."

No sense denying it. The truth was probably written all over her face anyway. "Yes, he does."

"He isn't apologizing, is he?"

"No. Antonio has nothing to apologize for, and he knows it."

"Arrogant."

"Confident," she countered.

"A keeper?"

"It can't last, Laura."

"Why, in Heaven's name, not?"

"He's new to the team, and he needs a friend right now. As soon as the season begins, he'll have women all over him, and he won't need or want me anymore."

"Hon, have you lost your ever-loving mind?" She scooted to the edge of her chair and leaned over the desk. "Men don't send flowers like this," she said and cocked her head in the direction of the bouquet, "unless they're apologizing or begging."

"Maybe he's just being nice."

"Nice, my ass. He wants you. Nice is a mixed bouquet. Something seasonal. Red roses represent blood. His. Either he's bleeding to show how sorry he is, or his blood is running hot for you."

Clare stood. She'd heard enough. "You are way off base, my friend. I've got a class in ten minutes."

Laura took the hint. At the door, she paused. "I'll see if I can find a geranium for you while you're out."

"Why a geranium?"

"They represent true friendship as well as stupidity. I'm your friend, no matter what, but you're stupid if you believe that man doesn't want you."

She stared at the empty doorway long after the other woman left, her parting words running an endless loop through her brain. She made it through her early class and cancelled her later one. Her brain refused to think about any kind of theory other than the one Laura had proposed. Was she underestimating Antonio's feelings for her?

She pulled the stuffed rabbit out of her drawer and set it, facing her, in the middle of her desk. Laura had to be wrong. All that mumbo jumbo about the meaning of certain flowers was something only a woman would know. There wasn't a man on the planet who knew the difference between a rose and a daisy. Antonio had simply called the florist and ordered the most expensive flowers available. The floppy-eared bunny was evidence enough the flowers were thoughtful and nothing more.

Still holding the unopened card, she slipped it from the envelope. Expecting a typewritten note, she was startled when she recognized Antonio's bold scrawl. She amended her earlier thought. He had taken the time to walk into the florist shop and write a personal message.

The next time you wear bunny slippers, we're going to do what rabbits do best.

See you on the bunny slope.

Bring the rabbit, he has the tickets.

I'll bring the carrot.

A wave of heat began low in her stomach and rose like the tide at full moon to warm her face and the tops of her ears. She clutched the card against her fluttering stomach.

Wait.

She read the card again. The rabbit has the tickets? Tossing the card aside, she reached for the stuffed toy. A closer examination revealed a zipper running along the bunny's back. Clare squeezed and, sure enough, caught the sound of crinkling paper. She carefully pulled the zipper down and slipped the folded envelope from the hidden compartment.

Inside were two first-class airline tickets to Aspen for Thanksgiving weekend.

Propping her elbows on the edge of the desk, she dropped her face into her upturned palms and groaned. She'd allowed herself to forget about the one remaining bid item, hoping against hope he would forget about it, too.

No such luck.

Along with the tickets was another handwritten note with every travel detail outlined down to the minute. He'd included a packing list, that if followed to the letter, wouldn't allow her past the front door of the condo booked for their use, much less onto the bunny slope.

Bases Loaded

Clearly, he had no intention of skiing.

Her desk phone rang, and she almost jumped out of her skin. It had to be a colleague or one of her students. Everyone else called her on her cell phone. For a half-second, while she stuffed the plane tickets back in their envelope and stowed it in her desk drawer on top of the Bases Loaded charm, she considered not answering the call. But she had a job to do, so she slammed the drawer shut and reached for the phone.

Tony faltered. Clare sounded out of breath, like she'd raced to get the phone before the caller hung up. Or shit…that's the way she sounded right after she came. The thought rocked him, and it took a second for him to recover his equilibrium.

"Hello?" she repeated. "Is anyone there?"

Get a grip, Ramirez. "Clare. It's me, Tony. Did you get the flowers?"

A sigh then a creaking sound. Her desk chair. He remembered the noise it made when she'd leaned back in it the day they fucked in her office. He'd gone down on his knees and put his hands on her thighs. As his hands went up her skirt, she'd tilted back a bit. Yeah, that was the same sound.

"Yes, I did. Thank you. They're beautiful."

"Not as beautiful as you."

Silence.

"Clare?"

"Please, Antonio. You don't have to keep doing this."

"What? Telling you you're beautiful or sending you flowers?"

"All of it."

"No. Unacceptable. What did you think of the bunny? Do you know how hard it is to find one of those this time of year?"

"He's cute, and I appreciate the thought—"

"Did you find the tickets?"

"I did, but I can't go with you. I've already made plans for Thanksgiving."

"Cancel them. You said you would do the auction items with me. This is the last one, babe. Spend the weekend with me."

There was the creaking again. He could imagine her sitting in her office, her skirt hiked up to her hips, stroking herself through her panties.

"What are you wearing," he asked.

"What?" she shrieked. The chair squeaked again.

"I asked what you're wearing?"

"Um…a skirt and blouse. Why?"

He wedged his cell phone between his ear and his shoulder, awkwardly standing to open his fly before his jeans strangled him.

"Lock your door."

"Antonio," she warned.

"Just do it, okay?"

"I shouldn't."

"You should. You don't have another class this morning, do you?"

"No. I had an early class. I need to work on the lesson plans for a new class I'm going to teach next semester."

"Good. Then do as I say. Lock the door."

The chair creaked again, and a loud thump came over the line when she dropped the receiver on her desk. He held his breath until she picked the handset up again.

"Okay. Door is locked. What's this all about?"

"It's about convincing you to spend Thanksgiving weekend naked with me."

"And I need the door locked for that?"

"Yes, you do. What kind of skirt are you wearing? One of those loose swirly things or is it tight on your hips?"

"I don't see what that has to do with anything," she protested.

"You'll see. What kind of skirt?"

"It's a pencil skirt," she said with an exasperated sigh.

"I like those. They show off your ass."

"Antonio."

He could see her plain as day. When she lost her patience, her lips thinned and her eyes narrowed. Sexy.

"Are you wearing pantyhose?"

"What century do you think this is?"

"I'll take that as a no. Good. Stand up, pull your skirt up to your waist then sit back down."

He could hear her breathing on the other end. Good. If he could hear her, then he was getting to her. After a long pause when he wasn't sure if she might hang up on him or see where this was going, he finally heard a loud *thunk* indicating she'd dropped the receiver on her desk again. That and the creaking of her chair told him she was following his instructions.

His heart beat so hard it could power a jackhammer. Unable to sit still, he stood and paced the confines of his hotel room, waiting for her to return. He double locked the door to prevent interruptions then crossed to the bank of windows and pulled the sheer panels closed.

There was a telltale sound—God bless that chair—on the line then she picked up the receiver. Tony closed his eyes and said a silent thank you to the universe. He'd rather be in her office doing his convincing in person, but he had been more than a little afraid she wouldn't have listened to him.

"I feel stupid," she said.

"Don't," he commanded. "Now, tell me about your panties. What color are they? Describe them in detail."

She sighed and after a long pause where he again imagined she was going to hang up on him, she said, "They're light blue. Lace in front with a thong back."

"You're wearing thong underwear?" His dick, already hard, throbbed as he imagined the scrap of blue lace covering her and nothing else.

"Yes," she drew the word out, so it was a question and an answer. "I didn't want panty lines to show under my skirt."

"So you wore nothing so every guy on campus who sees your ass will think you aren't wearing anything under your skirt?"

"No. I wore a thong so they wouldn't see the outline of my underwear and know how big my ass is."

She was exasperated, but he didn't care if he was pissing her off. She was pissing him off, too. "Your ass is *not* big. And I can assure you, with or without panty lines, every man who sees your ass in a tight skirt is going to be imagining what it would feel like against his crotch. The only difference is when they don't see an outline, they think there's nothing but air between their dick and your pussy, and that's a fantasy all its own."

"You're impossible," she huffed. "I'm hanging up now."

"No!" He tempered the panic gripping him. "Don't hang up. Please."

"Are you going to stop criticizing my choice of

undergarments and tell my why I'm sitting here with my skirt around my waist?"

Tony swiped a hand over his face and stared sightless at the city filtered by gauze-thin curtains. He'd gone way off track and almost lost her. It was time to back off and refocus on the reason for this phone call.

"I'm getting to that."

"I don't have all day," she said.

"Are your knees under your desk?"

"Yes."

"Good. Spread them wide so they touch the panels on either side."

"Okay."

"Touch yourself. Put your hand on your stomach and slide it lower, but don't go under the lace. Keep your fingers on top of the fabric."

"Antonio."

He ignored the protest in her voice. "Do it for me. I want to touch you, but I'm not there, so you'll have to do it for me."

Her chair creaked again, and he closed his eyes, imagining her fingers sliding over the blue lace panel. "Tell me what you feel."

"Um…the lace is rough on my fingers."

"And your mound? How does it feel?"

"Tingly. It sort of hurts, in a good way."

"That's the blood flow filling your tissues, getting you ready for my cock."

A hissing sound filled his ear. Her sucking in a breath?

"Two fingers now. Use them to part your lips. Press the lace into the crevices, so the fabric puts pressure on your clit."

Another unintelligible sound came from her end.

"You're doing good. Now, move your fingers up and down. Go lower. Are you wet?"

"Yes," she breathed.

"If I close my eyes, I can smell your arousal. If I was there, I'd put my mouth on you and taste you. But since I'm not, you'll have to imagine it. Close your eyes and imagine my face between your legs, my tongue gathering up your juices, flicking over your clit, rough like the lace of your panties."

God, he was going to die for wanting her. "Rub yourself.

That lace panel is my tongue."

"Mmm…."

"That's it, babe. I'm right there with you, tasting you, making you feel good. You're so wet, and now your pussy is swollen and even more sensitive. You want me inside you, and I want to be there more than anything. Move your fingers lower. Press the lace inside."

Her moan made his knees buckle. He stumbled to the nearest chair and sat.

"I know. That feels good, doesn't it, sweetheart? But you need more. I can feel it in the way your hips are moving. You need me inside you, not just my tongue."

"Yes." The word was nothing more than a gasp.

"Move the lace aside so I can see you." He continued as if he were there. "I love your pussy, especially when you're horny for me, like now. You're all pink, and slick with your own juices. I can't wait any longer, I know you want it, too."

"Please, Antonio."

He was dying. His cock had passed aching to downright painful. He needed release as much as she did, but his hand had recently become an unacceptable substitute for her pussy. Hell, her mouth ran a close second, and if she ever trusted him enough, he'd add her ass to the list and bump his hand completely out of the running.

"I'm here, babe."

She had long, slim musician's fingers. "Find the rim with your index finger. Trace it all the way around."

Another one of those sounds that came straight from her gut nearly did him in.

"That's it. Two fingers, babe. Put them inside. As far as you can get them."

"Ooohhh." A whimper followed the breathless moan.

"Oh, God. You feel so good. I have to move now. Out. In again. Hard."

"Aahhh."

Tony moved to the edge of the chair and braced his elbows on his knees. Cradling his forehead in one hand, he held the phone to his ear with the other and listened to the erotic sounds of her finger fucking herself.

Shit.

Why had he thought this was a good idea? She was getting off all right, but he'd be in pain until he could sink inside her again. And that would be days, at best.

"So good, babe. Feel me fucking you. Squeeze my cock. Yeah, just like that."

Another whimper told him how close she was.

"Use your thumb, Clare. Touch your clit. You're almost there. Reach for it."

Torture. Pure torture listening to her, imagining being inside her and knowing she was pretending her fingers were him.

"I can't stand it any longer. I've got to fuck you hard. Do it for me. Hard. In. Out. Harder. Shit. I'm going to come. Come with me."

Tony gripped his forehead hard enough to break bones. His fingers tightened on the phone, threatening to turn it to dust. Sweat trickled down his jaw and along his spine, and he was going to need dental work to repair the molars he'd ground to nubs.

"Come for me, Clare."

She made that little choking sound in the back of her throat—the one she made when she came. Then a string of sounds he had no words to describe, but were exclamations of intense pleasure. In the background, her desk chair creaked in rhythm with the short jerky movements of her hips as she rode out the orgasm.

Every muscle in his body trembled with the effort to remain still, when all he wanted to do was drive his cock into anything available. His hand. Sofa cushions. Throw pillows. Hell, he'd fuck a keyhole if he could find one. He needed a cold shower. Or a swim in the nearest frozen lake. Maybe he'd call room service for a couple of buckets of ice and fill the bathtub. That might do it.

"Antonio?"

Ah, God. The vulnerability in her voice nearly broke him in half. "I'm here, babe. I'll always be here."

She sighed.

"Are you okay?" he asked.

"Mmm. I'm good."

"You're perfect." He almost told her then, but when he said the words, he wanted to see her face. It was the only way he could be sure she believed him.

"I'm a mess."

"A beautiful mess. Your skin glows for hours after an orgasm."

"Oh!"

He almost laughed, imagining her lifting her cum coated hand to her face. "Don't worry. No one will know," he lied.

Every male, no matter what the species, would recognize the soft expression on her face, the flush of her skin. But he wasn't going to tell her. Every man she encountered today would instinctively understand she'd been claimed. The thought made him feel marginally better.

"Take the panties off," he said, "and put them inside the rabbit's pocket. They're mine now."

"Antonio." No warning, just a hint of acceptance.

"You're going to love Aspen."

"We aren't going to see a single thing in Aspen, are we?"

"We're going to see plenty, but it will all be inside our condo. I'm going to look all I want, explore every nook and cranny."

"That's what I thought."

"I'll allow you to do the same."

He held his breath until she sighed. "Okay. You win. I'll cancel my plans for Thanksgiving."

"Where are we going?" Clare peered out the limo window. This was not the way to the airport.

"We need to make a stop first. It won't take long," Antonio said.

She shrugged. If they missed their flight to Aspen, she wouldn't exactly be disappointed. Sure, she wanted to spend time with Antonio, but the man still had blinders on when it came to what she really wanted. He'd managed to deflect the conversation about Bases Loaded every time it came up, and somehow he'd convinced her to go on this trip with him. Not one of her finer moments.

They exited the freeway and, after several miles, turned down what appeared to be a private driveway.

Old growth trees lined the roadway and dotted open pastureland as far as she could see. They approached the end of the street, and a house came into view. Clare sat up. From the outside, it was everything she'd wanted in a home, and she envied whoever lived there.

"Where are we?" she asked as they followed the drive to the back of the house.

"Home." He exited the car, not waiting for the driver to come and open the door. He extended his hand to assist her.

Her spine tingled—whether from his touch or the implication of that one word, she had no idea. "Who's home?"

"Ours," he said, smiling.

"What are you talking about?"

Heading toward the house, he pulled her along behind him. "I bought it. Signed the papers yesterday." Stopping at the back door, he stuck his hand in the front pocket of his jeans and pulled out a Mustangs key ring with two keys hanging from it. He held them out to her. "These are yours."

He dropped the keys in her palm and closed her fingers around them. "I have a set, too." He produced another key ring from his pocket and fitted a key to the lock. The tumblers fell, and he turned the knob.

"Come on," he urged her through the open door. "See what you think."

The backdoor opened into a large, eat-in kitchen. Acres of granite countertops gleamed in the light shining through the multi-paned bay window that looked out over a beautifully landscaped backyard and created a natural alcove for a table. Oak cabinets and restaurant quality appliances were enough to make a gourmet chef weep with joy. She'd never seen a more perfect kitchen.

"What do you think? Can you see yourself in here? Not that I'm insinuating you belong in the kitchen or anything, but you know what I mean." He walked to the windowed alcove and turned to her. "Can you see it? A big round table here where we can eat our meals and the kids can do their homework while they snack."

Huh? The mention of kids, snacks, and homework snapped her back to her senses. "Have you lost your mind?"

"No, I don't think so. Remember when we were looking at

apartments? You said none of them were me. You were right. Maybe they were the old me, but the new me wouldn't be happy in an apartment. I was very specific with the real estate lady about what I wanted…well, what you said *you* wanted, in a house. Come on. Let me show you the rest of the place."

"Antonio." She crossed her arms and glared at him. "Explain yourself. Now."

"I thought I just did."

"If you did, it sounded like you bought this house for *me*, not for you."

"I bought it for *us*. I thought you would like it," he said, pitifully.

Between the look on his face, and the dejected tone in his voice, she caved. What would it hurt to see the house, then she would break the news to him—he would be living here alone.

After touring upstairs and down they made their way to the front of the house where they stood in opposite doorways opening into the limestone-tiled entryway.

"It's lovely," she said, meaning it. If she could have picked her dream house, this would be it.

"I'm glad you like it. I wasn't sure about the inside, but you can change anything you want."

"I'm not going to live in this house with you. We've been over this before. I'm not the kind of woman men like you keep around."

"Yes, you are." He crossed to stand in front of her, his broad shoulders blocking everything but him from her view. "What can I do to convince you?"

"How many times do I have to tell you? You say you love me, but I've only ever asked one thing of you, and you refuse to give it to me."

"That's because what you want is something completely insane. I love you. I want to marry you. And I don't want other men touching you, much less running the bases with you. You're mine."

The deep timbre of his voice sent a thrill down her spine while the voice of reason told her to beware of silver-tongued devils. He was so close the heat radiating off his body reminded her of a furnace. His scent drew her in, called to her in a way no other ever had. Her heart tripped and slid to her toes. It would be so easy to believe his pretty words. But not today.

She sidestepped, intending to put the necessary distance between them before the horny, love-struck idiot inside her told the stubborn man how she felt about him.

He moved fast. She gasped. Pinned between a wall of solid muscle and, well…a wall, she had nowhere to go and nowhere to look but up.

"Tell me what you want me to do, Clare. I give up. I'll do whatever it takes to convince you my feelings are real. I want you. I love you." He punctuated each declaration with a kiss that was neither quick nor friendly. His body pressed against hers, making his physical state clear. With anyone else, she would have been frightened, but she was certain Antonio would never hurt her.

"I want to run the bases. Please, let me."

His gaze burned through her skull—straight to her gray matter. Refusal was written in the creases fanning out from his eyes and along the chiseled line of his jaw. He ground his erection against her stomach.

"You're mine," he growled.

"Please, Antonio. I have to do this."

He spun away from her, raking both hands through his hair as if to keep from strangling her. "It means that much to you?"

"I told you before. It does. Running the bases may be wrong, but it will make all the difference in the world. Can't you see?"

"Hell no, I can't *see*." He fisted his hands on his hips and stared her down. "I've tried. I really have, but it doesn't make any sense to me at all. I guess it all boils down to one thing— I'm not enough for you."

She pressed her palms flat against the wall behind her for support and fought back the tears threatening to fall. "You're wrong. You're everything I've ever dreamed of."

"Make me understand, because nothing you've told me so far has made any sense at all to me."

She nodded, swiping moisture from her eyes with trembling fingers. "Did you know I was at Julliard when the Marauders brought you up from the minors?"

"No. Damn it, you haven't told me anything about yourself."

"You're right." She choked back a sob and swung for the bleachers.

He leaned against the far wall, one knee bent, his foot bracing him. He listened while she told him of her time at Julliard and how she had, in her words, worshiped him from afar. She looked anywhere but at him. When she wound down, her gaze landed on her feet.

"I've been living my fantasy these past weeks, but I'm a nobody. Just a silly girl with a crush on a professional athlete, and everyone knows it. So, you see, it's *me* who isn't enough for *you*. I never have been."

He let her words sink in. He admired her for having the guts to tell him how she felt. Most women would never admit to having a crush on a guy—not to his face anyway. But there was more to her telling than admitting to a young woman's obsession with a celebrity. With her connections, she could have arranged to meet him long ago, but she hadn't because deep down inside she hadn't thought she was good enough for him, or for any man, he suspected. Yet, she'd opened up to him, admitted her insecurities, and in her own way, begged for his help.

He had a savage urge to strangle the bullies who had made her feel that way about herself. Realizing what he needed to do made his stomach churn. He tasted bile in the back of his throat and swallowed hard.

"Running the bases means so much to you that you would tell me all your deep, dark secrets?"

"I wouldn't call my crush on you a deep, dark secret. More like a silly memory."

"Why me? Why not A Rod or Jeter or someone more famous?"

She shrugged. "I don't know. There's something about you I liked from the first time I saw you."

"That's the way it was for me, too." He paused, waiting for her to look up at him. When she didn't, he continued, "I don't know why you won't believe me, but I can see you don't."

"I want to…."

"Clare, look at me."

She raised her chin, and slowly, her eyelids lifted until her gaze locked with his. The despair in her eyes nearly brought him to his knees. He gave one last thought to his decision. Was there another way? Had he missed anything that might change her mind? He'd made love to her, shown her all the tenderness he possessed, and shown her the depth of his feelings for her.

He'd ignored the need clawing at him to give into his desires, believing what *he* wanted couldn't possibly be in her best interest.

He'd told her he loved her. But that wasn't enough.

He looked at the ceiling and prayed for divine guidance. When none came, he sighed and cradled his face in his hands.

Dropping his hands, he clenched them into fists at his sides. Never in his wildest moments had he thought he would ever say these words to the woman he loved. "Okay. I'll call some friends and arrange for you to run the bases."

CHAPTER SIXTEEN

That went well. Not. He'd hoped to win Clare over with the house of her dreams and ended up consenting to letting her run the bases.

He was an idiot. Nothing to do now but accept the inevitable.

She was going to do it.

He needed to wrap his fucked up head around the idea and make damned sure it was, if not the best experience of her life, at least a memorable one. That meant choosing her team wisely and making sure she was prepared. The woman had no clue what she was getting herself into. It was up to him to remedy the situation.

They made it to the airport with time to spare, so while Clare shopped in one of the you-won't-find-this-anywhere-else shops, he made a few phone calls. He had three days to show her what to expect, and he would need every minute.

He turned, locating her at the checkout counter of a nearby store. Leaning his shoulders against the wall, he watched her pay for her purchases. Unlike most travelers, she took the time to converse with the cashier, offering her a smile before she moved on to the next store. Tony pocketed his phone and crossed his arms and ankles, content to watch her without her knowing.

Just like the first time he saw her, she took his breath away. Every luscious curve of her body promised a lifetime of passion. She dipped her head to look at something, causing her hair to fall across her shoulder. He flexed his fingers, remembering the way those silken strands felt against his skin. She tucked the wayward locks behind her ear, framing her in profile. Why she didn't believe in her own beauty was beyond him.

Another traveler paused next to her, and she appeared to be unaware the only merchandise the man had eyes for was hers. He pushed away from the wall and headed in her direction. Before he could weave his way through the throng of passengers rushing to and from their gates, the man spoke to her. She was about to respond when Tony stepped up behind her, wrapping his arms around her waist and pulling her tight against him.

The interloper took a cautious step back, eyeing him. Tony recognized the look. Confused recognition. He knew Tony's face, but had no idea why. And Tony felt no inclination to help him out, not after the way he'd looked at Clare.

"Babe, we need to go," he said.

Instantly, her hands covered his at her waist, and she glanced over her shoulder at him. Her smile was like a jolt of electricity that went straight to his groin, with predictable results.

"Okay." She allowed him to steer her out of the store without a second glance at the other man.

Several stores down, with his hand at the small of her back, Tony turned her into a coffee shop. There was one unoccupied table in the back, and once he'd settled her in the dimly lit recesses and admonished her to stay put, he went to the counter to procure drinks.

He needed the time standing in line to wrestle his body under control. What was it about Clare that made him act like a caveman protecting his woman? He'd never felt this way about anyone else. Hell, most of the women he'd been out with, he'd actually hoped would find someone else to go home with. But Clare? He couldn't stand the idea of her talking to another man, much less....

Ah, hell. No way around it. He'd promised her she could play the game, and he was going to make good on it. First, though, she needed to prepare, and that was one thing he silently vowed, he would enjoy.

Tony returned to the table with two steaming cups of coffee and a couple of chocolate chip cookies.

"Thanks," she said, reaching for one of the cups.

He took the other chair at the table for two and handed her a cookie and napkins. "We need to talk."

"Oh?" She pried the plastic lid off the cup and with pursed lips, blew across the hot brew "I thought we were in a hurry."

He bit into his cookie to keep from tossing coffee, cookies, and everything else to the floor, so he could drag her across the table and taste those that mouth of hers. And the hell of it was, she hadn't done it on purpose. She'd been cooling her coffee, which wasn't anywhere near as hot as he was at the moment. His dick had begun to feel like a pogo stick. Up. Down. Up. Down.

"I made it up to get you out of there. That guy was hitting on you."

"He was not."

"Was, too. And we do need to talk. I was going to take you to the V.I.P. Lounge, but the place is like a morgue. We couldn't have any kind of conversation in there without everyone hearing."

"The guy wasn't hitting on me," she repeated. "And I'm fine with this coffee shop while we wait. What do you want to talk about?"

Tony sipped his coffee. "He was, and we aren't going to talk about him anymore. We are going to talk about this weekend."

She shrugged, took a big bite of her cookie, and chewed. He had to look away or risk arrest for doing indecent things in public.

"What about this weekend? I'm a lousy skier."

"We aren't going to be skiing," he said, trying not to notice the way the muscles in her throat worked when she swallowed. "I made some calls. A buddy of mine is going to meet us at the airport in Colorado. I asked him to purchase some things for me."

"What kind of things?"

"Let's just say they're training equipment. You have a big game coming up, and you need to get in shape for it."

Her face turned Mustangs red then ghostly pale in the space

of a heartbeat.

"No need to worry. I'll make sure you're ready." He reached across the table and covered her hand with his. "I can't let you go into the game unprepared."

"He's coming with us?" she asked in a startled whisper.

"Hell, no. He's just bringing the stuff to the airport for me."

Her color evened out, but she still could pass for a vampire. She slipped her hand out from under his, grabbed a napkin from the stack he'd put on her side of the table earlier, and balled it in her fist.

"You still want to play, don't you?"

She nodded.

"If you've changed your mind, then we won't need all the stuff. As a matter of fact, if you change your mind at any time, just say so. I haven't made any arrangements yet, and even if I had, I could cancel. All you have to do is say the word." *Please say the word. Please don't make me go through with this.*

"I want to play. But I'm a little intimidated by your plans for this weekend. Do we have to…?"

"Practice?" he supplied.

She turned bright red again.

"Yes, we do. You've only been to two of the bases, haven't you?"

If he hadn't seen it for himself, he might not of believed a person could turn that particular shade of red.

With a shaking hand, she raised her cup to her lips and sipped. "Only two bases, and you know which ones they are."

"Then you need to experience the third one before you commit to the rest. That's what this weekend will focus on. That third base and loading all the bases at once."

"How?" She wrapped both hands around her drink then squared her shoulders, hanging onto the cup as if it was an anchor.

"Don't worry. You know I won't hurt you, but the game is difficult, especially if you haven't had any experience with all the aspects. You can't go into it without experience, Clare. You'd never finish if you did."

She lifted and repositioned her fingers a few times in silent thought. His pogo stick was currently stuck in the up position, impossible to be otherwise with thoughts of how he was going to coach her this weekend rolling around in his head. He finished his cookie and gulped down the rest of his coffee while she sat tethered to the table by a cardboard mug of fowl tasting liquid.

"Think about it. Like I said, you can change your mind any time."

He pried the cup out of her hands and held the rest of her cookie up in question. She shook her head He stuck the remaining bite in his mouth and gathered their trash in one hand. With the cookie hanging from his lips, he deposited the garbage in a nearby receptacle and returned to the table.

"We should go now. Pick up our carry-ons from the V.I.P. Lounge."

Silent, she stood, allowing him to escort her along the concourse. They claimed their luggage and boarded their flight. Once the plane was in the air and the interior lights lowered for those who wanted to rest on the evening flight, he reached for her hand and found it cold as ice.

"Clare, look at me."

Her eyes were dark pools of turmoil that mirrored what he felt inside.

"It's going to be all right. I promise."

One of the perks of first-class was the use of a thin blanket. Tony retrieved hers and his from the seat pockets in front of them, removed them from their plastic wrapping, and draped one over her shoulders and the other over her lap. "Spread your legs, babe."

"Why?"

"Just do it. No one will see. That's why I gave you the window seat."

"We shouldn't," she said in a conspiratorial whisper.

"Maybe not, but we are. You need to be reminded how good it feels."

Her gaze darted around the darkened cabin then she eased her legs apart.

"Recline your seat." Tony tilted his to match hers and slid his arm across the console separating them.

She lifted the edge of the blanket, and he slipped his hand underneath. A glance her way, a lifted eyebrow, and she undid the fasteners on her slacks and pushed the zipper down.

Like a compass seeking true north, his hand found the triangle of skin and dipped lower. He hadn't noticed panty lines earlier, which meant she wasn't wearing any, or she had on a thong. When his fingers found heated satin, he wasn't at all disappointed. The outline of the fabric scrap indicated it was ornamental as opposed to a functional garment.

"For me?" he asked.

She nodded, a Mona Lisa smile on her face. He couldn't help himself. He shifted so he could kiss her. What should have been a thank you kiss quickly turned to a pre-orgasmic experience with tongues and teeth and maybe a groan or two. Thank God, the droning of the engines muffled everything but the sharpest of voices. A ding brought them to their senses.

The fasten seatbelts light had gone off. Tony wasted no time unbuckling first Clare's then his. In a move that would have made Gumby proud, he scooped her into his arms and swung his ass beneath her, bringing her atop his lap in her seat. One arm anchored her to him—the other was on a mission.

"Put your head on my shoulder," he said. "Wrap both hands on my forearm. If it feels good, squeeze. If not, let go."

She curled her fingers over his arm and dropped her forehead into the crook of his neck. His cock throbbed against her soft hip pressing into his groin. The big boy was going to have to wait. Clare needed reassurance, and in the cozy cocoon of first-class, he could give it to her.

"Close your eyes, babe, and relax. Just feel."

He found the scrap of satin again and, with sure fingers, pushed it aside. He swallowed hard, feeling the heat between her legs. Her pussy lips were tight, engorged, and inviting. A little pressure from his hand and she allowed her legs to slip a little farther apart. Tony took advantage, parting her folds to stroke her.

"You're wet," he whispered, against her ear. "I like that."

She wiggled, and he held her tighter.

His fingers stroked and played in her damp heat until she whimpered with need. He loved the way she responded to him, the way she told him what she needed without ever saying a word. He found her clit with his thumb and pressed down, using a circular motion that earned him another whimper and wiggle.

She was so damned wet, he couldn't wait to get inside her any way he could. He shrugged his shoulder, and she lifted her head to look at him.

"Kiss me," he said.

Her eyelids dropped, and her lips touched his. In that instant, he entered her. Two fingers sank to the third knuckle. She tightened her hold on his forearm until he was sure he would need surgery to repair the damage from her fingernails, but he didn't stop. Their mouths and tongues dueled while he kept up a steady rhythm with his fingers, plunging in as deep as possible then retreating. His thumb kept firm pressure on her clit.

She was close or coming. He could tell by the way her limbs stiffened, and the way her fingers clawed at the muscles in his forearm. Her breathing became labored, stealing oxygen from his lungs until he grew lightheaded. And maybe a little crazy.

Withdrawing from her, he swallowed her frustrated gasp with his lips over hers. His fingers, dripping with her natural lubricant, explored lower, finding her tight back entrance. She stiffened, but her grip on his forearm never wavered.

"Babe, it's going to be so good." He went back for more lube, returning to rim the prize. "Just a sample. Let up on my arm. If it feels good, dig those fingers back into me. Okay?"

She nodded, rested her forehead against his, closed her eyes, and loosened her grip on his arm.

"Here we go," he murmured against her lips. "Relax. Let me in."

"I don't know how," she said.

"Yes, you do. Concentrate, Clare."

Her shoulders lowered, then slowly, her entire body relaxed. It was now or never. Tony pushed his middle finger past the ring of muscles guarding her inner sanctum. She became a stone statue.

Tony froze. Every ounce of willpower he possessed went into maintaining the status quo while he waited for her to adjust to the new invasion. Then slowly, one by one, her fingers clamped down on his forearm, and his heart began to beat again.

Her pussy fit perfectly in his palm. He applied pressure with the heel of his hand and, with as much restraint as he could muster, he moved his middle finger in and out a few times.

"Perfect. You're so damned perfect." He found her clit

again and rubbed his thumb over it in tandem with his finger entering her. "Still feeling good?"

She dug her fingers into his forearm in answer.

"You need to come, don't you, babe?"

A wiggle confirmed the need he sensed building again.

"Then let's do this."

Making a cradle with his arm bent at her back, his free hand came up to cup her head, pressing her face into his. He drove his thumb into her vagina, plunging his middle finger as deep as he dared into her sweet ass.

The miracle broke over her in shuddering waves. Tony took her moans into his mouth while her body squeezed his finger and thumb so hard he was glad he still had months before he needed his hand again. He'd trade the rest of his career to feel her doing the same thing to his dick.

When she quieted, he slipped his fingers from her, gathered more of her juices, and with a tender touch, moistened the tissues he'd just abused. "Shh," he said, soothing her. "This will help so you won't be sore later on."

She allowed him to take care of her, relaxing in his arms, her head once again buried in the crook of his neck. Eventually, her fingers released their grip on his arm. A few minutes later, the soft brush of her breath against his skin told him she slept.

Tony closed his eyes, absorbing into his consciousness the wonder of her power over him. He'd do anything to make her happy. If she needed an orgasm during a plane trip or to fuck the night away with his teammates, he would see she wasn't disappointed.

Call him a crazy fucker, but he was in love with her, and whatever she wanted, whatever she needed, it was his duty to see she got it.

Too soon, the flight attendant made her way through the front cabin, quietly reminding them they would arrive at their destination soon. Tony kissed Clare awake then, in a reverse Gumby move, went back to his own seat, settling Clare in hers. He watched her hands move beneath the blanket, adjusting and refastening her slacks. As primly as you please, she folded the blankets and stuffed them into the seatback pocket in front of her.

Tony leaned over and kissed her again. "Just because."

Bases Loaded

The cabin lights came on. Flight attendants worked the aisles, collecting trash and making sure everything was in order for landing. Clare held her hand out palm up, and Tony placed his on top, lacing their fingers together. His heart landed with a harder thump than the wheels on the runway. He'd won a victory bigger than any other. Her trust.

I've lost my mind.

There was no other explanation for why she was freezing her ass off in the dark while Antonio looked for the door key supposedly hidden near the condominium's front porch.

"Sorry about that," Antonio said, reappearing from behind what looked like a giant snowball but apparently was some sort of shrubbery. His black wool jacket was dotted with clumps of white stuff, and even in the dark of the porch alcove, she could tell his lips had taken on the hue of frozen blueberries. "I forgot which window ledge they said it would be on." He held up a key. "Mission accomplished."

"Just get the door open before I freeze."

"No problem." The door opened under his touch, much like her, she mused then they were inside. "Let me find the lights."

Antonio slapped at the wall to their right a couple of times, looking for the switch. When he found it and flicked the lights on, Clare gasped. It was cold enough to hang meat, but other than that, the place was fabulous. There was no entryway. They'd stepped right into the main room. There was wood everywhere—walls, floors, furniture. An enormous rock fireplace took up one whole wall. Cozy plaid fabrics draped the windows and covered the man-sized furniture.

"Heat. We need heat." Antonio went in search of the thermostat.

Clare headed for the faux fur throw draped across the back of the sofa. Teeth chattering, she curled into the far corner of the couch and pulled the blanket over her like a tent.

"Found the thermostat," he announced and proceeded to bring their luggage in.

She did her best to ignore the new black duffle delivered to them at the airport. It, and the man who'd delivered it, were tangible proof they were moving forward with her invitation.

Besides Antonio, she now knew another club member. He'd introduced her to Keith who had been waiting for them at baggage claim. He'd grabbed Antonio in a guy hug, handed him the bag, and turned his attention on her. He looked her up and down, smiling knowingly.

"This the one?" he'd asked Antonio.

"Yes. Clare Kincaid, meet Keith O'Brian."

"Nice to meet you, Clare," he'd said, extending his hand.

Automatically, she'd extended her own. It had only been a handshake, but knowing he knew she would soon be running the bases, perhaps with him, made it more intimate.

"I look forward to seeing more of you."

"Back off, man. She's mine," Antonio had butted in. "Thanks for the stuff. I can take it from here."

"Okay, okay. I'm out of here. Call me when you're ready," Keith had said and left to collect their luggage from the carousel.

Just thinking about the way Keith had looked at her—like he would be happy to fuck her right then and there, if only she would ask—warmed her insides. Maybe she *was* being too hard on herself. Keith's perusal reminded her of the way Antonio looked at her—except when Antonio did it, she was helpless to resist. Keith's interest was flattering, but she hadn't been tempted to take him up on the offer.

"Now, let's see about a fire." Antonio's voice brought her thoughts back to the present. She trusted him to take care of her. He'd said she needed more experience before running the bases, and he was right. The black bag sitting inside the front door was evidence of her naiveté. She had no idea what was inside or why he needed those things to prepare her for the game.

Huddled beneath the warm throw, she watched him bend to the task, his broad shoulders straining the seams of his coat. With economical movements, he checked the damper, stuffed some tinder between the pre-stacked logs. *Capable.* He did everything with the same, no room for error, efficiency.

Using a butane lighter, he coaxed tinder to flame.

Clare held her breath. He remained where he was, watching to make sure the logs caught. She might be naïve about some things, but she'd come to know Antonio surprisingly well. "Antonio?"

"Hmm?"

"Is something wrong?"

He turned and sat on the raised hearth. "No. Not really."

"Then why are you over there instead of under this blanket with me?"

Bracing his elbows on his knees, he hung his head. "I don't know. I need a minute to process, I guess. The way Keith was looking at you…I've seen guys look at you…the one in the gift shop in the Dallas airport…others. But Keith? That was different. He knows."

"Will he be one you choose for my team?"

"Yeah. We've played the game together before, and it worked out for us."

A shiver, having nothing to do with being cold, tripped along her spine. Running the bases was no longer a fantasy. It was a reality. And she now knew two of the three men on her team. Soon, she would spend an entire night fucking with both of them.

"I see."

"No, you don't see. I'm having a hard time with this. I'm going to do it. I mean…I'm going to do my best to prepare you for it, and I'm going to make the arrangements like I said I would. It's just…I don't know…. You're mine, and Keith…."

"Is your friend," she finished for him. "I understand."

"I trust him. I do. I've never shared a woman who meant anything to me. This will be a first."

She didn't know what to say, so she sat quietly, waiting for him to get past whatever was eating at him. The fire had caught, casting a warm glow around him like a halo of flames.

"If things go as planned, he's going to come here on Saturday."

It took a second for her brain to process what he meant. But when his meaning finally registered, she straightened and clutched the throw tighter to her throat. "To…?"

"To fuck you. You. Me. Him. A trial run, of sorts. That's the most difficult part for the women, taking two cocks at the same time. It will be better for you if you've done it before, and I thought it would be easier later on if you had already built up some trust with Keith, too."

Even though he'd mapped out the plan himself, he struggled with it. Despite her inexperience, the idea melted her insides.

"You think I'll be ready by Saturday?"

"You'll be ready," he said, lifting his head to make eye contact with her. Desire blazed hotter than the fire at his back. He stood, removed his overcoat, and tossed it on the nearest chair.

She fisted her hands in the fabric clutched to her throat.

"Here's how we're going to do this." His tone brooked no argument, and she had none anyway. "There's a big tub in the bathroom. We're going to get naked and take a nice, long, hot bath together. I'll start working on your ass then. We'll start with a small butt plug and work up in size until you're able to take a large one without too much pain. I'm going to fuck your ass. If you don't want me to do that, you better say so now, otherwise, it's a done deal."

Good Lord. His brisk, matter-of-fact approach rocked her to her toes, and she had to admit, made her horny as hell.

"Saturday, Keith will be here. He's going to fuck your ass, too. If you do well with both of us at the same time, I'll make the arrangements for you to run the bases as soon as I can get everyone together."

She swallowed hard, trying to think of something to say that wouldn't make her out to be an idiot. He looked so damned good standing there, talking about fucking her, she could hardly think at all. She shifted her gaze to the far wall where a pair of vintage skis doubled as artwork.

"Clare," he said, his voice deep, and sounding like it had been dragged over broken glass. "Look at me."

She shook her head, all her bravado gone.

"I need you to look at me," he repeated.

Heart thumping, she faced him.

"You've been honest with me about what you wanted…make that *need*, from me, and I admit it has taken a long time to get through to me. I won't say I completely understand why you want to run the bases, but you do, and I've come to accept that."

He scrubbed his palms over his face. The gesture of frustration matched the way she felt inside. He'd twisted her up so many ways, she wasn't sure of anything except that she wanted him.

"What I need to say is," he continued, "I'm sorry. I've put you through a lot, and I haven't been honest with you, or with myself. I know how hard it was for you to open up with me back at the house. You spoke from your heart, and I appreciate that." He paced from one end of the massive hearth to the other.

But I've changed my mind about the invitation. She heard his non-verbal retraction in her mind, prepared for it. What else could he be about to say?

Antonio stopped pacing and faced her. "I owe you the same honesty."

"You don't—"

"Yes, I do. Please, just let me say this."

"Okay," she said, cautiously. She'd never seen him so agitated. The nerves of steel he appeared to have on the baseball field seemed to apply to his personal life as well. Up until now.

"I fell in love with you the moment I saw you walk into Jason's fundraiser. I was consumed with figuring out how to make you mine. But that wasn't all I was thinking about. I *wanted* to be traded to Texas. I asked my agent to approach the Mustangs to see if they would be interested."

"What has that got to do with me?"

"I wanted to get out of New York. I wanted a fresh start. Most of the members of Bases Loaded play for the East Coast teams, and there was a lot of pressure to participate in the…activities, let's say. I admit I enjoyed being on the teams I was on. I've tried hard to convince myself I didn't, but I did. Maybe I'm a pervert, but it's fun, especially when the woman makes it all the way."

"How often did you play?"

"That's something I lied to you about, too. I told you I'd only done it a handful of times, but that isn't true. I've been on more teams than I can count."

She sat up straighter. "What happened? Why did you ask for the trade?"

"It finally hit me one day. I only have so many years left in the league, and all I had to show for it was an apartment in the city and a tattoo on my ass. All the women in my life were either my relatives—who don't figure into this equation—or women my friends invited to run the bases. I didn't have anyone I could call my own, and as long as I hung around with the same crowd, I wasn't likely to meet anyone either. It was time to make a change."

"Why Dallas?"

"I've always liked the city. People are friendly, and it's a big city without being a *big* city, if you know what I mean. The population may be large, but there's still a small town atmosphere." He waved that discussion away. "Anyway, I didn't expect to find my soul mate, but I did hope I'd find someone who wanted to be with *me*, not...*everyone*."

"Antonio," she whispered his name.

"No, let me finish."

She nodded.

"Then I saw you, and I lost my shit. I mean I knew you were *the one*." He curled his fingers, making air quotes around the last two words. "Anyway, I always thought when I found *the one*, I wouldn't want the same things I'd wanted for all the years I'd been in the club. I thought I would want her all for myself. Don't get me wrong. I do want you all for myself. I lay awake at night and think about being with you, but almost from the beginning, I saw you with others. Friends of mine. I tried to get the images out of my head, Clare. I really did, but then you asked me about the tattoo and, God help me, I damn near had a heart attack."

"I'm sorry," she said.

"Don't be. It wasn't your fault. I was shocked you knew what it meant, and the part of me that wanted to keep you all to myself stood up and bared its teeth. But the other part of me, the part that had been dreaming of you running the bases? That part tore at my gut. I've been battling it out internally ever since. I do love you, and I want you all to myself. But at the same time, I'd give just about anything to see your sweet body taking all of us at once."

Her mind raced. What was he saying? He wanted her to run the bases, but he *didn't* want her to? Antonio turned around. He grabbed the poker and nudged a few logs until the flames roared.

He faced her again. "So, I owe you an apology. While you've been trying to convince me to invite you to run the bases, I've wanted the same thing. Only, I've been denying it to you and to myself. If it makes me a pervert, then I guess that's what I am. Today, when we were at the house and you told me why running the bases meant so much to you, I finally accepted it was what I wanted, too. Part of me still wants you to want me and *only* me, but there's another part of me that can't wait to get you on the field. I'm a fraud, Clare. I don't deserve a woman like you. But I love you. I can't imagine my life without you. Can you forgive me?"

She stood, letting the throw drop to the floor. She skirted the slab of tree that doubled as a coffee table and separated her from the man she loved. He didn't encourage her, just stood stoic as if he expected her to reject him. But how could she? She understood about wanting to re-invent herself, knew how the desire to do so ate at her.

Coming to a stop in front of him, she flattened her palms against his chest. "Antonio," she implored, looking up into his troubled eyes. "Do you really think there is anything to forgive?"

"I've been an idiot. I *wanted* to change, but one look at you and I knew it wasn't going to happen."

"Do you know what it means to me that you envision me running the bases? It makes me tingle inside. It makes me feel beautiful and desired." Tears blurred her vision. "That's all I ever wanted. I love you."

She rose to her tiptoes and pressed her lips against his. He remained stock-still.

"I shouldn't want the things I want with you," he finally said.

"I love that you do. You aren't a pervert, Antonio."

"I feel like one. I want you to be my wife, and still I can't get the images out of my head."

"Do you think less of me because I want the same thing?"

"God, no!" He grabbed her, framing her waist with his palms. "I never thought that. Not for a minute. I've always respected the women who played the game, but for whatever reason, I never thought I'd find someone I wanted to invite. It's hard to explain, but my family is ultra-conservative. My desires, my sexual inclinations, are so far from what I was taught was normal, and for once, I was trying to fit into that mold. Then I met you. You're beautiful. You're smart. You're a college professor, for crying out loud. I started thinking about dragging you into my less than normal world, and I was determined not to do it. I know it doesn't make any sense. Yes, I wanted you to be different, to be totally innocent of the kind of things I desire, but deep inside I desperately wanted you to accept me for who I am."

He tugged, and she folded herself against him, her cheek to his chest. "I was going to use this weekend to convince you to forget about playing the game, but after what you said back at the house…I couldn't do it. I finally realized you have your reasons, and I understood why you want to do it. You need to do it."

"I do, Antonio. It's as crazy as it sounds, but yes, I need to do it."

"I know that now, and I'm going to make sure you get what you need. That's why I called Keith. He's a good guy, and he'll treat you right."

"We're really going to do this, aren't we?"

"You bet we are." His thumbs traced the waistband of her slacks beneath her sweater. "Just as soon as we get you out of these clothes." His head lowered, his lips hovering above hers. "Are you up for this? I know I am." He held her tight and pressed his erection into her belly.

"I want everything you promised. I want you. My body is yours."

The thin coat she wore joined his on the chair, and soon she stood before him in nothing more than a blue satin thong. Her nipples were twin points of pain, reacting to both the cold and Antonio's heated gaze.

"God, you're beautiful." His hands warmed her skin everywhere he explored, and he left not an inch untouched. "I know I keep saying that, but it's true. Did you see the way Keith looked at you tonight? I thought he was going to fuck you right there on the baggage carousel, and God help me, I probably would have helped him."

"I wanted him to," she admitted.

He froze. Had she said too much? He lifted his lips from the curve of her breast and straightened, towering over her.

"Did you?"

She nodded.

Antonio smiled. "Damn, woman. Why didn't you say so? We could have given him a ride in the limo. He's good in tight spaces, if you get my meaning."

She giggled like a schoolgirl. "I know what you mean. But as exciting as it all sounds, you're right. I'm not ready. I trust you. Consider this winter training for rookies."

"There's only one rookie I'm interested in, and that's you, babe."

He lifted her in his arms and, holding her much like he had on the airplane, he kissed her. Tongues tangled, plunged, and explored until the pressure built between her legs, and she thought she might die if he didn't fuck her soon.

"You said something about a bath?"

"I said a lot of things."

"And I want you to do every one of them."

He didn't deserve her. She was too damned perfect. There had to be a catch. No one was as perfect as Clare was without some flaw. But running his hands over the curve of her bubble-covered back, staring at her sweet, heart-shaped ass raised and open for him, he couldn't conceive of a flaw big enough to change the way he felt about her.

"Tell me if it hurts," he said, rimming her with his finger first. He'd warmed the lube and smallest butt plug Keith had supplied by dropping them into the bathwater earlier. An added bonus was Clare had the opportunity to examine the toy and get used to the idea of allowing him to insert it.

After bathing each other, he judged the time had come. The way she opened for him, trusted him to get her through this humbled him.

He folded a towel on the ledge at the end of the tub. With her head resting on her folded arms, her breasts floated in the bath water. The caress of warm water on them would add to her pleasure. He'd played with her nipples enough that they had to be sensitive.

"I'm ready, Antonio."

He squeezed lube on his finger and spread the warmed gel over the tight rosebud. A little more on his finger and he flattened the palm of his left hand on her left cheek to steady her. His finger slipped effortlessly past her barrier. He felt her tense, saw her body react.

"Okay?" he asked.

"Uh huh," she said with a slight nod of her head. "I'm okay. It feels good. Strange, but good."

His cock could hoist a mainsail it was so primed to take over the job. Ignoring his erection was impossible, but he did his best to focus on what was important. Clare.

"Relax for me." He stroked over her ass cheek to the small of her back, massaging until her muscles gave way. "A little more now. Just my finger, babe. Nothing to worry about."

God, she was tight, but he managed to wiggle his finger a bit, twist it around, move in and out enough to give her pleasure. After a while, she began to move her hips, showing him what felt good.

"Oh, yeah. You like the way it feels, don't you?"

"Yes. Oh, God, Antonio. It feels so good."

"Hang onto that thought. This is going to feel good, too."

He wasn't much good with his left hand, but he managed to locate the warmed butt plug and coat it with lube, all with one hand while he continued to pleasure her with the other. She moaned, moving with the slight motion of his finger. The plug was bigger around and longer. She would feel it, that was for sure.

Withdrawing from her, he immediately pressed the tip of the plug against the slight hole he'd created. She gasped but managed to keep her muscles relaxed. He pushed harder. The plug dilated the ring of muscles, slipping inside easily. Seated, she closed around it, holding it in place.

Tony saw stars, remembered he needed to keep breathing or he would pass out. He sucked in much needed oxygen, and when his vision cleared, he grabbed the rim of the tub to steady himself. His cock throbbed, and his balls felt like hot coals. The urge to replace the plug with his dick was so strong he was reaching for the rubber toy before he came to his senses. She wasn't ready for him yet. She would take him in if he insisted, but it wouldn't be as good for her as it could be if he did this right. And he was damned sure going to do it right, for her. His Clare.

"How's that, sweetheart?"

"Good. Antonio. I'm so horny."

"I know, babe." Her pussy glistened. "Let me take care of that."

"Please," she begged.

He used his thumbs to part her folds. Her clit peeked out, all pink and plump, and he couldn't resist. He arched his back to get lower and flicked his tongue over the needy bud. She moaned and pushed her ass toward his face.

"I've got you." He pressed his face to her pussy and allowed his tongue free rein. She tasted better than any meal he'd ever had, and the added bonus was this dessert was his. He was going to enjoy every minute of watching her take pleasure from his friends, but this part of her was his. He'd fucking kill any man who put his face between her legs.

She was on the edge. He'd made sure to drag the foreplay out as long as possible, knowing the higher her level of arousal, the easier it would be for her to take the plug and enjoy it. He could sit right here, eating her pussy for the rest of his life, but he'd kept her on edge for a long time, and he couldn't wait for her to experience her first orgasm with a solid object up her ass.

Man, was she in for a surprise.

He speared his tongue inside her, twisted it, sipped her juices. She wiggled her ass, earning her a tiny swat on the rear that stilled her long enough for him to give her one final, long tongue sweep. Then he covered her clit and sucked. His tongue flicked against it a couple of times. She ground her ass against his face, and with a keening wail that echoed off the tiled walls, she came.

Tony held her ass tight, keeping her cheeks apart so she would feel the maximum impact on the plug, all the while he continued to torment her clit. A fresh wave of her arousal coated his cheeks, and he couldn't help thinking next time he wouldn't shave before he ate her. See how she'd like the way his beard felt against her pussy.

When he'd wrung the last spasm from her, and she'd practically flattened him, falling onto his face, he wrapped his arms around her and pulled her trembling body against him.

"Tell me how it feels right now. Any pain?"

"No. It makes me feel full, but no pain."

"And the orgasm?"

"Oh, God, Antonio. There are no words."

"Good?"

"The best."

CHAPTER SEVENTEEN

Her body had turned to putty. That first night, Antonio had carried her to bed. He'd made sure the plug was properly seated then spread her legs and filled her with such tender care she'd wept.

"Soon, that will be Keith's cock in your ass while I fuck you. Does that make you hot?"

She tentatively moved against him. "Yes."

Already, the tension coiled inside her, and the images his words brought to mind only escalated her need. But, he wouldn't be rushed. Each stroke was measured and deliberate.

"Slow, babe. So you get used to the feeling. If it hurts, say Miners, and I'll stop."

She hadn't needed the code word that night or through the next two days. He had changed the plugs regularly, each increasing in size. With each one, he gave her time to adjust to it then he made love to her slow and gentle.

She was about to go out of her mind with anticipation. She leaned over the granite-topped kitchen island and watched him grill steaks on the indoor grill. She hadn't worn a stitch of clothing since he'd undressed her for the bath their first night in the condo. He insisted she would feel less self-conscious playing the game if she got used to being naked, as the game was a no clothes zone from the first inning to the last.

He seemed perfectly at home wearing nothing at all, and she was perfectly fine watching his tight ass in the kitchen.

"You doing okay?" he asked.

"Fine. This is the last one, right?" Sitting down was doable, but not desired.

She'd had her doubts when Antonio had brought out the plug she currently wore, certain there was no way it would go inside her. He'd taken her to the kitchen, bent her over the counter, and proven her wrong.

He turned. The apron he'd donned for safety's sake tented in the front. "You can stand at the counter and eat dinner. Then I'll take the plug out, let you rest for a while before I fuck you there. Do you think you're ready?"

"You aren't going to fuck me with the plug in, like we did with the other ones?"

"No, but I'm going to fill your pussy with a life-sized dildo. Keith will be here tomorrow, remember? You need to feel what it's like, be certain you can handle it, before then."

Moisture leaked down her thighs. "Are you hungry?"

He smiled. "Babe, you know I am." He flicked a knob, turning the grill off.

Watching him cross the room to stand beside her, her heart raced. He tweaked the plug, causing her to gasp.

"This is about trust. I'm humbled you've given me as much as you have, but allowing me to plug you is one thing. I don't think you understand how much more trust you'll have to give up to let me fuck your ass. And it will require even more to let my friends have you there." He pressed against the plug with the heel of his hand, his fingers dipping into her wet folds. "Are you ready?"

Her knees, already weak from two days of almost non-stop sexual arousal, nearly gave out on her.

"Whoa, there." His arms were around her in an instant then she was in his arms being carried to the bedroom.

"I'm fine."

"You almost fainted or something," he said, laying her gently on the bed, rolling her to her stomach. "Let me see."

She buried her face in the covers and relaxed her ass cheeks. He knew that part of her better than she did. He'd certainly seen it more than she ever had. After applying more lube, testing the fit, and assuring himself she wasn't in any pain, he placed a kiss on her right cheek and pulled the comforter up to her shoulders. "Don't move."

He left her there, horny, and weak with need. He returned a few minutes later, disappeared into the en-suite bathroom. She listened to the sound of running water for what seemed like forever. The next time he appeared in her sight, he had lost the apron. His erection was at full-mast, and he had a washcloth in his hand.

"We need to speed this along," he said, uncovering her. "Time for this to come out. I've got the dildo warming in the bathroom sink. I'll give it a few minutes to warm up then I'll make sure it fills you properly. It will take some getting used to."

Her head spun. He parted her cheeks. There was pressure against her anus then the large plug popped free, and she sighed with relief.

"Jesus, look at your ass." Something else enter her. "I can get three fingers in there without any resistance."

He played for a little while until he forced a groan from her. He withdrew, draped the warmed washcloth between her cheeks, and held them closed with one hand.

"You remember your word, right?"

"Miners," she said.

"Yeah, I hate that team, but I'd hate to hurt you even worse, so don't be afraid to use it if you need to."

"I'm fine. Really. I got weak-kneed in the kitchen thinking about what you said, about putting all my trust in you." She rose to her elbows and looked over her shoulder at him. "Get the thing…the dildo, please. I want to feel you inside me."

"It's different, you know? I'm not sure how to explain it, having not been on the receiving end, but I know it's different. I want to do it to you, but you have to understand, the trust goes both ways. I trust you'll tell me if you hurt or if there's anything else going on I need to know. It's emotional. That's all I'm sayin'. And you have to tell me if it's too much for you."

He brushed a lock of hair behind her ear, his knuckle trailing along her jaw, over her shoulder and arm then to her nipple, puckered and hard, begging in the shadows for attention. She let him play, the distraction just what they both needed at that moment.

His furrowed brow eased as her body responded to his touch, and she was glad she could alleviate his concerns.

"I promise to tell you if I feel…anything. Please, Antonio. I'm aching."

He rolled her nipple between his thumb and forefinger, held it prisoner while he spoke. "You're sure? I was going to give you more time, an hour or two, at least."

"Can you last an hour? I know I can't. I'll probably come as soon as you get inside me."

He tugged on her nipple. A ripple of pain/pleasure shot straight to her pussy. "I want it to be good for you. I want that more than anything."

"With you, it's always good."

His smile was tender. He palmed her breast and leaned down to place a kiss on her forehead. "Rest. I'll get everything we need and be right back."

Clare dropped down on the mattress. He checked to make sure the cloth was still in place then pulled the comforter over her again. She closed her eyes, idly wondering if he took this much care with the other women he'd been with.

She woke to his hands on her, stroking her ass and thighs beneath the comforter. His weight was a solid presence along one side of her body.

"Wake up, sleepy head."

"Mmm…that feels good."

"Spread your legs for me, babe."

Still on her stomach, she did as she was told. One large hand cupped her, his fingers probing her sex. "Did I sleep?"

"A couple of hours." His hand roamed upward, gently explored her nether hole. "Any soreness?"

"No. That feels good."

"I need to see you to get the dildo in properly. I'm going to uncover you now."

"'kay." She opened one eyelid enough to see the room was dark except for a few candles flickering around the room.

"I'm going to lift you. A pillow under your stomach will make this easier for both of us."

She didn't have a cooperating muscle in her body, but he had enough for both of them. He lifted her hips easily and slid a pillow underneath, tilting her ass up and open. She couldn't even find the control to fist her hands as he patiently explained his every move.

Lube. All over. Her pussy, her ass, her thighs. She would need a bath after this.

"This dildo has a cup on it." He brought it to her face so she could see it. "This part fits over your mound. Holds it in place."

She nodded at the enormous rubber toy. "'kay." *Whatever you want. Fill me. Fuck me.*

Between her legs again, he inserted the head, inquired about her comfort then, assured she was handling it, eased it fully inside her. The front piece applied pressure in just the right spot and the length and girth of the phallus stretched her fully. He had her attention.

"Relax, babe." He massaged her thighs, her hips. "Use your word if you need to."

"It feels…good. Big, but good."

"If you can do this, you can take everyone I know."

"It's big."

"Yeah, it is. But no sense using anything smaller. You have to know what the real thing will feel like. That's why so many women don't complete the game. They aren't prepared for the reality."

"It's better now. Will they take it slow like this?"

"If you ask they will, otherwise, no. I told you, this isn't easy. It can be a brutal game if you aren't up to it."

"I need…more."

He chuckled and kissed each ass cheek. "And you're going to get more. Ready?"

"Yes, please, Antonio. Fuck me."

"Legs together," he said, urging her to close over the dildo, increasing the perceived size.

He straddled her thighs, spread her cheeks with both hands, and seated the head of his cock at her entrance. "I put a condom on while you were still asleep. Can you tell?"

"No."

"Good. It's a thin one, so it shouldn't interfere with your pleasure or mine." He rocked his hips, nudging at her anus. "You're still open a little from that last plug. I'm going to take it slow. Real slow."

She closed her eyes and, as she'd learned to do with the plugs, relaxed her body. He entered her. Stopped, allowing her time to adjust. "Tell me what you feel."

"It feels good. Kind of scary, you're big all at once, not tapered like the plug."

"Yeah, I know. I thought about using a dildo on you, but didn't want to ruin the experience for you."

"I like this."

She took another inch then he rose up over her, keeping his weight off her by bracing his hands on either side of her head. His thighs bracketed her hips, and she could feel heat radiating off his body. And suddenly, understood what he had been trying to tell her.

This was different.

"Here we go, babe. I'm counting on you telling me how you're doing."

His hips flexed, and he slid inside her, lowering his chest to her back. His hands found hers, pinning her to the mattress from head to toe.

Impaled.

Conquered.

Dominated.

Her brain scrambled to keep up with the sensory overload. For a split-second, her body kicked in to fight mode.

"Shh, sweetheart. It's me. I've got you. You're safe."

His words got through to her, and she relaxed.

Submitted.

He filled her, body, soul, and heart. Her body was no longer hers, but his, and her faith, her trust in him, was not misplaced. Warmth flooded her, tears pooled behind her eyelids, and liquid desire gushed between her legs.

"God, you're magnificent. Clare. My Clare. Mine."

"Antonio," she breathed.

"I'm here, love." He wove his fingers with hers, curled her fists into his.

"Love me. Please."

He withdrew almost all the way and filled her again. "I love you, Clare. I love you so much."

She absorbed his words, certain the emotion behind them was equal to what she felt for him. She gave herself to him, fully. With every motion, he claimed another bit of her heart. Pleasure spiked each time he drove into her, pressing her clit against the cup covering her mound. Tiny rubber fingers inside stroked her sensitive nub, making her crazy, driving her up and up.

His body, flush against hers, demanded her total submission. She gave it, unable in this position to do anything but submit. If she said her word he would stop, would let her up, but she wouldn't, couldn't. He'd tried to tell her, but no way could he completely comprehend what a mind-fuck this was for her. He owned her. By refusing to say her safe word, she gave everything to him. God help her if he broke her trust because she'd have nothing left.

Tension coiled in her center, and the last puzzle piece fell into place. He wanted one final piece of her, her orgasm. Once he claimed that, he would have it all. Again, her body contemplated fighting, but as if he sensed her reserve, he demanded her complete surrender.

"Give it to me, Clare."

And she gave it to him. She gave him every last gut-wrenching spike of pleasure. She screamed his name and silently begged him to give her something of himself in return.

"Holy, Mother...." He slammed into her in short, hard thrusts. He rocked against her, giving her a piece of himself with every spasm.

He relaxed his arms, and his full weight came down on her, pressing her into the mattress. Impaled, she was helpless beneath him. Weak with surrender, her heart soared with an empowering realization. He'd given her all of himself—his body, his soul, his love, his protection. Buried deep inside her, his heart beating a rapid rhythm against her back. He was as much hers as she was his.

"I wish we didn't ever have to move," she said.

"Me, too, sweetheart." He kissed the crown of her head. "Are you okay?"

"Yes. You?"

"I'm in Heaven. Did you go there with me?"

"I did. I didn't know…."

"What didn't you know?"

"That it would be like this. You said it would be emotional. It is…and more."

"Am I crushing you?" He started to move, and she squeezed his fingers entwined with hers to stop him.

"No. Don't move. I want to remember the way I feel right now."

"How do you feel?"

"Cherished. Loved. Safe."

"I'll always cherish you. Love you. Keep you safe."

"I know."

He hated to, but he needed to move off her, take care of her. Easing from her, he rolled to her side and pulled her back to his front, so he could hold her a little longer. He never wanted to let her go. No woman had ever claimed so much of him.

No woman had ever trusted him the way Clare had.

She snuggled her ass against his groin, and he gently nudged her upper leg forward. "Time for this to go." He removed the dildo as gently as he could and tossed it on the bed behind him, returning his hand to cup her. "Sore?"

"Tender, but not sore. I could use a long soak."

"I'll fix a bath for you in a few minutes. While you're soaking, I'll see if I can salvage those steaks."

She lay in his arms for long, silent minutes.

"The others. Will it feel that way with them?"

She didn't have to elaborate. He knew she referred to the other team members. "I don't think so. I don't know what the women feel. Mostly, I think it's just sex for them. They don't have an emotional attachment to any of the players. For the guys, at least for me, it's always been about the pleasure. A woman's ass has a different feel than her vagina. Same as her mouth feels different. We're all about the pleasure."

"So, I won't feel this…attached to the others?"

"You feel attached to me?"

"I feel like I belong to you. When you pinned me to the bed and filled me…it was scary at first, then you told me I was safe, and that's when it changed for me. It was like I gave you everything. My body, my soul, my heart."

"It's all safe with me, sweetheart." He kissed her shoulder, humbled she was so open with him. Open with her body, her soul, and her heart. He'd do anything to deserve it.

"Then, when I thought I'd given you everything, you asked for more."

"I did?"

"You demanded my orgasm." She sighed, and he felt like crowing, and laughing, and doing it all naked on the rooftop for everyone to see.

"You gave me that, too."

"I did. You own me, Antonio."

"And you own me. Forever."

CHAPTER EIGHTEEN

"He's on his way." Antonio dropped his cell phone on the coffee table. "You can still call this off. Anytime, babe."

Clare curled her feet under her on the sofa and wrapped her arms around a throw pillow as if it could save her from drowning in her own thoughts. Her toes peeked out from under the blue robe Antonio had wrapped her in following their leisurely bath.

Everything in the room, from the blazing fire to the furnishings, looked normal. On the outside, she did, too. She knew this thanks to an extended session of look and touch this morning with Antonio in front of the full-length mirror on the back of the bathroom door. But she was different on the inside. She'd given everything she was to him, and in return, he'd filled her heart, mind, and body with a new reality.

"Keith will understand if you want to call it off."

"You said it would be different…with him." Giving herself to Antonio had changed her in a fundamental way, and it was hard to imagine the experience being different with someone else.

"It will be. I promise. I'll be making love to you. Keith will be having sex with you. That's all it is for him, and I'm sure that's

172

all it will be for you. Your heart and mind won't be engaged, just your body. Casual sex."

That's something she hadn't had much of, and she wasn't at all sure she knew what it was. She hadn't been with many men before Antonio, but she'd had at least a small emotional investment in each of them. Keith was a virtual stranger. She'd only met him once, and conversation had been non-existent.

"You want him to...?"

"To fuck you? Yes, I'd like to see that. I want to see your eyes when we both fill you. But I understand if you've changed your mind. I can live with either decision."

"Why do you want this?"

He shrugged. "I told you before, I've fought with myself over this ever since I met you. I want you all to myself, but I've seen how much enjoyment women can get from dual penetration, and I want you to experience that level of pleasure. I have all kinds of ideas about ways to make your magnificent body sing, and anal play is one of them. Since you asked to run the bases, I thought perhaps you might be one of the fortunate women who play the game and enjoy it. A trial run with Keith will answer that question."

Clare stared into the flames behind the wrought-iron fire screen. This shouldn't be a difficult decision. She had been ready to jump into the game without any preparation at all, and he was offering her the perfect opportunity to try it on for size—so to speak. The thought brought a smile to her face.

"What are you so happy about?" Antonio asked. Leaning back against the opposite arm of the sofa, he'd brought his sock-clad feet up, too. He nudged the sole of her foot with his toes.

I'm crazy. Certifiable. "I want to try it. I think."

At the muffled sound of a car door shutting, she stilled.

Antonio stood and reached a hand out to help her up. "He's here."

She took the offered hand and allowed him to pull her to her feet.

"Do you trust me?"

She nodded though her stomach fluttered with nerves. "Yes. I trust you."

He tugged her around the sofa to a place facing the door. "No matter what happens, all you have to do is say the word, and we'll stop. You understand that, don't you?"

"I understand."

"Good. You're mine, and I'm in charge as long as Keith is here. He'll only touch you if I give him permission to. Do not argue with my decisions. I won't let him hurt you. He's here to give you pleasure. If you do as I say, you won't regret it."

The doorbell rang, and he moved to stand behind her, his hands firm on her shoulders. "Will you allow me to bring you pleasure through Keith?"

"Yes." Her whole body trembled, and her stomach felt like it was twisted in knots.

"The only way we stop is if you say the word. Otherwise, you follow my orders."

"Yes," she nodded weakly. "I'll do anything you want me to do."

He placed a kiss on her neck, below her ear. "You won't regret it, love."

His fingers dug into the shoulders of her robe and tugged. He walked around to examine his creation. The blue fabric framed her breasts, held her arms tight to her sides, her shoulders bare. He lifted her breasts, so they rested on the bunched fabric at her ribcage.

Away from the fire, the room was cold. Her nipples tightened to hard nubs. He licked each one, returning to suckle gently. She loved the contrast of his dark hair and skin against her fair complexion. He took her in his mouth, and she shuddered with arousal. When he was finished, her nipples were red and glistened.

"Watch his eyes, sweetheart. I want you to see how desirable you are to him."

She braced herself. Antonio was confident Keith would look on her with lust. She wasn't as sure, but he'd asked for her trust, and she had given it. He opened the door. A blast of cold air felt like ice on her damp nipples tightening them painfully. She bit her bottom lip to hold in a groan.

Antonio closed the door behind his friend who took two steps inside and stopped.

"Holy Mother of God," he exclaimed, looking straight at her.

"Give me your coat," Antonio said, "then you can touch her tits."

She thought she might faint. Her vision clouded, and then she remembered to breathe. She sucked in a breath, which thrust her breasts straight at Keith who had shrugged his coat off and crossed the room to her. She forced herself to look at his eyes.

Heat. Desire. Lust. It was all there, barely banked. He raised a hand to her right breast. His finger was ice cold as it traced a line around her areola. She shivered at his touch but quelled the urge to jerk away.

He did the same with the other then, having put Keith's coat away, Antonio came to stand beside her, one strong arm supporting her at the waist.

"She's beautiful, Tony."

"I know." He slipped his free hand beneath her right breast, lifting it. "Taste her."

Keith's gaze met hers, silently asking permission. She inclined her head, granting his request. He bent his head and took her nipple in his mouth. His cheeks hollowed out, sucking hard on her tender flesh.

Antonio tightened his hold on her, providing the support her knees refused to give. Moments ago, she had looked down at Antonio's dark head at her breast. The sight of Keith's sandy pate and faintly tanned skin held her in thrall.

She fisted her hands in the fabric covering her thighs.

Keith devoured her like she was his last meal on earth. Antonio's hand kneaded her breast, increasing her pleasure. God, she was going to die. The two of them together were a team she wasn't sure she could handle, but desire and arousal coursed through her body, and she wanted to feel everything they could make her feel. Even if it killed her.

"Enough, Keith," Antonio said.

He released her at once, straightening to his full height.

"Candy," he said, capturing her gaze. "The sweetest candy." His tongue swept over his lips, curved into a satisfied smile.

"Then you will enjoy seeing more." Antonio swung her around to face him. His gaze commanded hers, holding her captive for a moment of unspoken communication. He silently offered her the opportunity to say no, to put an end to what was to come.

She refused to look away while his fingers worked the knot loose at her waist. Her robe parted, slid to the small of her back.

He held it there, the question still in his eyes.

She placed her hands over his and together they released the fabric to fall at her feet. Cool air tightened every follicle, but she wasn't cold. The admiration, approval, and desire burning in Antonio's eyes warmed her.

His hands rested on her hips, his fingers flexing in a possessive caress. "This is what you want?"

"Yes." She nodded. "I want to do this."

"Okay, then. There's only one way to stop this from now on."

"I know."

They stayed that way, absorbing the import of her decision, for the space of several heartbeats. Then his gaze moved to Keith who stood behind her.

"Let's make this good for her," Antonio instructed. Pressure on her hips made her turn to face their guest.

Her heart almost leapt from her chest at the hungry expression on Keith's face. His gaze raked over her, pausing at her breasts, and again at the juncture of her thighs. All the while, Antonio's hands swept over her hips and buttocks, massaging, reassuring, arousing.

Keith looked his fill. "She's exquisite, Tony."

"Yes, she is. She's agreed to let us pleasure her." Antonio's touch warmed her lower back.

"I can't think of a thing I would enjoy more." Keith looked right at her when he said it. His voice was deep and resonated with desire, setting every cell in her body on alert.

They retired to the bedroom where both men disrobed and joined her on the bed. Keith kept his distance, touching her only with his hands while Antonio pressed close along her side.

"Close your eyes," he said. "Just feel, sweetheart." He leaned over her, capturing her lips in a kiss that sealed her eyes shut and loosened every ligament in her body.

Together, the two men set her skin on fire and reduced her to a quivering mass of need. They touched, they kissed, they tasted, so when Antonio pulled her on top of him, her mind felt drugged with pleasure and her body primed.

Beside them, Keith stroked her back from nape to the crease spread wide as she straddled Antonio. His fingers explored lower, flicked over her clit and slid effortlessly through her wet and swollen folds.

She was beyond embarrassment at their handling of her. Every touch brought nothing but pleasure just as Antonio had promised. They were offering her fulfillment of that promise.

"She's ready for you," Keith said.

"Ready, sweetheart?" Antonio asked, his gaze intent and searching.

Her heart swelled with love for him, knowing they'd come this far, and he still offered her the chance to say no.

"Yes." She put her hands on his shoulders and pushed herself to a sitting position on his belly.

"Take me in," he urged.

"Let Keith help you."

He moved between Antonio's legs, and with his hands on Clare's hips, helped her rise. Antonio guided his cock to her entrance, and with his free hand on her thigh and Keith's on her hips, they eased her down until she had taken him completely inside her.

"How's that?" Keith asked.

Antonio gazed up at her, the same question in his eyes.

"Good," she said. *More than good. Perfect.* It was like he filled a part of her she hadn't known was empty. Love swelled her heart until it took up so much room in her chest she could hardly breathe.

With one hand on her hip, Keith reached around them for a condom and lube off the nightstand. Antonio stroked her breasts, providing a distraction while behind her, her other lover suited up.

"Your ass is beautiful," he said.

Antonio had warmed the lube, but they'd taken their time getting to this point. The gel had grown cold while they played.

"Fingers first," Keith said, working two heated digits past her barrier, spreading the cooled lubricant liberally.

She closed her eyes and searched the same feeling she'd had when Antonio had done this to her. Then she'd felt like she was giving him a part of her, but Keith's touch was different. She felt anticipation and desire, but that was it. His fingers felt good, stretching her, preparing her for more.

"Hold her for me," Keith said.

Antonio's hands moved to her ass. His fingers dug into her cheeks, spreading her.

"Perfect." Keith rose to his knees and fitted his cock to her entrance.

She dug her fingernails into Antonio's shoulders.

"Relax," he coached her.

She made an effort to do as he said, aware any tension in her body would make the other man's entry more difficult and potentially painful.

Keith nudged forward and the barrier gave way. "Christ, that feels good," he hissed, holding still. His hands went to her hips holding her immobile as he inched deeper inside.

Her heart raced. Everything she had felt when Antonio took her there, the overwhelming emotion, was absent. The physical pleasure was the same. She felt full, taken, but not possessed as she had with Antonio.

"Open your eyes, Clare." Antonio's voice was hoarse, commanding.

She looked down at him, and the raw hunger in his eyes heated her blood.

Keith gripped her shoulders hard. "A little more," he said. With one final thrust, he seated himself deep inside her. His groin was hot, pressed against her ass. "That's it, darlin' We're in, and Christ Almighty, you feel like Heaven."

"Give her a minute," Antonio said. He turned his attention back to her. "You okay?"

"I'm fine. What now?" she asked.

"You got the gag?" Antonio asked Keith.

"What?" she gasped. He hadn't said anything about a gag.

"Right here." Keith passed him a contraption that looked like a dildo with straps attached.

"Last chance to say no." Antonio held it up for her to see. "This will give you an idea what it's like to run the bases. Open up, sweetheart."

He placed the head of the dildo against her lips. "Suck it in," he commanded.

She sucked and with a little help from Antonio, the dildo filled her mouth.

"Okay?" he asked.

She nodded, and he held it in place while Keith fastened the straps around the back of her head.

"God, that looks hot," Antonio said. "I can just see you with your face pressed against Mike's crotch, his balls banging your chin.

His words conjured a vivid image in her mind, and her pussy clenched.

"Shit," both men said at the same time.

She clenched her inner muscles again and would have smiled at their reaction if she'd been able.

"Let's give it to her," Antonio said.

They began to move inside her, slowly at first, but as they established a rhythm, the tempo increased. She was consumed with the way they felt inside her, and after some time she realized her suction on the dildo was in rhythm with their thrusts.

Her arms trembled, supporting her weight against Antonio's shoulders. He said something, and Keith's arm wrapped around her waist, pulling her against his front. It felt strange, another man's bare chest against her skin, but soon Keith was crooning sexy things in her ear, nibbling on her neck while his hands lavished attention on her breasts.

Pulling her upright changed the angle of penetration for both men, and it seemed as if both were going deeper. Antonio moved his hands up the inside of her thighs and soon his thumbs double-teamed her clit, alternating between a smooth circular motion with lots of pressure and a quick flick that made her crazy.

Her head fell against Keith's shoulder, and she clung to his arms. The feel of his corded muscles moving as he loved her breasts reminded her of the strength her lovers possessed. She was safe, protected. They only wanted to give her pleasure, and they were doing it so well she didn't want it to end. If they could just hold her this way forever....

A familiar tension built low in her belly, and soon, her body was reaching for something, for the promise of something bright and so wonderful she couldn't imagine it. The reward was there, just beyond....

"Give it to me, Clare." Antonio's voice reminding her she was his, her orgasms were his, pushed her over the edge. Into a super storm of sensation.

Her body wasn't her own. Wave after wave of intense pleasure consumed her, heightened her senses so even the slightest touch added exponentially to her pleasure. Antonio's hands stroking over her stomach, her ribs, left trails of fire on her sensitized skin. Keith secured her, his hands cradling her breasts in a firm grip.

"Beautiful," he murmured in her ear. "God, that feels good. Suck that cock just like you're sucking mine and Tony's."

Her breath came in short, desperate pants. Her nostrils flared, drawing in the heavy scent of sex, and the unique musk of her lovers. She sucked hard on the dildo filling her mouth, unable to do otherwise, and let the sensations tumble her through the storm.

The tempest calmed, and she went limp in Keith's embrace. He whispered in her ear, "So damned beautiful." With one hand beneath her chin, he turned and lifted her face to his. He covered her cheek, her jaw with kisses. "Just a little bit more, darlin', then we'll release you."

Keith gently eased her down to lie atop Antonio whose arms came up to surround her with his love.

"You okay?" he asked, cradling her head to his shoulder.

She nodded, loving the feel of his solid body beneath her, inside her, a foundation of safety she trusted implicitly. His fingers trailed along the bands crossing her cheek securing the dildo in her mouth. She shivered and moaned as he traced her lips stretched thin around the artificial cock. "You're doing so good, babe. We're going to finish it now. Hang on to me."

She curled her fingers into his shoulders, and they began to move inside her again. Slow at first, then faster as they established a rhythm, retreating and thrusting as one. Keith remained upright, his hands spreading her ass, holding her still. She wanted to move, but was helpless to do anything but let them take her.

Her pussy throbbed, every sensitive nerve ending wired. After the orgasm she'd just experienced, she didn't think it was possible to feel that way again, but it wasn't long before the familiar tension began to build again. Hyper-aware, she sensed them growing harder, if that was possible, inside her, and in a matter of moments, she tumbled into the eye of the storm again, pulling both her lovers with her.

CHAPTER NINETEEN

Clare snuggled against Antonio while they waited in Dallas for the luggage carousel to spit out their bags. With one arm slung over her shoulder, he held her tight as if he needed her attached to him in order to breathe. He'd been glued to her side ever since Keith crawled out of their bed, dressed, and left the day before. And truth be told, she felt the same way. Coming back home was a given, but she wasn't ready to end the connection they'd made over the long holiday weekend.

She didn't understand what had happened, but somehow, the interlude with Keith had created a bond between her and Antonio that went beyond anything she could ever have imagined. She loved him, but for her, it encompassed her body and soul.

Soul mates.

The term was used to describe people who were meant for each other, but it didn't seem to be an adequate description of what she felt for Antonio, and what she thought he felt for her. They hadn't talked about the new depth of feeling, but let their bodies carry on the discussion with touches, glances, and constant contact.

Bases Loaded

In a few minutes, out of necessity, they would go their separate ways. Her job waited for her, and Antonio…well, surely there was something he needed to do. They couldn't remain in the cocoon of sensual bliss they had lived in for the last four days.

His arm tightened on her shoulder, and she squeezed him back with her arm wrapped around his waist. She shifted, turning into his side, so she could press her mound against his hip. She ached to have him inside her.

"Stop that," he said, placing a smiling kiss on the top of her head. "I can't do anything to help you here."

"I know," she said, nuzzling his shoulder, inhaling his scent. "I can't get enough of you."

"You're not sore?"

"A little," she admitted, "but I still want you." She pressed up against him again to emphasize the point.

"Behave," he admonished playfully. "I'll massage your aches away later."

Their bags plopped out onto the carousel. She reluctantly let him go so he could grab their luggage. He returned, setting the suitcases at her feet.

"Clare!" A familiar and unwelcome voice made her freeze. "Tony Ramirez," the woman said, her heels clicking across the tiled floor as she approached. "What are you two doing here?"

Clare grabbed Antonio's coat sleeve and silently prayed she was having a nightmare. She wasn't really standing in the DFW Airport in a sensual haze brought on by a weekend of the best sex ever, with the worst bully in the world bearing down on her.

He straightened from having set Clare's suitcase down, and faced the woman approaching with a determined stride.

Jessica Roach came to a stop in front of them. It took less than a second for her gaze to sweep from Antonio to Clare to the suitcases between them, and come to the obvious conclusion.

She turned her evil eyes on Antonio. "You're with her?" She pointed one perfectly manicured claw at Clare.

Antonio wrapped his arm around her. "I am. And you are…?"

"Jessica Roach. We haven't had the pleasure yet." She thrust out her hand.

Antonio ignored the offer of a handshake, perhaps picking up on what she thought was obvious—Jessica was bad news.

"We're in a hurry," he said, reaching down to release the spring-lock handle on Claire's suitcase.

Jessica would not be dismissed that easily. Something evil flashed in the witch's eyes, but before she and Antonio could wrangle their suitcases into moving, she realized they were too late.

"Tell me you didn't take *her* to run the bases," Jessica said. The emphasis she put on the word *her* made it plain she believed Clare to be a lower life form.

Antonio stopped arranging the luggage and straightened. He looked at Jessica, studying her like one would study a potentially dangerous bug, deciding between squashing it and letting it go on its way.

Clare held her breath. Did he remember Jessica from the Press Dinner? There's nothing she would like more than to see someone squash this particular roach. But the saying, no good deed goes unpunished was coined for vermin like Jessica. There would be a price to pay for crossing her.

"Not that it's any of your business, but we went skiing. We're tired, and Clare has work tomorrow, so you'll excuse us…." He reached for a suitcase handle.

"My, oh my." Jessica laughed her witch's laugh, and having been dismissed by Antonio, turned her attention back to Clare. "Does he know?" She tossed her head to indicate Antonio.

"Know what?" she asked.

"That he's—" She leaned in and whispered loud enough for half the terminal to hear. "—*fucking* Doyle Walker's niece?"

Antonio stilled. He looked at the roach, who wore the satisfied look of a predator going in for the kill. Then he looked at Clare.

"What did she say?" he asked.

A blast of cold slammed between her and Antonio. He actually took a step back, creating more distance between them than any time in the last twenty-four hours. For the span of a heartbeat, she considered denying it, but despite all her precautions, Jessica had discovered her connection to the team manager. Which meant everyone knew because the woman wasn't capable of keeping a secret.

Bases Loaded

She opened her mouth to confirm the damning information, but the words never made it past her lips.

Jessica jabbed the barb further in. "How's that moral's clause working out for you, Tony? Did you give it a thought when you were fucking her? Do you think your career will survive when *Uncle Doyle* finds out you went *skiing* with his precious niece?"

When Jessica turned her vicious grin on her, Clare blanched. "Did you earn the charm? I think not." Her gaze went to the crotch of Clare's jeans. "The piercing is a bitch. You wouldn't be wearing those this soon. But you'll never know. Will you?"

"That's enough," Antonio said. "Leave Clare out of this. What do you want?"

Jessica smiled at Antonio as if she hadn't just shattered Clare's world and put his career in jeopardy. "Nothing. Nothing at all. I like you, Tony. I think you'll be a great addition to the outfield this season. The last thing I want is to see you throw it all away on the likes of someone like her." She stepped up, placed her palm flat on his chest. "I'll show you my charm, if you show me your tattoo." She winked at him, turned on her heel, and walked away, dragging a Louis Vuitton roll-on behind her.

Her body had become a solid block of ice. Any movement might cause her to shatter into a million pieces. She should have told him about her uncle, but keeping the secret had become so natural it hardly ever occurred to her to mention the connection. And in her own defense—not that she really had one—he had started all this by coming up to her at Jason's fundraiser. If her being the team manager's niece was a problem for him, then the fallout from his pursuit of her was his fault. She would have gone on crushing on him from afar, perhaps wouldn't have ever gotten closer than an introduction if he hadn't outbid her on all the auction items.

"Is that true?" he asked, turning to face her.

"Is what true?" The spiteful witch had thrown out so many shocking revelations, Clare wasn't sure which one he wanted verified first. Not that it mattered. They were all true.

"Doyle Walker is your uncle?"

"Yes."

His shoulders squared, and he looked away from her.

She rushed to put his concerns at ease. "But I have no intention of telling him about us or…anything."

"Come on." He grabbed the handle on his bag and started walking. She followed, pulling her bag along with her.

The limo driver who met them when they'd first deplaned stood at the curb holding the rear door open for them. They left their luggage with him and ducked into the car.

He didn't speak again until the door closed, sealing them inside the private compartment. "I can't believe you told that woman I'm a member of the club." His gaze was as cold and sharp as his accusing words.

Clare reeled. After all they'd done together….

"You think *I* told her?" Her voice was unsteady, but disbelief was steadily growing into anger. "What kind of idiot do you take me for? Jessica is a mean, vicious woman. I do my best to be civil to her when I have the misfortune of running into her in a public place, but I. Do. Not. tell her anything—much less something I don't want the world to know. She feeds on gossip. And spreading it is why she gets out of bed in the morning, or crawls out of her cave."

She sank back in the seat, exhausted from…everything. The weekend, the sex, the emotions, the travel, meeting up with the one person in the world she truly hated. And now this. Arguing with Antonio, and knowing deep down Jessica had accomplished exactly what she had intended. She'd driven a wedge between her and the man she loved.

She couldn't take much more.

"Well, she had to find out somewhere, and there aren't that many people who know," he accused.

"Read my lips," she said, sitting up to face him. "I. Did. Not. Tell. Her." She collapsed back into her seat. "Maybe it was one of the women you ran the bases with. Did you think about that? Or maybe one of the guys on her team told her. I don't care how she found out, but I know this, it wasn't me."

"When were you going to tell me Doyle is your uncle? After you ran the bases? Is this some sort of sting? Wrangle an invitation, get inside the club, so you can hand over our names to team management?"

"What are you talking about? *You* came on to *me*. I had no idea you were a member of that club until…."

"Why didn't you tell me the night we met?"

No longer afraid of breaking, she was just plain mad…and hurt. "*Really*? Did you hear *anything* I said to you? I had a crush on you for years, so yeah, the *first thing* that entered my head when you came on to me was to tell you about *my uncle*." She put as much sarcasm as she could muster into the statement. "You wouldn't have come near me if I had, and call me pathetic, but I wanted your attention."

She vibrated with anger and a pain so deep it was a wonder she wasn't bleeding all over the seat. Tears welled in her eyes, and she turned her head so he wouldn't see.

The car moved out into traffic and, with each silent passing mile, carried her further into herself and away from Antonio. She was right, and he couldn't deny it. He didn't even try. He wouldn't have given her a second look if he had known.

When they arrived at her apartment, she paused before stepping out of the car. "I suspect Uncle Doyle already knows we're seeing each other. You took me home from the Press Dinner. Remember? He's not the kind of man who would deny his niece her happiness, and he isn't the kind of manager to hold it against you that things didn't work out between us. I wasn't going to tell him about your involvement with the club, and I won't. I'm the least of your worries. If you value your career, don't turn your back on Jessica. She knows, and if she thinks hurting you will hurt me, then she'll sell you out in a heartbeat."

Tony clenched his fists around the edge of the seat to keep from grabbing Clare and dragging her back inside. He felt like a part of him was leaving with her, and the possibility scared the shit out of him. She'd gotten under his skin, and stolen his heart.

She's Doyle's niece.

"Shit," he mumbled as the car pulled away from the curb.

That bit of news sent shockwaves down to his toes, but he'd had nearly an hour since the bombshell exploded to get used to the idea, and he'd come to one conclusion. He didn't give a flying fuck if Doyle approved of him associating with his niece or not. Clare was a grown woman. The decision was hers.

And he was pretty sure his own stupidity had just insured he would never see her again.

He didn't know what made him blurt out the sting operation thing. It was the first stupid thought that had popped into his head—and like the first pitch, good or bad, he'd swung without thinking. Stupid. He deserved to strike out.

She was right—he had approached her, not the other way around. No one, least of all him, could have anticipated the way he'd felt the instant he saw her at Jason's fundraiser. For all the world knew, he liked his women pencil thin and gum eraser dumb. If anyone was setting up a sting, they most likely would have employed someone like Jessica Roach to approach him.

Which brought his thoughts around to the most disturbing news. His secret was in the hands of a woman he didn't trust. It hadn't been necessary to warn him. He'd decided Jessica was bad news at the Press Dinner when she'd rattled Clare. The woman had venom in her veins, and she was on a mission to destroy someone. Bullies always were.

They zeroed in on people they perceived wouldn't fight back and asserted their authority over them in heinous ways to boost their own sense of self-worth. Funny how bullies didn't see for every notch their self-worth went up, their human worth went down ten. As far as he could tell, Jessica's human worth was somewhere around zero.

He'd have to find a way to, if not stop the woman's bullying entirely, deflect it from Clare, and at the same time insure she kept her mouth shut about Bases Loaded. She had no real proof of his connection to the club. Maybe she knew one of the women he'd played the game with, but it would only be hearsay, not solid evidence. But in a world that lived for rumors like Major League Baseball, it could be enough to do serious damage to his career and the careers of every other member of the club.

The press would have a hay-day with the information. One report based on what Jessica did know—presumably the names of the players in her game, plus the players, like him, she believed were part of the club—and no telling how many more women wanting their fifteen minutes of fame would come forward. No doubt, innocent athletes would be dragged into the scandal as well. They always were.

Bases Loaded

Look at what happened to Jason Holder. He'd been wrongly accused of using performance-enhancing drugs, and the accusation had come close to wrecking his career.

He would have to find a way to silence the cockroach and end her bullying before she unleashed a shit storm of bad press for everyone. The only problem was, he didn't have the first clue how to go about it.

Too bad he couldn't just spray a can of insecticide on her and be done with it.

Clare canceled her classed for the Monday following Thanksgiving. Most of the students wouldn't be back anyway, and she was in no shape, mentally or physically, to teach. She was sore all over. Even her jaw hurt. The pain could have been a delayed reaction to sucking on the dildo gag or from clenching her teeth all night long. She didn't know which, and what did it matter? The result was the same. She was miserable. And dehydrated from crying.

She'd held it together the night before until she passed the threshold of her apartment, and then the floodgates had given way. After collapsing to the tiny square of tile that constituted her entryway in a heap of sobbing misery, she'd made her way to the bedroom, eventually crawling into bed where the tears continued through most of the night.

The mirror told the ugly story all too well. Her eyes were puffy, red, and as fuzzy as tennis balls. Her lips were swollen, and a streak of dried drool trailed from the corner of her mouth down her chin. She'd wiped her sniveling nose on whatever had been handy—her sleeve, the bed sheets—and the abuse was obvious.

Turning from the painful visage, she stumbled her way to the kitchen. She needed coffee and ice. The first to kick-start her defeated body and other to ease the throbbing in her temples.

It took two cups of caffeine before she had enough strength to pop two slices of bread into the toaster. The combination of food, aspirin and the ice pack helped ease the headache and the soreness in her jaw. A shower was beyond her ambition, but she managed to get out of the clothes she'd had on since the day before. Wearing her second most comfortable set of clothes—the most comfortable being the ones she'd put on to dissuade Antonio on the night of the Press Dinner, and thus not an option today—that memory was too much to bear—she plugged her iPod into the speaker system and curled up on the sofa.

If ever there was a day she was entitled to a pity party, this was it. As horrible as last night had turned out following the confrontation with Jessica, she couldn't stop thinking about the weekend before.

It had been perfect, and then Jessica had shown up at the airport—Clare's rotten luck—and ruined everything. Antonio hated her now. She had a list of should'ves, would'ves, and could'ves as long as her arm. That's where her stupid fantasies had led her, into a sea of regrets without a boat, or so much as a life jacket.

No matter how she twisted the last few weeks with Antonio, it all came down to her fault. Sure, she'd laid the blame on him last night, but she never should have agreed to do a single one of those things with him. From the outset, she'd known it wouldn't end well. He might be her perfect man, but she wasn't his perfect woman, and she never had been.

She woke to ringing of the doorbell. She had no idea how long she'd slept, but what did it matter? She walked softly to the door and looked through the peek-hole. Her friend and fellow professor, Laura, stood outside. Clare dropped her forehead against the door and sighed. She didn't want to see anyone, but knowing her friend, she wouldn't go away unless Clare opened the door.

She wiped sleep from her eyes and turned the knob.

"Hi," Laura said, sweeping past her hostess without invitation.

Clare shut the door. "Did I invite you in?"

"No, but look what I brought you." She stood with her left hand behind her back. Bringing it around, she held out a thin crystal vase containing one perfectly beautiful long-stemmed red rose in full bloom.

Clare automatically reached for it. "You didn't have to do that," she said, taking in the lovely fragrance with a long sniff.

"I didn't. I mean, I'm the delivery person, but I didn't buy it for you." She dug in her purse, pulled out a white florist's envelope. "Here. This came with it. It was the same delivery guy, and when I told him you called in sick today, he wasn't going to leave it. But we're old buddies now, he and I, so I told him I would make sure you got it. He was okay with that."

She rattled on, and Clare only half-heard what her friend said. There was only one person who had ever sent her flowers. Antonio.

"Is it from the same guy? The baseball player? Oh, man. He must have done something really stupid. If that's not a cry for forgiveness, I don't know what is."

Her uninvited guest plopped down on the sofa and Clare joined her.

"Why do you think that?" she asked.

"It's in full bloom—his heart is open. What else could it mean?"

"I have no idea." After the way they'd parted last night, it could mean anything, but she didn't dare hope Antonio was asking for forgiveness. No, that was too much to wish for.

"Well, open the card. I'm dying to find out."

Clare looked down at the forgotten envelope in her hand. She placed the vase on the coffee table and slipped the card from the envelope. Her heart split wide open, and though she had been certain there wasn't another tear left in her, one slid down her cheek.

"What is it?" Laura placed a comforting hand on Clare's arm. "Let me see that." She grabbed the card from Clare's numb fingers. "I hope you like roses," she read aloud. "There's one for every day until you forgive me. I'm an ass. Love, Antonio." She turned the card over as if expecting to find more on the back. "Oh, hon. What did he do?"

Clare leaned into her friend's offered embrace and let the tears flow. Laura patted her back and murmured soothing things until Clare finally found some control.

"He…I…we argued. It was my fault. Mostly." The whole story spilled out, minus the secret club, and that he had accused her of setting him up. She left Keith's involvement out as well. It was one thing to tell your girlfriend you'd had the most spectacular sex of your life, but mentioning a third party to that sex might be going too far.

Laura made herself at home, fixing a fresh pot of coffee and rummaging until she found a half-eaten box of cookies while Clare filled her in on the weekend. As her friend bustled around her apartment, taking care of her without having been asked, Clare thought she really did need more friends like Laura in her life. She was as different from Jessica as a person could be.

"Thank you," she said when she brought coffee and cookies and sat down beside her. "You didn't have to come over and do all this for me."

"Yes, I did. You should have called me, and I would have been here sooner." She sipped her coffee. "So, are you going to forgive him?"

"Probably, but it won't change anything. It's over. He won't trust me again since I lied to him. I don't blame him. I should have told him the night we met."

"Clearly," she said, waving a hand toward the bloom, "he doesn't think it's over."

"He will. He just hasn't thought this through very well. Once he does, he'll come to the same conclusion I have. A relationship between us can go nowhere, so ending it now is the best thing for both of us."

CHAPTER TWENTY

Tony pocketed his car keys and entered the stadium. He'd called ahead, and Doyle had agreed to carve out a few minutes in his schedule for his new centerfielder. It had been three days since Jessica Roach dropped her load of shit on his head in the airport. Three days of hell.

Clare hadn't spoken to him—and rightfully so. He'd stepped into the shit and compounded the problem by spreading it all around in places it had no right to be. Like on Clare. And their relationship.

He'd spent the last two days replaying the encounter in his mind, and just like a blooper reel, it never got any better.

Blame it on lack of sleep, a sex-addled brain, or just plain stupidity, but what it added up to was he'd behaved like an ass. Oh, he'd thought he was handling it well. He hadn't yelled at anyone in public. He hadn't confirmed or denied his involvement in Bases Loaded. And, he'd gotten Clare out of the airport before that Roach woman could say anything else or cause a scene.

She'd said plenty—enough that he was voluntarily going to put his career on the line rather than wait for her to throw another load of shit at the fan. From what little he knew about her, she might be the type to do just that. Sixty hours of contemplation, and his best option was to be forthright. Get it out in the open, and in so doing, diffuse the shit-bomb hanging over his head.

"Doyle," Tony extended his hand. "Thanks for agreeing to see me."

The Mustangs manager clasped Tony's hand in a firm grip then ushered him to the comfortable arrangement of sofas and chairs on one side of the room.

"Can I offer you anything? Coffee? Water?" he asked.

"No, but thanks." His palms were sweating so much he would need batting gloves to hold onto anything breakable right now. Back when he'd joined Bases Loaded, he'd sort of known it could come back to bite him in the ass someday, but he'd been green, and horny, and young enough to believe himself invincible.

He'd changed over the years and come to realize a few things—one of which was his career existed at the whim of team management. He could have the best stats in the League, and if management wasn't on his side, he could be watching the next season from a barstool in Brooklyn and selling insurance with his old man.

The team manager settled into one of the plush armchairs while Tony chose a seat in the center of the sofa. A large wood and glass coffee table topped with a pottery bowl filled with baseballs separated them. Over Doyle's shoulder was a plate-glass window overlooking the baseball field. He couldn't help but wonder if he'd be wearing a Mustangs uniform come spring or if he'd be lucky to be selling hotdogs in the stands. It could go either way.

"What brings you here today?" Doyle asked.

Tony took a deep breath and stepped into the batter's box. "I've got a bit of a problem. I'm hoping it won't evolve into a public scandal, but there is a possibility it will. I thought I'd better give you a heads up, just in case."

The older man sat forward, his elbows resting on his thighs. "What sort of problem are we talking about?"

"I'm sure you're aware of Bases Loaded, the not so secret club?"

He nodded. "I've heard of it. The members do a good job of keeping it quiet, but if you spend any time at all in the clubhouse, you hear things."

"Yeah, well…I'm a member. I have been since my first year in the Majors."

Doyle sat back, crossing one ankle over the opposite knee. It was a relaxed pose, but there was nothing relaxed about the man. "Not news to me."

Tony raised his eyebrows at the statement. He'd suspected Doyle knew of his involvement with the club since the night of Jason's fundraiser when he'd warned him to be on his best behavior with Clare. Knowing now about their family relationship, Doyle's comments made more sense.

"Apparently, you aren't the only person in Dallas who knows. There's someone else, and I'm not sure they're going to keep it to themselves."

"One of my players?"

"No. A fan. I've heard through a third party she's been to one of the club meetings…and she insinuated the same to me while implying she knows of my membership. She's not a nice person, and until I came here, I'd never seen her before, but she seems to have an agenda."

"What kind of agenda?"

"I haven't got a clue. She's been…unkind…to a female friend of mine. I think seeing this woman with me has set the crazy woman off."

"Jealousy?"

He shook his head. "No. I don't think so. As I said, I'd never met the woman until I came here. She doesn't like the woman I've been dating. That much I know for certain. If she does anything, it will be to hurt my girlfriend. Unfortunately, the Mustangs could become collateral damage."

Doyle propped one elbow on the arm of his chair and stroked his thumb over his bottom lip. Tony had seen the gesture a million times. It was team manager sign language for *I'm thinking.*

The tension in the room seemed like a living, breathing thing. Silence stretched between them.

"This girlfriend of yours. Would she by any chance be Clare Kincaid?" Doyle asked.

Yep. He would be hawking peanuts and hot dogs for a living. It beat selling insurance in Brooklyn. "Yes, sir. I understand she's your niece."

Doyle's eyebrows rose. "She told you that?"

"No. This witch of a woman told me. Recently, I might add."

"How recently?"

"Last Sunday." Tony related the official story—that he and Clare had gone skiing over the Thanksgiving holiday, ending with the scene at the airport.

"Does this woman have a name?"

"Jessica Roach. Clare says she attends most of the local charity events."

Doyle stood and paced to the window overlooking the field. He crossed his arms over his chest, stretching starched white fabric across his shoulders and back. Tony remained where he was, hardly daring to breath. At least he was still alive.

"I know her." Doyle turned, sat on the wide ledge spanning the length of the window. "She dated one of my players a few years ago. Traded him to Minnesota."

Tony didn't have a clue what to say, so he kept his mouth shut. He didn't mind cold weather, but Minnesota was beyond cold, and he did not want his career to end playing on frozen tundra.

"Before the trade, he dated Clare for a while. Not long. I think they went out a few times—nothing serious."

"That could explain why she goes out of her way to make Clare's life miserable."

"It could. Tell me, Tony. What is the nature of your relationship with my niece?"

Here's where it could get dicey, but he decided before coming to see her uncle, honesty was his only option. "I'm in love with her, sir. And I think she loves me, too, but at the moment...she isn't speaking to me."

Doyle smiled. "Pissed her off?"

"Yes, sir. I wasn't as understanding as I could have been when I found out she was your niece."

"She knows about this club you're a member of?"

"She does."

He nodded. Sitting there with his back to the field, his arms and ankles crossed, he looked every inch the formidable manager he could be during a game. He had a reputation for being fair on and off the field. Tony prayed it was true.

"What happens to her if Ms. Roach goes public with this knowledge she has?"

"She would be caught in the middle of a nasty scandal." He scooted to the edge of the sofa cushion. "The thing is, all Jessica has is second-hand knowledge of my involvement in the club. When she…was *there*…I wasn't. Without divulging what goes on within the club, I can say she and I were never in the same place at the same time. She seems to believe I'm a member, but she couldn't possibly have proof."

"Is there proof?"

"I have a tattoo."

"The baseball field? Bases Loaded under home plate?"

"That's the one."

"Generic enough for a baseball player. It can be explained away."

"That's the idea, sir. We…the members…try to be discreet, but when there are women involved…."

"You can't always insure they'll keep your secret."

"That's the way of it."

"I take it there are women who can vouch, with certainty, for your involvement?"

"Yes, sir. Quite a few."

Clare's uncle fell silent again. Tony studied the bowl of baseballs in front of him. He could see autographs on a few. He picked one up, turned it over to see the signature."

"Home run balls," Doyle said. "I collect them."

Tony nodded. "Nice collection. Some big names in here." He placed the ball carefully back on top.

"I think I have one of yours from a few seasons back. It's one I didn't have to buy. You hit it into center field," he said, pointing over his shoulder, "right out there. It landed under the scoreboard, out of reach of the fans. That's when I decided I wanted you to play for us. I had to wait until you were a free agent, but I got you."

He remembered that one. Someone brought the ball to the clubhouse for him to sign after the game. Now, he knew where it had gone.

"And I'm glad to be here. I want to stay here." Tony stood. Perhaps he might walk out of here still employed, and alive. "I love Clare. I want to marry her. If I can get her to talk to me again, I think I know a way to keep this Roach lady quiet. It will take Clare's cooperation, but I think it might work."

"What kind of plan are we talking about?"

"I really don't want to say, sir, given that Clare is your niece, but suffice it to say, it would mean the end of my involvement with the club, and elevate your niece to a position of strength where Jessica Roach is concerned."

"Why are you telling me all this if you have a plan to fix it."

"Because there is the very real possibility Jessica could go to the press before I can carry out the plan. And, I admit, the plan might not be enough. I'd really like to keep my job, sir, if there's any way to make that happen."

Doyle nodded. He remained on his window perch. "I don't want to see my niece involved in a public scandal any more than I want the Mustangs to be. I understand the nature of Bases Loaded, and I'm not going to pretend I like the idea of my niece being involved with the club in any way. However, she's an adult, and I wouldn't presume to meddle in her personal affairs. That's one of the reasons we've tried to keep our family relationship out of the public eye. I don't know how this Roach woman found out, but that's not the end of the world—unless Clare's name gets dragged through the mud along with yours. Then all this comes back on me and the team."

"I understand, sir. That's why I thought you should know what's going on. In case I'm not able to stop the train before it leaves the rails."

"If you fail, your career is over. You know that." It wasn't a warning, but a statement of fact Tony couldn't argue with.

"I know. I can live without playing baseball, but I can't live without Clare. I'm doing this for her, not to save my career."

Doyle stood. "Then your plan better work, son."

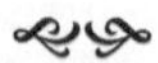

Bases Loaded

The roses were lovely. And every time she looked at them or caught a whiff of their soft scent, her heart ached. There were six so far, each one in full bloom with an accompanying note written in Antonio's hand. The latest had been delivered to her apartment that morning.

Clare lifted the vase, swiped the dust rag across the table, and replaced the vase. This was housecleaning Saturday, the one day a month she reserved for the things she hated most—dusting, vacuuming, and cleaning out the refrigerator. None of them required much thinking, which left her brain free to reflect on Antonio and his daily pleas for forgiveness.

Against her better judgment, her resolve to cut all ties with him had begun to weaken. Maybe it was the roses or the handwritten notes. Or perhaps she was coming to her senses. She ran the dust cloth over a lampshade and let that thought sink in.

No. Her good sense was long gone, overpowered, and overruled by love. She was in love with Antonio, and no matter how hurt or angry she was, her love for him was here to stay.

She finished the dusting and moved on to the refrigerator. As she pulled container after container of fuzzy leftovers out, she wondered why she'd bothered saving them in the first place. Keeping them made as much sense as loving Antonio. Holding onto something she didn't want or couldn't have took up room in her heart or her refrigerator she could use for something useful, something nourishing.

She turned her face away to avoid flying spores and dumped slimy, green goo down the whirring garbage disposal. Gone. Flushed down the drain and out of her life.

If only getting Antonio out of her life and her heart was as simple.

She stuck her head back in the fridge and moved the filtered water carafe out of the way to reach the last of the questionable containers. The doorbell rang and she jerked, banging her head on the freezer door.

A glance through the peephole revealed a vase of red roses that obscured the face of the delivery person. But Clare knew those hands.

Antonio.

Her heart raced, and the fresh knot on the back of her head throbbed. Every cell in her body went on high alert.

She could pretend she wasn't home. Yeah, that was best. She took a step back and stared at the door as if it might dissolve any second and reveal her for a liar.

"Come on, Clare. Open the door. I know you're in there. Your car is out front and your blinds are open. I saw you in the kitchen."

Shit.

She'd opened the blinds in order to dust them and forgot to close them afterward. Not a smart thing for a single woman living on the first floor to do.

Knock. Knock. Knock.

"Clare. Please."

Maybe it was the breathless way he said her name, or perhaps it was the desperation she sensed behind the word please, but she gave in. Taking a deep breath and exhaling, she opened the door.

"Thank God." He held out the bouquet. "These are for you."

She reached for the vase and, stepping back, allowed him to enter. "New job delivering flowers?"

"No, but it's not a bad idea. It might pay better than hawking peanuts in the stands."

The flowers were spectacular and artfully arranged. She made a mental note to use his florist the next time she needed to send flowers. They clearly knew what they were doing. She made room on the coffee table for them and went to the window to close the blinds. Lesson learned.

Her apartment seemed adequate for her, but with Antonio taking up most of the floor space, her living room felt crowded.

"Thanks for the flowers," she said, inviting him to have a seat.

He sat at one end of the sofa, and she took her one and only chair. She could barely see him over the flowers. Thanks to good genes, she supposed, his face was normally free from worry lines, but today he looked both tired and worried. She knew the signs, saw them every time she looked in the mirror.

"Why are you here? Is something wrong?"

He fidgeted, scooted to the edge of the sofa cushion. "I came to see you and apologize. There's no excuse for the way I behaved at the airport and on the way home. I won't make excuses because we both know there aren't any that would make it all right. I screwed up. I hurt you. I'm sorry."

She nodded, twisting her hands together in her lap. Her love for him felt like a river coursing through her, branching out in a million different directions, bringing life to every part of her body. It was all she could do to keep from leaping over the coffee table and tackling him. Her skin tingled with the need to touch him, to feel his body pressed against hers, inside hers.

"Apology accepted. Was there anything else?" she asked.

"Yes." He rubbed his hands on his thighs. "I talked with your uncle, and I have a plan."

She sat up straight. "You what?" she shouted.

"I talked to your uncle. I told him about that Jessica woman, and…everything."

Her head spun, and she gripped the armrest to keep from tumbling face first out of her chair. "Everything?" she squeaked. *Please, God, no.*

"Well…not *everything*, but I told him enough that he understands what's at stake. I had to tell him, in case my plan fails. All kinds of shit could come back on the team, and him specifically, if my plan to shut that woman up doesn't work."

She couldn't speak, couldn't process what he was saying. He continued, and she did her best to keep up. When he wound down, she remained silent.

"So…what do you think? Are you willing to give it a try?"

"Can you give me some time to think about this?" Her brain still felt like it was a few sentences behind in comprehending.

"How much time? I've made all the arrangements. There's a plane waiting for us at the airport."

She closed her eyes and pressed her lips together. She'd inhaled too many mold spores or it was the bump on the back of her head, but she was having a hard time keeping up.

"What do you say? We'll be back in a few days, as soon as you're…up to traveling."

"My classes. Finals are in two weeks." Was she seriously thinking about going to New York with him and…?

"Cancel them, or ask someone to take them for you. You'll be back in plenty of time for finals week."

She searched her brain for a response and came up blank.

"Oh yeah." He stood and reached into the pocket of his jacket. "I can't believe I forgot."

He was on one knee beside her chair in the blink of an eye. Capturing her hand in one of his, he held an open ring box aloft with the other. The biggest diamond she'd ever seen flashed fire around the room.

"I love you, Clare Kincaid. And no matter what happens, even if I end up delivering flowers or selling popcorn in the stands, I want you to be my wife. Forever. Please. Say you'll marry me."

She tore her gaze away from the ring that seemed to have the power to hypnotize and looked at Antonio. His gaze met hers and held. She looked for any hint he had another motive besides not being capable of living without her, but found none.

"You love me?" she asked.

"More than anything in this world. More than my career. More than my own life. If this whole thing blows up in our faces, we'll go live somewhere no one knows us and start over. Even if I lose my contract with the Mustangs, I've got enough money for us to live on the rest of our lives. Please, Clare. You're killing me. Will you marry me?"

"What if I don't want to carry out this plan of yours?"

"Then we'll just wait and see what happens. Maybe Jessica will forget about us. I don't care. I just want to be with you for the rest of my life. This week has been Hell on Earth without you. I can't go on like this. I can't play baseball unless the organist playing my intro is you—my wife."

Her heart felt like a balloon filled to bursting. She didn't know if the hallucination was the result of mold spores or inhaling too much furniture polish and she didn't care. The man she loved was asking the question she never thought she would hear from him say. She bit her lower lip, savoring the sharp bite of pain that meant she wasn't dreaming. This was real. And there was only one answer.

A bead of sweat glistened on his forehead before it lost its grip and slid down his temple. The balloon inside her burst wide open, unable to contain her love for him. She'd brought Antonio Ramirez to his knees. Her. Clare Kincaid.

"Yes," she said.

His eyes sparkled, but he wasn't smiling. "Yes, what?"

"Yes. I'll help you with your plan, and yes, I'll marry you. Yes to it all."

Antonio smiled. The hand holding the ring came up to her nape, urging her down. His lips captured hers in a kiss that promised a lifetime of love, and at least a few hours of immediate pleasure. His tongue plunged deep, freeing all the pent-up passion she'd tried to deny since they'd argued. Her nipples grew hard, begging for his touch. Between her legs, she was embarrassingly wet and ready for him. He ended the kiss a moment before she would have slipped off her chair and thrown herself into his arms.

"First things first." He took the ring from the box and, lifting her left hand, slipped the diamond onto her finger. "The next time I make love to you, I want you to wear this."

She could barely see it for the tears in her eyes.

Antonio used his thumbs to remove the ones spilling onto her cheeks. "I wish we could do this now, but we have a plane to catch."

"Now?" she asked, completely thrown off balance.

"How fast can you be ready to go?"

CHAPTER TWENTY-ONE

It was past midnight when he ushered her into his Manhattan apartment. If what they'd done on the plane to Colorado hadn't qualified her for the Mile High Club, what they'd done on the flight to New York certainly had. Private planes were a lot more conducive to sexual activity than commercial flights, but so were cars. If his plan didn't work, then there would be a lot less private planes in their future and a lot more four-wheel road trips.

"You live here?" she asked, seeing the stark bachelor pad for the first time.

"Used to. Almost ten years."

She walked around the room, looking for anything that would indicate a human lived in the apartment. Three apartments the size of hers would fit in the living room alone. "Decorator?"

"How can you tell?"

"There's not a single thing in this room that looks like something you would pick out for yourself, and there aren't any pictures."

"She told me I couldn't mess up her work of art with my junk." He shrugged. "I have some stuff in my office, down the hall." He pointed.

"I'd like to see that but later. I'm exhausted."

He smiled and pulled her close for a kiss. "I'll never get enough of you, but you need your rest. You know, you don't have to do this. The guys will go along with anything I want. Jessica would never know one way or the other."

"I want to do it. But if you would rather I didn't...."

His hands roamed from the small of her back to her hips and up to massage her breasts. "You know I would love to see you go through with it, but it's totally up to you. I'm okay with whatever you decide."

She kissed him, letting him know how much it meant that he insisted the decision be hers. "I want to do it. For you, for me. For us. Besides, I don't think I'm a good enough actress to pull your plan off otherwise."

"I understand that. You won't get any argument from me. I'm through pretending I don't want you to run the bases. I'm so hard right now, I could go for a swim in the Hudson, and the cold wouldn't faze me."

"No swims tonight. Let's go to bed."

The following day, she woke alone in Antonio's bedroom. Like the living room she'd seen the night before, the bedroom was as impersonal as a luxury hotel room. To say it was uncomfortable would be wrong. The bed was like sleeping on a cloud, and the furnishing were, if not what she would have chosen for him, beautifully sleek, modern, and expensive.

He'd told her to sleep as late as she wanted, explaining he would be gone most of the day, finalizing the arrangements for tonight, and staying away so he wouldn't be tempted to get a head start on the evening's activities. As much as she would have loved to spend the day with him, he was right. She needed to rest.

After a light lunch, she used the spa appointment Antonio had thoughtfully made for her. When she left three hours later, her skin was soft as silk, her nails—all twenty of them—sparkled, and her hair gleamed, bouncing in fat curls around her shoulders. Her makeup was perfection. She'd even swallowed her embarrassment and allowed the esthetician to tidy her pubic hair. She now sported a neat triangle pointing the way to her secrets. She couldn't wait for Antonio to see it.

Back at the apartment, she undressed and slipped into the one garment she was allowed tonight—Antonio's Mustangs jersey. She'd brought along a pair of high-heeled sandals in case they went some place dressy before they returned to Dallas. She sat on the edge of the bed and slipped them on.

Standing, she caught sight of herself in the mirror on the back of the open closet door.

Sin.

She swept a dark curl over each shoulder and cocked one hip so her knee peeked out from between the tails of the shirt. Pursing her lips, she made kissing sounds at her reflection.

Switching sides, she hitched her other hip out and fluffed her hair at her nape in an effort to find the inner vixen she felt sure was hiding somewhere inside her. Wherever it was, it was trembling like a leaf.

Would they take her wearing Antonio's jersey? That would be hot. He would like that, and so would she.

With one hand on her leg, she scooted the shirt hem up an inch. An inch more. She couldn't wait to feel Antonio's hands on her, slowly creeping beneath the fabric to find her naked bottom.

His eyes would go dark like they always did when he wanted her. He would back her against the wall, and his hands would find all her lady parts while his lips kissed her senseless. Then he would hand her over to the others.

He'll be here, she reminded herself. *Antonio will be here.*

She took a deep breath and forced her reflection to smile back at her.

Relax. You can do this.

"Clare?" Antonio called from the living room.

"I'll be right there." She dried her sweaty palms on the jersey and said to the woman in the mirror. "I'm as ready as I'll ever be."

"No jersey has ever looked better."

She jumped at the sound of his voice at the door. He wore a black suit coat with a white shirt tucked into faded jeans. The shirt was open at the collar, revealing a hint of bronze skin that made her mouth water.

"I feel...."

"Sexy?" he supplied. "Because you look good enough to eat." The gleam in his eye told her he wasn't kidding.

"Antonio," she warned.

"No worries. It's all part of the game." He took her hand in his and drew her to him. "The guys are waiting for us in the living room."

"Oh." Reality hit. The game wasn't hypothetical any longer. There were three men in the other room prepared to spend an entire evening, or as long as it took, to fuck her senseless.

"You can still say no," he reminded her. He nibbled her neck while his hands found her bare ass beneath the heavy game jersey.

"No. I mean, yes. I want to do this."

He lifted his head, and his gaze met hers. "You trust me?"

She nodded.

"If you are uncomfortable at any time, physically or otherwise, you have to say something. We can't feel what you're feeling, and we don't read minds."

"I understand."

"We'll do our best to make sure you're aroused and ready, and we'll use plenty of lube. We don't want to hurt you."

"Okay."

"I've talked with them. They have my permission to touch you, but your permission is the only one that counts."

She nodded again, afraid to try to form words. Her legs were shaking so badly she was afraid she might topple off her high heels.

"Okay, then. Let's go." He stepped back, and the jersey fell into place over her ass. Looking her up and down, his eyes blazed. "Nice shoes."

If he hadn't supported her with an arm around her waist, she might not have made it to the living room without tripping. Her legs were jelly. Couple that with the heels and nearly ankle-deep carpet and unsteady was an understatement.

They paused inside the living room. Three of the most gorgeous men she'd ever seen in her life stood in a line with their backs to the gas fireplace.

"Clare Kincaid," he said. "May I introduce your team?" He

swept a hand toward the man to his left. "You know Keith O'Brian. We played on the Marauders together."

Keith smiled. "Clare. Good to see you again. I'm looking forward to this."

Her skin prickled, and her face flushed.

"This is Mike Waverly from the Sidewinders." Antonio indicated the man in the middle. He was the shortest of the three, but he still had several inches on her. His hair wasn't as light as Keith's or as dark as Antonio's.

"Clare," Mike said with a half smile that would have made her swoon if she'd been capable of reacting, but she was a ball of fire on the inside and frozen solid at the same time. "You're more beautiful than Tony said."

She nodded. Or at least, she thought she did.

"Last, but not least," Antonio said, "is Conner Ostenhouse from the Claimjumpers."

She shifted her attention to the last man. Conner was perhaps the youngest of the four men, but it was difficult to tell. Norse gods didn't age, did they? They were all big men. Not fat. No. There didn't appear to be an ounce of fat between them. They were all shoulders, and legs, and rock-hard muscle. Athletes in their prime.

"Pleased to meet you, Clare," Conner said. "That jersey will have to go. It's criminal to cover a work of art."

Could she possibly blush any brighter? She nodded, accepting the compliment. This is what she'd wanted for so long, for men to look at her and tell her she was beautiful, find her desirable. Their approval satisfied the deep-seated insecurity that had plagued her since her teenage years when her body had shown signs of being curvy instead of fashionably thin.

As flattering as it was to be desired by strangers, the reality of what was about to take place scared the living daylights out of her. All she had to do was say the word, and it would end here.

She tried to swallow, but her mouth felt like it was filled with sand. She turned to Antonio. He smiled, squeezed her hand reassuringly, and all thoughts of ending the game evaporated in the heat of his desire.

"Rules of the game," he said. "Three on base, one plate umpire. The plate umpire can touch Clare anywhere, with any part of his body he chooses, as long as he doesn't interfere with the players. All four men have to come each inning. We play four innings instead of the usual three, with an hour break in between each one. Longer if Clare needs more time. I'll umpire first. If Clare also comes all four innings, she earns not only the clit charm, but the diamond necklace as well. That's our goal, team. She needs that necklace."

"We'll do our best," Conner said.

"Not a problem, Tony," Keith said.

"Ditto. What they said," Mike added.

Antonio turned to her. He still held her hand in his, and the heat of the connection steadied her. "Your word is Miners. Say it and we stop. We end it. If you need a minute to adjust, cross your fingers," he said, demonstrating the universal sign for luck, "and wave your hand in front of someone's face. You may not be capable of speech, but your hands will be free. You may touch any of us, anywhere, or yourself at any time."

Her brain was on overload, but she managed a nod.

"Do you understand and consent to having sex multiple times tonight with these men?" He squeezed her hand again. "We need a verbal response, Clare."

She opened her mouth to speak, but nothing came out.

"Get her a glass of water," he said.

Keith broke away from the group and returned with a filled tumbler he pressed into her hand. He held the glass steady while she sipped the cool liquid.

"Thanks," she said. "I…. Yes, I want to do this."

Antonio squeezed her fingers again. She squeezed his in return. If he was touching her, she could do anything. His strength was her strength.

Keith smiled at her response then rejoined the others, setting the water glass on the fireplace mantle behind him.

Antonio put himself between them and her. With one more reassuring squeeze, he released her. "As Mike said, this has to go."

He slipped the first button on her jersey free, then the next. His gaze held hers until the last button came loose. He kissed her while his hands pushed the shirt open, using her breasts to hold the two sides apart. Cool air brushed her exposed skin, but soon his hands warmed her, sweeping across her sensitized flesh, arousing and teasing. Her nipples peaked beneath his palms. She almost forgot the others were there, but then he ended the kiss, gave her one long, assessing look, and stepped away.

Three sets of eyes blazing with desire took in her body framed by Antonio's jersey. The scarlet fabric should contrast nicely with her cream skin, but she feared her entire body was an embarrassing shade of puce.

"Holy shit," Conner said. "I knew she was a work of art."

"Oh, man," Mike chimed in. "You're one lucky son of a bitch, Tony."

Keith smiled and chuckled beneath his breath. "Clare." He waited until she looked directly at him. "We are honored to be of service to you tonight."

Memories of his gentle, caring touch allowed her to return his smile. Antonio urged her forward. She followed him to the large, square ottoman that was both a footrest and a coffee table for the sectional sofa. When she was seated on the edge, he went to his knees in front of her and spread her legs.

Her breath caught, knowing four men were now privy to her most intimate secrets. He stroked along the tops of her thighs, comforting her. She focused on him, and only him.

"Lie back," he said, "and let us love you."

Her gaze locked with his, and the storm of passion in his eyes fueled a fire within her. His hands on her legs were her lifelines. She lay back, raising her arms over her head, offering herself to them.

"Players." Antonio called his friends to the field. "Let's play ball."

His hands slid beneath her thighs, lifting and parting her. Fingers closed over her ankles, and she looked up to see Mike standing over Antonio, holding her legs aloft. Keith and Conner knelt on either side of the ottoman. They reached for her breasts, and she closed her eyes as they caressed her. She tilted her head and arched her back, inviting them to taste her. A heated mouth closed over each aching nipple, forcing a moan from her throat. Then Antonio claimed her pussy. Claimed her. Her brain short-circuited. She lost the ability to think, leaving herself at the mercy of her senses.

She was on fire. Her skin burned, and the blood racing

through her system felt like molten lava, searing everything it touched. Nerve endings fired like a pyrotechnics show gone wrong, haphazard, random, wherever her lovers touched her. Between her legs, Antonio detonated one explosive after another, sending shockwaves of pleasure through her body. Mike cradled her left leg between his shoulder and his neck, kissing anywhere he could reach while holding her right leg aloft, stroking fire from the back of her knee to her ankle.

Her head rolled from side to side, one moan after another falling from her lips. It wasn't long before tension coiled tight and low inside her. She was vaguely aware of all the hands on her—everywhere. From the top of her head to the arch of her feet, rough palms and fingers explored her every curve and found secret places where a touch could drive her insane with need.

The tension built one caress, one questing tongue flick at a time until she couldn't stop the inevitable. Like a pebble dropped in still water, shock waves radiated out from her pussy, along her legs and torso all the way to her toes and fingertips. Even the tops of her ears tingled as her first orgasm of the night unleashed its power in a shower of light and moments of complete and utter darkness, catapulting her from one to the other so fast she could do nothing but ride the waves of pleasure like a rubber raft adrift in a hurricane.

The storm seemed to go on forever, but slowly her body calmed, and feeling as if she'd drowned and washed up on shore, she became aware of being lifted by strong arms and held.

Safe.

Her mind drifted in her post-orgasm haze. Around her, she sensed activity, others, but she couldn't make it all out. Voices, soft but firm. Then she was being passed from her safe cocoon to another place of safety. How she knew she was in no danger she didn't understand. She just was.

Time meant nothing. Her lovers positioned her boneless body, stroked, and molded.

"Clare, baby. Look at me."

She opened her eyes and was face to face with Keith. He smiled, and she smiled back, too happy and sated to do anything else.

"That's our girl. Hold onto my shoulders." Someone

helped her lift her arms, curved her fingers over Keith's shoulders. "Here we go. Remember to cross your fingers if we're going too fast."

Hands on her ass, from somewhere behind, lifted her. The pressure between her legs was like a jolt of electricity to her brain. Suddenly, she was alert and completely aware of her surroundings. A quick glance around confirmed the tidbits of sensory information coalescing into reality in the fogged recesses of her mind.

Her lovers had shed their clothes. She still wore Antonio's jersey, but instead of lying on the ottoman, she sat astride Keith's lap. Over her shoulder stood Mike. Conner and Antonio stood on either side of her.

"Take me in, baby," Keith crooned.

Her mouth form an O as Keith's cock impaled her in one slow but steady slide.

"She's so damned wet. Tight and hot," he said to their audience. Then to her, "Christ, baby. I don't know how long I can last."

"Lie back," Mike said.

"Come with me." Keith wrapped his arms around her and with incredible abdominal control, lowered his back to the ottoman, taking her with him so her breasts flattened against his rock-hard chest.

Fingers probed her ass, gentle but firm. "Oh, man. This is going to feel so good."

"Use this." Antonio's voice.

"Thanks," Mike said.

She bit down on her lower lip and closed her eyes, embarrassed and anticipating what she knew was coming. The lube wasn't as cold as she expected, but Mike's fingers slathered it on and in her with quick efficiency that left her little time to react.

"Ready, Clare?" Antonio asked.

She nodded, and instantaneously Mike pressed against her. With one hand at the small of her back, he breached her barrier, filling her completely. Clare crossed her fingers and waved her hand around.

"Slow down," Antonio warned. His face filled her vision.

"Okay?" he asked.

Her head spun, and she quickly realized it was because she was holding her breath. She exhaled and dared to draw in another breath. She nodded. "Forgot to breathe."

Antonio smiled, and she gave him a weak one in return.

"You're doing fine. Conner is ready whenever you are, babe." He stroked her cheek, his thumb hanging on her lower lip for a second. "Raise up on your elbows when you're ready to take him in. Everything okay below?"

"Yes. It feels good."

"For them, too. Mike is turning purple trying to keep from coming."

She smiled at that. "Let's do this, then." Pushing to her elbows, she looked down at Keith. His jaw was clenched tight, and the muscles in his neck looked ready to rupture.

The ottoman dipped as Conner dropped to his knees at Keith's shoulder. He held his cock in one hand and reached for her with his other. Cupping the back of her head in his broad palm, he guided his cock to her lips. He was big. They all were, but when she glanced up at Conner and saw the raw lust in his eyes, she opened her mouth and took him in. Placing her weight on one elbow, she wrapped her other hand around the base of his cock and sucked.

Keith and Mike took that as their cue, and with ease, established a piston stroke rhythm that made it difficult to concentrate on the cock in her mouth. Then Antonio was there, stroking her spine, sweeping her hair off her face, encouraging her with erotic words whispered in her ear and kisses from her nape to her ass. The grunts and groans from the other three confirmed their pleasure. Clare's psyche soared.

She was doing it! And, God, it felt good! She'd never felt so empowered in her life. The words of a song popular decades ago but still relevant reverberated through her brain. "I am woman, hear me roar!" She might have even hummed the tune because Conner grabbed a fist-full of her hair and shoved his cock to the back of her throat.

"Christ almighty. That tongue…." And then he was convulsing, filling the thin condom worn to protect her. Conner's release triggered a chain reaction of creative curses and uncontrolled thrusts as one by one the others came inside her. She'd almost forgotten all four needed to come until Antonio's voice issue a hoarse curse.

Conner pulled free and behind her, Antonio grabbed her hair, yanking her chin to her shoulder. In her peripheral vision, she saw him fisting his cock in short, quick strokes. No condom. Hot cum shot across her cheek, random spurts making it into her open mouth. Her tongue lapped eagerly at the salty cream on her lips. She moaned when Keith and Mike withdrew, but then four sets of hands caressed her, and pride swelled her heart.

"I did it," she said in wonder, collapsing onto Keith.

"You did," Antonio said, his fingers tripping along her spine, sending shivers through her cooling body.

"That was fucking perfection," Mike said, his hands massaging her ass.

"God, what a mouth," Conner added. "You should have warned me, Tony."

Antonio chuckled.

"You sure you want Tony?" Keith asked, the words rumbling through his broad chest. "I think I love you, baby."

"Get your own damn woman," Antonio said, his voice carrying enough edge Clare understood he wasn't entirely kidding. "This one is *mine*."

"Can't blame a guy for trying," Keith said.

"Come on, let's get her into a hot bath."

She let her head fall against Antonio's shoulder as he carried her to the bathroom. He held her while Mike filled the tub with warm water and fragrant bubbles. Soon, the restoring water worked its magic on her body while from behind, Antonio held her safe in a cradle of arms and legs and chest.

Conner brought them ice water in crystal glasses, setting them on the wide ledge surrounding the tub. Keith added a plate of cheese, crackers, and grapes.

"I feel like a queen," she said, taking sustenance from Antonio's fingers.

The others had done their jobs, and left them alone for the moment.

"You are. And we're your willing slaves for the night."

"Just for tonight?" she teased.

"The others. Me? You've got me forever."

She lifted her left hand. Soap bubbles slid down, revealing the ring he'd given her before they'd left Dallas. "I can live with that."

"No matter what happens, I love you. You've proven you have what it takes to win this game. If you want to stop now, it's okay. I'm sure the guys will go along with a charade."

She dropped her hand to his raised knee above the waterline and let her fingers trail down his thigh. "If you don't mind, I'd like to finish what we've started." She glanced meaningfully at the counter where three spent condoms lay in an arch, representing first, second, and third base.

"Babe, you have no idea how hot it makes me seeing you with these guys. If we continue, I get to be inside you for the next three innings." He flexed his hips, making her aware of his growing erection. "That's something I'm always up for."

As if on cue, the rest of the team returned. She licked her lips at sight of them fully aroused—for her.

"She's ready," Antonio said.

And like the queen she was for the night, they helped her from the water, dried her, and coated her body in rose-scented lotion before Mike swept her up in his arms and carried her to bed.

CHAPTER TWENTY-TWO

Tony lay awake, watching Clare sleep. The fourth inning hadn't concluded until nearly dawn, and while he'd seen to her bath, the guys had changed the sheets on his bed. She'd been asleep before he'd pulled the covers over her exhausted body.

He'd drifted off for a while, but the need to touch her, to make sure she was okay prevented him from resting. The guys had all gone to Keith's apartment to sleep it off and wouldn't be back until evening when, if Clare was up to it, they would take her to receive the clit piercing she had earned.

She looked like an angel, her dark hair rumpled and sexy against the steel gray sheets. Her eyelashes formed crescent-shaped fans on her cheeks. He reached out to touch her still swollen lips and stopped short. He didn't want to wake her.

On the pillow beside her face rested her left hand bearing the evidence she was his. He'd staked his claim on this remarkable woman, and still couldn't believe what a lucky bastard he was. Why he'd fought to keep her to himself, he couldn't fathom. The night before he'd witnessed her metamorphosis from a beautifully shy rosebud to a flower in full bloom, confident of her place in the world.

That bitch of a woman back home had better look out! The

Clare Kincaid she was used to pushing around was gone, and he, for one, couldn't wait to see the new, confident Clare in action.

He was so damned proud of her. Not only because of what she'd accomplished the night before, but because of the way she'd done it. After the first inning, she'd had every one of them eating out of her hands. They'd called the pitches the first time, but after that, it had been all Clare. She'd told them how she liked it, where to touch her, how fast, how slow. And she'd touched them, exploring, giving as much pleasure as she took, and earning the respect and love of every one of them.

When they put the second phase of his plan into action, there wouldn't be any acting involved. Every word, every move would be genuine.

Tony rolled to his back and stared at the ceiling. Many floors below, the city teemed with life and energy, unaware a goddess slept above them.

"Mine," he whispered to the universe. With one last look at what was his, he slipped out of bed.

An uneasy feeling woke Clare with a start. She sat up, brushing her hair away from her face and clutching the sheet to her chest. Four gorgeous hunks of manhood stood at the foot of the bed, smiling at her.

"You're awake," Mike said.

"About time," Keith added.

"I'm hungry," Conner said.

"There's plenty of time," Antonio admonished the team. He walked around and sat on the edge of the mattress beside her. "How are you feeling?"

She took stock. She was undeniably sore in a few places, but otherwise…. "Not bad," she said. "I'll live."

"Sore?"

"A little."

"I'll get you something for that." Conner headed for the bathroom.

"Do you want a bath? Or a shower?" Mike asked.

"I think I can manage a quick shower to wake me up."

Conner returned with a glass of water and two over-the-counter pain relievers. "Here. This should fix you right up."

Antonio looked at Conner as if he was two pitches short of a full count. "You think? Give the woman a break, Ostenhouse."

Clare downed the tablets and handed the glass back. "Thanks, Conner." She put a hand on Antonio's arm. "I'm fine. Really, I am. If you'll give me a few minutes, I'll be ready to go. Do we have time for food first? I could eat a horse."

They assured her a meal was next on their agenda then left her alone to get dressed. Naked, she made it to the en-suite bathroom and turned on the shower. She looked around for a towel, found one, and hung it on the peg next to the shower door. She'd been avoiding it, but no longer could. She faced the mirror over the vanity. Lord, she was a sight. Her hair was going to take more than a brushing to wrestle under control. Several spots on her body showed signs of having been up close and personal with a five o'clock shadow—or four. She'd thought hickeys had gone out of fashion but apparently not. Thank goodness none of hers would show wearing normal clothing.

All in all, she looked pretty damned good considering the night she'd been through. She was about to step into the shower when a thought struck her, and she turned back to the mirror. In all her perusal of her naked, well-loved self, not once had she thought of herself in terms of fat or ugly.

"My body is beautiful," she whispered. "I'm beautiful!" She'd said it out loud and then laughed. "I really am." She turned this way and that, admiring for the first time the womanly curves that had kept four men enthralled for an entire night. And they were back, waiting to mark her as someone special to them.

Reborn, she stepped into the shower, unconcerned if the men waiting overheard her less than perfect rendition of *I Am Woman*. She emerged from the bathroom a good bit later, a woman in charge of her own destiny.

She felt like a queen holding court. Her escorts turned heads, but they only had eyes for her, even though they could have had their pick from the bevy of beautiful women in the trendy restaurant.

"Really, guys. Don't you want to try your luck elsewhere? If I see that I-wish-I-was-you, look from one more woman, I think I may just let her take my place."

"No you won't," Keith said. "Admit it. You aren't through with us yet."

She laughed. "You're right. I'm not through with you."

"Oh, yes you are," Antonio asserted. "These guys are along because this is a celebration. They can come along next weekend for the big event, but there won't be any more base running. Not with my woman."

Clare melted inside. She reached for Antonio's hand and laced her fingers with his. "The only bats and balls I want to play with from now on are yours. But I'll never forget what these three did for me. For us."

"You know, you can wear both charms on a necklace. You don't have to do this," he said.

She shook her head. "No. I want to wear your charm there as a reminder of who I belong to. No one else needs to see that one, but the other one…it will be on display for everyone to see. I'm never going to take it off."

"We want whatever you want," Conner said. "You're the most amazing woman I've ever met, and I'll do anything for you. All you have to do is crook your finger, and I'll come running."

"Same goes for me," Mike said. "Maybe you'll name your first kid after me."

"Not on your life," Antonio said, tossing a dinner roll across the table.

Laughing, Mike caught the flying bread using his napkin as a glove.

"Clare," Keith said, placing his hand over his heart. "None of these women hold a candle to you. I'm yours. Always."

"They're harmless," she said to Antonio. "Just kids coveting the new toy their friend brought to the ballpark. As soon as I'm out of sight, they'll find women of their own. You mark my words."

"Yeah, well." He tossed his napkin on the table and stood. "Let's get the piercing over with. I'm not looking forward to the long dry spell after this, so the sooner we get it done, the better."

She'd read the doctor's instructions about keeping the piercing clean for a period of time until it healed fully and understood what Antonio was talking about. Not that she'd be ready for more physical intimacy anytime soon, but the thought of not making love with Antonio for weeks was almost enough to sway her decision the other way.

The doctor was waiting for them, her practice long-since closed for the day. She greeted the players by name, giving them each a very unprofessional hug before turning her attention to Clare.

"How do you do," she said, extending her hand. "I'm Dr. Fiona Goldstein. You must be Clare."

She shook the doctor's hand. "Nice to meet you. You've done this before, I understand."

"More times than I can count," she confessed. "But this is the first time I've ever had a four player entourage."

"They're my knights in shining armor," she explained. "They all deserve to be here."

"Fine by me." Dr. Goldstein scanned the group. "So, which one of you gets to hold her?"

"That would be me," Antonio said, taking a possessive hold on her hand.

They followed the doctor down the hall, where she instructed Keith, Mike, and Conner to wait outside until she was ready for them. Once inside the exam room, she pointed to the exam table already prepped with a white sheet draped over the raised back. Antonio climbed on, letting his legs dangle over the sides.

"The skirt can stay on," she said. "But if you're wearing panties, they'll have to come off."

Clare held onto the table with one hand for balance and removed her shoes and her panties.

"I'll take those," Antonio said, holding out his hand for the scrap of lace.

She handed her panties over and watched them disappear into the pocket of his slacks.

A few minutes later, the doctor examined Clare and pronounced her fit to receive the piercing. Using a mirror so her patient could see what she was talking about, she explained to her what she was going to do and gave her instructions for keeping the area clean.

"Ready?" she asked.

Clare took a deep breath and let it out. "Ready."

Her team entered at the doctor's call, fanning out around the exam table. Antonio's arms banded around her waist, providing emotional and physical support. Keith held the mirror so she and Antonio could see. In the blink of an eye, the procedure was over, and she was able to admire the tiny gold charm hanging from a barbell piercing the hood of her clit.

"It's beautiful," she said, tears of joy blurring her vision.

"First is a sapphire. Third is a ruby. Second and home are diamonds," Antonio said. "Mustangs colors."

"I can't believe it's mine. That I'm yours," she said.

"Forever." Antonio, placed a kiss on her neck sending shivers through her body.

"None of that. At least not for a while," Keith said. "Now that that's done, we have one more gift for you." He held his hand out, and Mike placed a small box on his palm. "You're the first to earn this one, so wear it with pride because we couldn't be more proud of you."

She accepted the box and, with shaking hands, opened it. On a background of midnight blue velvet lay an exquisite gold chain, and on the chain, a pendant the same shape but a little larger than the charm she'd just received. All four bases winked in the bright overhead exam lights.

"All diamonds," Keith said. "For a Grand Slam."

"Thank you." She fingered the magnificent piece.

"That's a work of art," Dr. Goldstein said. "Wow! Color me jealous!"

"You should be," Mike said. "No one else has ever come close to earning one of those."

Clare looked over her shoulder. "Put it on for me," she said to Antonio, handing him the boxed jewelry.

He secured the chain at her nape, and Keith handed her the mirror again.

Her eyes filled with tears at the sight of the pendant against her skin. "It's the most beautiful necklace I've ever seen."

"But not as beautiful as the woman wearing it," Antonio said.

Then her knights in shining armor admired the queen's new jewels, above and below, and after each placed a kiss on her lips, they filed out. She took the aftercare packet the doctor offered, and a few minutes later, she and Antonio were in their modern-day fairy tale coach, headed uptown to his apartment.

CHAPTER TWENTY-THREE

Clare looked in the full-length mirror and swished her hips just to see the diamonds on her dress sparkle and flash one more time. Antonio came up behind her, wrapping his arms around her waist, his chin against her temple.

"You'll outshine everyone there."

"I can't even imagine what you paid for this," she said, meeting his gaze in the mirror.

He shrugged his shoulders, encased in burgundy velvet to match the cape she would wear over her snow-white, diamond-encrusted ball gown. "It's for a good cause."

The Costume Ball was held every year between Thanksgiving and Christmas to benefit the local food bank. Besides the price of admission, the costumes would be put up for auction after the event to raise more funds.

"I've never worn anything like it, and I suspect I never will again."

"You're the Queen of Diamonds," he said. "You can't show up wearing just any old thing."

She smiled at the picture they made together. Him—tall, dark, and handsome as sin in rich burgundy velvet, and her—not so tall, but regal in white threaded with gold and embellished with real diamonds. The strapless gown showed off her shoulders, and the sweetheart neckline drew attention to the pendant she hadn't taken off since her knights had presented it to her.

"You know what tonight is," he said, dipping his head to place a line of kisses from the tip of her collarbone to that soft spot behind her ear.

"Yes." She'd been counting the days, the hours, the minutes.

"I'd take you right now if your loyal subjects weren't in the other room waiting for you to make an appearance."

"I'd let you," she said, meaning it. "Can't they wait?"

"We're already going to be fashionably late. After all you've accomplished to get to this point, you wouldn't want to miss the show."

"No, I wouldn't." Reluctantly, she turned from the mirror. Antonio offered her his arm and escorted her from the room.

"There she is," Keith said, sketching a bow.

Mike and Conner followed his lead.

"My Queen," they all said in unison.

She regally inclined her head then burst out laughing. "Oh my! You're all so…pretty!"

"Pretty?"

"What?"

"I knew it," Mike said. "It's the lace." He tugged on the fall of lace covering his hands down to his knuckles."

"Clare, you never tell a guy he's pretty. They're…." Deep lines etched his forehead as he seemed to search for the appropriate word to describe the costumes his friends wore.

"Okay, striking. How's that?" she asked.

The fitted trousers were no more revealing than the pants they wore on the playing field every day, so they couldn't object to those, but the coats, complete with tails, brass buttons, and gold braid trim were over the top. Adding on the elaborate cravats and lace trimmed shirts might have been too much.

"Better," Keith said. "You know I'd do anything for you, my Queen, but this?" He waved a hand to indicate his attire. "Well, let's just say I wouldn't do this for anyone but you."

"Thank you," she said, including all three in her gratitude. "As Antonio reminded me, it's for a good cause."

"I can think of no better cause." Conner bowed to his queen. He referred to their other reason for attending the ball as a group.

Clare had almost forgotten amid the preparations. She and Antonio had spent the last two weeks thinking up creative ways to be intimate while her piercing healed. The challenge had been effective in keeping her from stressing over tonight.

She acknowledged Conner's comment with a dip of her chin. "Thank you. Which reminds me…Antonio, do you have the things we talked about?"

"Oh yeah! Glad you remembered." He hurried off, leaving her alone with her devoted minions.

"I can't thank you all enough," she said. "I owe you more than I can repay already. So, please, understand…tonight…isn't your fight. Antonio and I have decided it's the only course of action for us, but I would feel terrible if this backfires and the three of you are caught in the fallout."

"No worries," Keith said. "We understand, and though Tony thinks you belong to him, we feel like you belong to us, too. So…we're in this, no matter what."

"It could cost you your careers," she said, using her final, and most persuasive argument.

"We might all end up selling hot dogs in the stands after this," Antonio said, returning with the items Clare had sent him for.

"Hey, I'd look better in a hot dog vendors uniform than I do in this," Conner said. "And, I wouldn't have to go to another fundraiser for the rest of my life."

"Heck yeah," Mike said. "I'm all for no more fundraisers."

Antonio handed each man a sword in a scabbard. "Here. This should give you some more clout as her ladyship's knights." While they wrestled with how to strap the things on, Clare went down the line, pinning a large, ornate medal on each of their coats.

"You are officially, Sir Keith," she said, placing a kiss on the man's cheek. When she was all done, she stepped back to survey her entourage. "Perfect!" She beamed at them.

Antonio draped the heavy cloak over her shoulders, fastening the collar at her neck. "And, your scepter, my Queen." He handed her the ornate accessory.

"How does she look?" he asked, stepping aside so they could admire the whole picture.

Clare blushed. "I look ridiculous."

"She's almost perfect," Mike said.

"Just needs one more thing," Conner added.

Keith picked up a wooden box she hadn't noticed on the coffee table and, standing before her, lifted the top.

She gasped. "It's beautiful."

"Don't get too attached." Mike lifted the tiara from its box. "It's on loan."

"Those are real?" she asked as he put it on her head.

"More diamonds and rubies than you can count," Conner confirmed.

Clare hurried to the mirror above the fireplace. Talk about over the top! "This is…."

"Perfect," Antonio said.

She turned, and to her amazement, all four men dropped to one knee. "We pledge you our lives, fair Queen," Keith said.

Clare almost doubled over at the sight. "Get up," she laughed. "Didn't someone say we were going to be late?"

"Hold up a minute," Tony said as they approached the ballroom doors. "Let's give Clare a minute to collect herself and make sure we're all on the same page."

The limo ride from his hotel to the one where the ball was being held had been short, but as they'd passed the familiar downtown landmarks, he couldn't help but notice Clare's growing anxiety. Giving her a moment was essential to the success of their endeavor.

None of them could afford failure. The cost was too high. Clare's self-esteem and their jobs were on the line. In order to salvage all those things, they needed to present a united front against Clare's enemy, now their enemy as well.

"Last chance to save yourselves," Tony said, offering them the opportunity to change their minds.

The guys shared a look.

"We're in." Keith said. "How will we know which one she is?"

"As soon as we spot Jessica, we'll give you a heads up," Tony said.

"But we're going to wait until she approaches Clare, right?" Keith asked.

"Right," Tony confirmed. "That shouldn't be a problem. After she sees Clare's entrance, she won't waste any time before she tries her bullying tactics on her."

"Bring her on," Conner said.

"Remember, stay close to Clare. We are her minions, devoted to her," Tony said.

"That's easy, since it's true." Mike grinned at Clare.

"Ready?" Keith asked her.

She inhaled deeply and exhaled. "Ready as I'll ever be."

He was so damned proud of her he thought he might bust right open. The short interlude had given her the time she needed. She was once again a Queen. Her shoulders were back, her chin up, and the smile on her face brought back the twinkle in her eyes.

She's mine. The thought firmed his resolve. Their approach might have the wrong effect on the Roach woman, and if so, he would lose everything. Except Clare. As long as he had her, he had all he needed.

Tony offered her his arm. "Then let's do it."

Keith and Conner moved to the double doors and waited with their hands on the handles while Mike adjusted Clare's cape so it hung perfectly over her shoulders and down her back.

"Good to go," Mike said.

Tony placed his hand over Clare's fingers curved over his forearm. She glanced his way, her lips curved up on the corners, and he knew everything was going to be all right. They would come out of this the victors.

The doors swung open, and they moved into the ballroom, her on Antonio's arm, Keith, Mike, and Conner falling in behind them. Heads turned to survey the newcomers. Clare smiled and nodded at a few acquaintances, allowing Antonio to steer her through the crowd. They stopped often to converse, the five of them answering the expected questions regarding their costumes, and occasionally talking baseball with the attendees who knew the sport and recognized one or more of her entourage.

She'd have to find her Uncle Doyle in the crowd and thank him for getting them the tickets. Though the event wasn't affiliated with the Mustangs, it was a cause the organization supported year-round with food drives on game day and with public service announcements. Everyone who was someone in Dallas attended, which meant Jessica would be at the ball, too.

It wasn't long before Clare spotted the woman. Dressed as Cruella DeVil, complete with a stuffed Dalmatian tucked under her arm, she stood out.

"Unoriginal villainess at one o'clock," she whispered in Antonio's ear.

Her fiancé squeezed her fingers. "I think she saw us. A series of hand gestures informed the rest of their group to be on alert. Bending so only she could hear, Antonio told her, "Just remember, I love you, and so do the guys behind you. We've got your back."

"Thank you. I love you, too." Feeling the need to reassure them both, she placed her left hand over Antonio's where it rested on top of hers. Her engagement ring caught the light from one of the overhead spotlights and flashed a starburst of fire around the room.

She could see the moment Jessica noticed her ring. Her eyes widened, and her mouth fell open, but she recovered quickly, replacing disbelief with malice.

"Clare, darling," Jessica crooned, waving her long-stemmed e-cig around in a dramatic fashion.

Baring her teeth in what she hoped was a congenial smile, Clare acknowledged her enemy. "Jessica. Or should I call you Cruella?"

The evil woman ignored the question and went straight for Clare's throat. "The fake ring is really too much with that costume. Haven't you heard when it comes to accessories, less is more?"

Behind her, Clare sensed her protectors squaring for battle. She lifted her hand, presenting the back of it so Cruella couldn't miss getting a good look at the ring. "You mean my engagement ring? I couldn't very well not wear it, now could I? Antonio wouldn't like that very much. He's the possessive type." She turned to him. "Aren't you, sweetheart?"

It was hard to tell with Jessica's overdone makeup and the lighting being what it was, but Clare was certain the woman turned white.

"You know me too well," Antonio said. "I want you to wear all the jewelry I gave you, even if I'm the only one who will ever see it."

Jessica's narrowed gaze darted between the two of them then landed on the small army of champions over Clare's shoulder.

"So, you did it. How much did you have to pay them to do it?"

The wall of testosterone behind her took a step forward. "Be careful what you say about Clare," Keith warned. "We're *all* possessive types."

"Show her your new necklace," Antonio said.

She lifted the gold pendant. "It's lovely, don't you think?"

Jessica stared at the item then her gaze made the rounds of their little group, coming back to Clare's. "What is that, a consolation prize? Couldn't make it all the way?"

"Oh, she made it all the way," Mike said.

"And then some," Conner added.

Antonio took the pendant from her fingers, looking it over before replacing it against her skin. "Clare's the first woman in the history of the club to earn the Grand Slam pendant, as well as the Homerun charm. Four complete innings and not a single strike out. Watching her receive her trophies is a moment I'll always treasure."

"I was honored to have all of you there to share in the moment." She glanced over her shoulder. Her knights in shining armor took turns leaning in, kissing her on the cheek.

"She's our Queen of Diamonds," Keith said. "And we are her devoted servants."

"We'll do anything for her," Conner added. "All she has to do is ask."

"How are you?" Mike asked her. "If you need my special attention, *anywhere*…you have only to say the word."

She managed not to laugh at Mike's blatant reference to her new piercing, but she couldn't help smiling as she answered, "Thank you, Mike. I'm much better now, but perhaps you can check for yourself…later."

"No. I don't believe it," Jessica said. "It's not possible."

"Believe me, it's possible," Antonio said. "And Clare has the jewels to prove it. However, the only one you need concern yourself with is the one hanging around her neck, and the one on her finger. Clare is going to be my wife, and these men," he said, motioning to the stern-faced wall behind them, "are her sworn protectors, willing to do whatever it takes to see to her happiness."

"But…she's—"

"Watch yourself," Antonio warned.

"She's Doyle Walker's niece!" Cruella fell back on her last barb.

A familiar voice joined the conversation. "She's my favorite niece."

Clare turned and smiled at her uncle. "I'm your only niece," she countered.

"And my most beautiful niece." He extended a hand to Antonio "I understand congratulations are in order."

"Thank you, sir." Antonio shook Doyle's hand. "We were just sharing the good news with Ms. Roach. And I think you've met our friends…."

Doyle inclined his head in greeting. "Ms. Roach, pleased to meet you." Then to the players, "Gentlemen. I see Clare has bewitched you also."

She watched Jessica's power over her slide away, one smile, one handshake at a time. The casual conversation exchanged between the men, though veiled, made it clear her uncle understood the nature of their relationship, and approved. With a kiss to her cheek, her uncle excused himself.

Jessica clutched her stuffed dog hard enough it was a wonder stuffing didn't ooze from the seams. "This will ruin you, every one of you," she hissed.

"No, it won't," Antonio said. "You see it's our word against yours. We're all prepared to lie through our teeth, in a court of law, if necessary. The club you think exists is nothing more than a rumor."

"I have proof." She raised her chin defiantly.

Antonio arched one eyebrow. "A piece of jewelry? Feel free to show that to the world, if you so choose. I'm sure the press would love to have a photo, but before you go that far, you should know there isn't a man on the planet who will admit to helping you earn that particular piece."

"Club? What club?" Mike said.

"I don't know what they're talking about," Keith said.

"Would someone fill me in on what's going on," Conner added in a convincingly confused tone.

"Leave my fiancé alone, Ms. Roach. Clare is the Queen of Diamonds, in every possible way, and you? Well, you are nothing compared to her."

Was that steam coming from Jessica's ears? No, just a coil of fake smoke from the e-cig trembling in her hand. With one last hate-filled gaze around their group, she turned and stalked off into the crowd.

"Well, that went better than I expected," Keith said.

"She's a piece of work." Remarked Conner.

"I don't think she'll be giving you any more trouble, Clare." Mike placed a reassuring hand on her shoulder.

"It's not me I'm worried about. She can't hurt me now. I've out-done her in every possible way, and she knows it. But she could turn her venom on the club."

"What club?" Antonio said with a laugh. "I don't know what you're talking about."

Suddenly, Clare was overwhelmed, and moisture filled her eyes. Her knights formed a protective barrier around her, offering their lace cuffs as handkerchiefs and begging her to tell them what to do to make the tears go away.

"I'm fine, really." She wiped moisture from her cheeks with her fingers. "I guess it just hit me. All of it. I'm done with Jessica. I ran the bases. I'm going to marry Antonio. And it's been two weeks…."

As one, her protectors muttered their understanding.

"What do you want to do?" Antonio asked. "Your wish is our command."

"I want to go home. I want…."

Her fiancé's eyes twinkled. "I know what you want." He took her hand. "Gentlemen, our Queen needs me."

A few minutes later, Clare slid into the back of the limo and Antonio joined her. Her champions stood on the curb, waving as the car pulled away from the hotel. When they were out of sight, she turned and found Antonio kneeling on the floorboard.

He grabbed the hem of her dress.

"Let me see."

She shivered as he inched her voluminous skirt up to her waist, revealing her pierced hood to his gaze. She could barely see the top of his head over the bunched fabric. Then his head disappeared. His tongue flicked the gold charm, and her legs and mouth fell open at the same time.

"Antonio," she breathed.

"My Queen," he said. "Let me tend to your needs."

His tongue swept over all it could reach, and Clare's heart sprinted toward first base.

ABOUT THE AUTHOR

USA Today Best-Selling author Roz Lee is the author of over thirty romances. The first, The Lust Boat, was born of an idea acquired while on a Caribbean cruise with her family, and soon blossomed into a five-book series originally published by Red Sage. Following her love of baseball, Roz turned her attention to sexy athletes in tight pants, writing the critically acclaimed Mustangs Baseball series.

Roz has been married to her best friend, and high school sweetheart, for over four decades. They have two daughters and are the proud grandparents of three adorable grandkids. Roz and her husband live in the wilds of New Jersey with their Labrador Retriever, Bud which is code for Big Unruly Dog.

Even though Roz has lived on both coasts, her heart lies in between, in Texas. A Texan by birth, she can trace her family back to the Republic of Texas. With roots that deep, she says, "You can't ever really leave."

When Roz isn't writing, she's reading or traipsing around the country on one adventure or another. No trip is too small, no tourist trap too cheesy, and no road unworthy of travel.

www.RozLee.net